· Children's Games ·

This one is for the Wednesday Night Barracudas,
with deepest gratitude and affection

The human race, to which so many of my readers belong, has been playing at children's games from the beginning, and will probably do it till the end, which is a nuisance for the few people who grow up.

G. K. Chesterton
from "Introductory Remarks on the Art of Prophecy" in *The Napoleon of Notting Hill*

Port Silva, California, is a fictitious town. Stretch the Mendocino coast some twenty miles longer, scoop up Mendocino Village and Fort Bragg, toss in a bit of Santa Cruz. Set this concoction on a dramatic headland over a small harbor and add a university. Established 1885. Elevation 100 feet. Population 24,020, a mix of old families, urban escapers, students, academics, and tourists in season.

· Prologue ·

No siren, just a low rumble, and a bright glimmer in the fog. Then a red Porsche whipped in from the highway and snarled to a stop against the log barrier at cliff's edge. The driver was on his feet before the engine's echo had died, a square-shouldered, straight-backed man in boots, Levi's, and a dark windbreaker.

"Sorry, but no one is . . . ah." The speaker tugged his pale-blue sweatshirt into place over his belly and sighed as he extended a hand. "Chief Gutierrez, thank God! What took you so long?"

"Professor Anderssen." Port Silva's chief of police had a tight-skinned dark face made of straight lines: heavy brows, deep cheek grooves, long mouth. "Fog's still thick on the streets," Gutierrez remarked as he turned to survey the nearly empty parking lot. "Your BMW?"

"What? Yes, of course. But it—he—is down the cliff." Anderssen clamped his mouth shut as Gutierrez paused to survey the cream-colored sedan. Then the policeman set off for the flight of railed wooden steps that led to the beach, and the professor fell in behind him.

"I was . . . my God, I was just out for my usual morning run, a bit late today because it's Sunday," he said, raising his voice over the clatter of Gutierrez' boots. "The fog was beginning to lift, and I looked up for some reason, and . . . That way, near the north end," he directed as they reached the bottom.

"At first I thought it was just a pile of clothing someone

1

had discarded." He was abreast of the policeman now, broad-soled running shoes giving him the better purchase on the sand. "Then I could make out the vest, who'd throw that away? So I got closer for a better look, and saw it was, um, somebody in the clothes. Somewhere along about . . . yes, there."

Anderssen planted his feet in the sand, buried his fists in the front pockets of his sweatshirt, and stared up at the cliff. Gutierrez followed the other's gaze, shading his eyes with one hand. Then without a word he began to pick his way over the rubble of rocks and driftwood against the foot of the cliff.

The figure was spread-eagled, face down, perhaps three-quarters of the way from the top, at the point where the sheer cliff face eased outward. It was a puffy down vest that had caught Anderssen's eye, made of a denim-blue fabric with a muted sheen; the collar of the garment was rucked up against the back of a very blond head that seemed oddly misshapen.

"He's dead, all right, and getting stiff." Anderssen's voice was hoarse, a loud whisper.

Gutierrez reached the body and stood up straight to survey it from blue-and-silver Nikes to outflung arms, half-curled hands. An errant breeze lifted and dropped a lock of the bright hair. Gutierrez braced himself with his left arm and reached forward with his free hand to grip a dirt-streaked bare wrist. He released the wrist, moved a step to the left and leaned closer against the cliff to peer up at the half-buried face.

"It's the Tucker boy, isn't it?"

"Yes." He pushed upright, turned, and began the descent to the sand, placing his feet with care. "You knew him?"

Anderssen shook his head. "He was in his father's office one day when I had some business at the bank, and Mr. Tucker introduced him to me. His appearance was . . . memorable. That golden blond coloring seldom persists past childhood." Another head-shake, slow and sad; he glanced at the sky and then at his watch.

"If that's all, Chief Gutierrez? I'm sure my wife has had breakfast waiting for the past hour."

"Sorry. You can call her from the station. Where you'll go now to make your statement," Gutierrez added as the other's face lengthened in astonishment. "And you should probably tell her to draw the blinds and unplug the phone."

"I beg your pardon?"

"Port Silva is a small town, Professor Anderssen, an old town for this part of the country. David Tucker's great-grandfather founded the bank William Tucker still runs."

"Oh. Yes, I see. A nasty accident to a member of a prominent family . . ."

"People seldom get shot in the back of the head by accident." Mouth closed in a hard line, the policeman turned on his heel and set off for the steps.

◦ 1 ◦

Meg Halloran managed to refold the sheet of paper and push it back into its envelope. She shoved the envelope into her hip pocket, then wiped both hands on her Levi's. This one had not come via the postal service, but had been slipped stampless into her mailbox. Perhaps she could get the little bastard for improper use of government property.

"... so today, Wednesday, expect midday sun, with coastal low fog morning and evening," droned a familiar voice. "No shit," she muttered as she reached out to silence the portable radio beside her kitchen sink. Late last night, returning to Port Silva after a week in hot and dusty forest campgrounds, she had met the fog with pleasure; its gentle veil softened hard edges, made her small brown house seem snugly private on its wooded knoll.

Private, or isolated? She wrapped both hands around her coffee mug and stared at the gray mist hovering beyond the kitchen window. Probably it was the thick fog that had made Dave Tucker feel free to abuse her mailbox; she should be grateful he hadn't burned down her house, or at least defecated on her doorstep.

And that, you silly bitch, is the kind of attitude that gives license to vandals everywhere. She splashed more coffee into her mug and gulped a mouthful. The letters had moved from accusation to near-threat and could no longer be ignored. She could take Katy and run, or she could make a fuss, a loud demanding official fuss.

Right. And no mealymouthed sergeant this time, she'd insist on seeing the top man. Port Silva's chief of police had a hard brown Aztec face and a personality of corresponding warmth, but the locals spoke of him with respect. And in her sole personal encounter with the man, the memory of which still made her cheeks burn, he had certainly proved himself unflappable.

She jerked her reaching hand back from the wall telephone as a single high note rang out. The second bell of the door chime was lost in a burst of thunderous barking. Meg sighed, smoothed palms over her hair in a gesture both automatic and futile, and padded off toward the front of the house. "I'll get it, Katy," she called into the living room as she passed.

Her giant dog was upright against the front door, ropy grayish hair lifting along neck and shoulders as he rumbled deep in his throat. "Down, Grendel," Meg commanded, reinforcing the order with a sharp tug at his slip collar. "Down! Wait!" She herself waited while the dog reluctantly planted his rear; then, a finger still hooked through the collar ring, she pulled the door open to face a fog-shrouded figure standing well back.

"Yes, what . . . ? Oh." The dark face with its air of chilly authority might have come directly from inside her head. Her sense of time and sequence teetered alarmingly.

Port Silva's chief of police inclined his head briefly. "Vince Gutierrez, Mrs. Halloran, we met a few months ago. If I could talk to you . . . ?" He shifted his feet and the angle of his shoulders to move past her; at the dog's soft rumble he stiffened and took one quick step back.

Quite right, Grendel, you know unfriendly when you see it. Meg gave a flat-palmed signal to the dog, who lay down at once but kept his head up, alert. "Yes, Chief Gutierrez?" she said crisply. "What is it?"

A deep breath, a tight smile. "Your name has come up in the course of our investigation," he said, and turned wary eyes on the dog. "I need to talk to you about it, please, if your . . . whatever the hell he is . . . will let me in."

"He's a komondor, it's a Hungarian breed. What investigation?"

He straightened his shoulders and rearranged his expression: patience with fools. "The investigation of David Tucker's murder."

"Murder?" The fog swung and pressed, cottony-thick; a vivid golden image of Dave Tucker was followed by a sick lurch of displacement as reality seemed to mock her once again.

"Mrs. Halloran!" A voice in her ear, hard hands gripping her upper arms. And from very close, a high-pitched snarl that lifted the hairs on the back of her neck.

"Grendel, no! Friend, Grendel!" The policeman let go of her and stood absolutely still. She moved away from him and said softly, "Hold your hand out to him, palm down. Friend, Grendel."

The dog sniffed, grinned, and backed away with a wave of his tail. Patches of dull red marked Gutierrez' cheekbones as he took another deep breath. "Mrs. Halloran, don't you read the papers? Or listen to the news? Where have you been for the last three days?"

"In the mountains, camping. We got back to town just last night. When was he . . . killed?" Her throat tightened on the last word; she coughed and repeated it. "Killed. And how?"

"Someone shot him in the head with a small-caliber handgun late Saturday night. His body was found Sunday morning on the rocks above Tanbark Beach."

Saturday! Four days dead, and his presence had been nearly tangible in her kitchen this morning. Self-righteous Dave, so sure of his place in heaven, what a joke if he were now some kind of shade, a ghost condemned to wander . . . no, not a joke, there was nothing remotely funny about a ghost who could write letters and open mailboxes and . . . She registered the policeman's silence and tried to gather her scattered wits.

"Well, I certainly didn't shoot him, I don't own a fire-arm of any kind and I've never fired a handgun in my life." Her bright babble faded into silence, while his face changed not at all: no blink, not the slightest upward quirk of the long mouth.

Yes indeed, Maggie-me-love, and now we stand here and wait for the friendly policeman to take out his note-book and draw a firm line through your name. Which may be a very long wait.

She straightened to her full five feet ten, bringing her gaze nearly level with his. "Chief Gutierrez, I'll ask you to come through to the kitchen. My daughter is at home, and I won't have her involved in this."

"I understand." He stepped past her into the entry hall; she eased the door shut and turned to find Katy in the living-room archway, eyes round with curiosity. Her face was very young under its cap of thick dark hair, but a coltish length of leg suggested that she was beginning to make her way out of childhood. Now she cocked her head, frowned, and said, "Mommy? What's the matter?"

Meg could feel hair clinging damply to her temples; she knew her chilled skin must be greenly pale. She drew a shaky breath, stretched her lips into the semblance of a smile and felt the smile grow real as she looked at her daughter.

"It's all right, love. Katy, this is Chief Gutierrez of the Port Silva police; he's come to talk with me for a few minutes. Chief Gutierrez, my daughter, Katy."

"Did he show you his badge?" Sensible, city-bred child, thought Meg.

The policeman's eyes glinted as he pulled a wallet from his hip pocket and held it out for inspection. Katy flushed, but peered closely at it and at him before nodding and stepping back. "Good girl," he said with an answering nod as he flipped the wallet shut. "Between you and the dog, your mother is well-protected."

Meg drew in her breath with a hiss, but Gutierrez gave her no time for words. "Nice to have met you, Katy. I hope this won't take long."

"You stay by the fire with your book, sweetie." Meg pulled the little girl close and dropped a kiss on rumpled hair. She met the upturned blue gaze calmly; and after a brief hesitation Katy nodded and moved away, her only protest a barely audible sigh.

Kitchens were safe places, in some atavistic fashion having nothing to do with reason. Today gray-green shadows lurked in corners, but the air was tinged with the aroma of coffee and the scent of lemons from a heaped basket on the central counter. Meg led her visitor to the breakfast alcove, gesturing him to a chair at the far end of the long pine table where she did most of her schoolwork.

"Please tell me how my name came into this," she said over her shoulder as she yanked open the drawer beside the sink—formerly the cigarette drawer—to find it full of other junk. It's been almost a month, she reminded herself as she turned and propped her backside against the sink's tiled rim.

"Right." Gutierrez took notebook and pencil from a shirt pocket. "For the record. You are Mrs. Margaret Evans Halloran, widow, with a single minor child, a daughter aged ten. You came here from Arizona a year ago to take a position as English teacher at Port Silva High School."

"For the record" was even more ominous than "in the course of our investigation." As the comfort of the familiar room receded like an outrushing tide, Meg reached back to twist the handle of the dripping faucet and caught a reflection of herself in the window over the sink. Narrow, tanned face bare of makeup, badger-colored mane of hair restrained by a rubber band, she wore her oldest Levi's and a shrunken, once-red sweatshirt with nothing under it. She was even barefoot, chilly toes reminded her.

She folded her arms over her breasts and faced the policeman. "That information is accurate, Chief Gutierrez. Perhaps you will now outline with equal clarity just what has brought you here, so that I may decide whether or not I should have my attorney present."

Gutierrez slumped in his chair, teeth flashing white in what was more grimace than grin. "Okay, I sounded like a bad imitation of 'Dragnet.' Mrs. Halloran, this town's been on its ear for three days, and I've got irate citizens climbing me like a fence. Please. Just sit down and listen for a minute, and then you can call your attorney if you feel it's necessary."

Her own carelessly tossed word, lobbed neatly back. Meg knew two lawyers in Port Silva; they were married to each other and lived at the end of the block. Marcia—she thought Marcia's interests lay in social issues, counterculture stuff. Perhaps Mark handled ordinary criminal cases, she could call him and . . . Oops, let's run that one by again: ordinary criminal? Moving her feet with precise care, Meg crossed the room, lined up the empty captain's chair, and perched herself on its edge.

Gutierrez' face was expressionless. "Yeah, well, what happened is this. While Mr. Tucker was in the office this morning—he's naturally been there a lot—we got a report that his son was seen here Saturday night, right in front of your house."

Leaving his little love note, thought Meg, and pressed her lips tight to keep the words unsaid.

"Now, Tucker has been insisting that Dave had no vices, few bad habits, and absolutely no enemies," Gutierrez went on, "but suddenly he remembers that there was trouble, serious trouble, between you and his boy. So he demanded, or rather we decided, that further investigation was in order."

"I'm afraid Mr. Tucker's perception of his son was seriously flawed."

"That's possible. Even probable." He sat back in his chair but kept his gaze locked with hers. "But in three days—shit, in three days and three *nights*—my entire force has turned up nothing. Not only have we no witnesses, no evidence, and no solid leads; we haven't learned anything about Dave Tucker to tell us why anybody might have wanted—needed—to kill him."

"It's funny," Meg said slowly, "but I have this stereotyped notion of small towns as places where people know each other."

Gutierrez stiffened. "Port Silva isn't all that small anymore, Mrs. Halloran. Our population is over 25,000 when the university is in full session." He picked up his notebook, riffled its pages, found the one he wanted.

"I knew Dave Tucker to see him, knew who he was. And I know from checking the records that he has never come to the official attention of the police. No juvenile vandalism, no speeding tickets, never picked up drunk or stoned, apparently never got anybody's daughter pregnant. Zilch. To all appearances Dave Tucker was just your average semiperfect eighteen-year-old."

"That's bullshit!" snapped Meg, but Gutierrez wasn't finished.

"That is, until he ran into you. Something Dave did made you angry enough to come to the police, but you let it drop, no complaint filed. So I'm left with only Mr. Tucker's side of the story." His voice was soft, the black eyes now wide in friendly, sensible appeal: Trust me.

She tucked her feet back under her chair, squared her shoulders, folded her arms close. "Chief Gutierrez, that's very good," she murmured, and watched with satisfaction as his official mask settled back into place. Let's just keep the roles straight around here.

"What you're asking," she said after a moment, "is that I rebut a serious charge before having heard it. If I'm to continue this conversation without legal advice, I insist on knowing what Mr. Tucker has accused me of."

In a room suddenly small, its heavy air pressing at her temples and constricting her breathing, she stared at the policeman's bent head and listened to a noisy silence. A click and then a creaky hum from the old refrigerator, a slow splat, splat from the dripping faucet, the relentless tunk-tunk-tunk of the battery clock. A thread of distant music. A whoof of morning breeze, to set branches a-scrape against the kitchen wall and bring a faint groan from the house itself, old bones.

"When did you leave town?"

Meg jumped, met the black gaze, flung an answer. "Wednesday morning."

"And you went where?"

"Into the Mendocino National Forest and then the . . . Trinity, I think it was. We have a van rigged for camping; we stayed in forest-service campgrounds through Monday night."

"Receipts?"

"Um—yes, I should have gas station charge slips from Covelo, and Red Bluff and . . . Rio Dell. And Katy always saves the little numbered tabs from the campground fee envelopes, they're probably in the glove compartment."

Gutierrez leaned back in his chair and grinned; mouth wide, eyes aglint, it was a two-second revelation of the man's basic, crackling vitality. Meg sat straighter, startled by the flicker of some long-dormant nerve. "Will that do?" she snapped.

"Come worst case, you could always subpoena the Department of Agriculture; I'll bet they put all those numbers in a computer someplace." He jotted quickly in his notebook. "We'll take it as understood and go on from there. But I'd suggest you find the receipts and hang on to them."

◦ 2 ◦

Half a dozen tiny, vital pieces of paper, and where are they? "I'm going to have a beer," Meg said abruptly, pushing her chair back. "Would you like one? Or would that constitute drinking on duty?"

"I think I just went off duty." The last words were spoken through a yawn; she returned from the refrigerator to find that he had stretched his legs out and let his head fall back. In the brightening light from the windows, his face was tired and sad, with bruiselike smudges around the closed eyes, a faint stubble riming jaw and chin.

At the pop of a pull-tab he pushed himself up straight, blinking. Meg set one can before him, then returned to her seat with the other. "Mr. Tucker?" she prompted.

"Mr. Tucker, right." He took a sip of beer, set the can to one side and donned a milder version of his policeman's face. "Mr. Tucker's remarks boil down to this: one, you disliked the boy from the start because he was too bright. Two, you therefore persecuted him, refusing him credit for work he'd completed. Three, when he tried to talk to you after school about his grades, you, ah, made sexual overtures to him." Ignoring Meg's exclamation, he

kept his head down and went on. "Four, when the boy
went to your house in one last attempt to straighten
things out, because he needed your course for graduation, you set your dog on him."

"Holy sweet Christ on a crutch!"

Gutierrez put his notebook down. "Not true?"

"Not true." She took a deep breath. "And what did Mr.
Tucker suggest for point five? Why was I supposed to
have killed Dave?"

Gutierrez hunched his shoulders. "Uh, well, he thought
. . . he said you were excitable, an unstable woman living
alone. And Dave might have come to you for some reason
of his own, or maybe even just by accident. And . . . look,
Mrs. Halloran, Tucker is hurting, and it's obvious that he
needs somebody to punish. But he did produce some
specific information, and I couldn't ignore it."

Poor Mr. Tucker was simply a bereaved father. Poor
Gutierrez was simply a hard-working cop. And be damned
to both of them.

"Mrs. Halloran?"

"Yes." Elbows on the table, she pressed the heels of her
hands against her eyes, waiting for the surge of anger to
abate. "Yes. Point one: he was not nearly so bright as he
thought, and I didn't dislike him, not at first. I simply
found him . . . odd." She paused, trying to capture an
image.

"A cat. Dave would pad into the room like a big golden
cat, puma or something, not lion. He'd choose a seat apart
from the others, and watch everyone with those strange
yellow eyes; he never seemed to blink. And handsome as
he was, he was an isolate . . . no crowding up against the
pretty girls, no joking around with the other boys. There
was always space around Dave Tucker." She looked up to
meet Gutierrez' intent gaze.

"Point two: he was failing because he was not doing the
work. Whatever we read, from Sophocles to Faulkner,
Dave judged only on its moral stance, and for him that

meant fundamentalist Christian morals. His essays were always little sermons, using the assigned topic as a springboard or not using it at all. He disputed my every grade, of course." With a subtle landowner-to-serf manner that had both irritated and unnerved her.

After a moment of silence, Gutierrez said, softly, "Point three?"

"Point three is a vicious lie." Meg took a drink of beer, set the can aside, lifted her chin. "Teaching is my profession, Chief Gutierrez, and our only means of support, mine and my daughter's. I do not make sexual overtures to teenage boys, nor send any sexual signals. Dave Tucker came to my classroom late one Friday afternoon to complain about his report card. When I refused to change his grade he became abusive, and Mr. Johnson, the head custodian, heard the noise and removed him." With one enormous black hand gripping the boy's shoulder and the other hovering near the seat of his jeans, she recalled now in momentary pleasure. Mr. Johnson was a widower who had raised five sons; he took no nonsense.

"But he'd told his dad . . . look, even an experienced teacher can't read every adolescent. Is it possible he'd come to make a pass at *you,* and blew up when he realized how far off base he was?"

As Gutierrez raised questioning eyebrows, Meg felt her face flame. "Damn it, that's just the kind of look I got from the counselor when I told him about Dave. 'All them ol' boys'll try to get some any way they can,' according to ol' Coach Eason. I think he felt I should be flattered.

"I was sitting at my desk," she said more softly, "and Dave stood over me, inches away." She closed her eyes briefly, remembering the scarlet face, the bulging eyes, the fine spray of spittle. "But he made no effort to touch me. And he was not sexually aroused."

"Ah," said Gutierrez. "Well, a cop has to start with the obvious. So what real thing, besides a better grade, did he want from you?"

Meg clasped her hands tight and pressed them against her chin. "He yelled at me, but not about grades. About a jealous God and how He would punish unbelievers, sinners, the ungodly. 'The sword of the Lord and of Gideon,' reading 'David' for 'Gideon.' "

"But I don't see—"

"I have given this a great deal of thought, Chief Gutierrez. I've decided that Dave Tucker was looking for power. He'd picked me as vulnerable, somebody he could manipulate."

The yawn which had caught him tailed off in a squeak of amazement. "Vulnerable?"

"For real living-on-the-edge, Chief Gutierrez, try being a forty-year-old woman on her own with a child." Especially a woman, she added bitterly but silently, who made a neat balance sheet of advantages/disadvantages before moving to a small town but gave not one serious thought to the matter of religion.

Gutierrez was the first to pull his gaze away. He leaned back in his chair, balanced his pencil between thumb and forefinger, sighed. "Okay. Better cover point four; remember point four?" He waited for her to nod. "Right. Unfortunately, I was out of town at the time. All Sergeant Nelson remembers, he says, is that you phoned to say Dave Tucker had threatened your daughter; and then Mr. Tucker stormed in yelling that you'd set your dog on his son."

Meg rose, picked up her beer can, and went to stare out the kitchen window. The fog was thinning; timid little fingers of sunlight were reaching for the garden. "It was exactly a week later, Friday afternoon. Dave had been in class all week, quiet and polite and offering no challenges.

"He didn't threaten her, not quite. He frightened her." Silly word, frightened, a word for stories. "It was a minimum day at school for the kids; the faculty had a series of meetings scheduled. I asked to be excused early, because Katy was home in bed with a cold."

She blinked at the beer can, then tilted it for a long swallow. "He'd come in through the front door somehow, perhaps it wasn't locked. Katy woke up, heard a noise in my bedroom; she thought it was me and went in to find him rooting around in my dresser drawers. And he . . . he backed her into a corner there, and told her that people were watching, that everyone knew her mother fornicated in that bed with a Jesus-killer, at the very least I was sure to go to hell even if someone didn't shoot me first."

Gutierrez made a sound like a low growl, but Meg didn't turn.

"A Jesus-killer and a child of Satan. Sammy, I suppose." A gust of wind swept the backyard, rattling the springy deodar cedar against the board fence and shaking droplets of condensed fog from the big Monterey pines. "Our friend Sam Goldman spent a week with us at the end of February. He drove me to school in my van a couple of days, while his Volks was being tuned. Sam would be the first to admit that he's the living image of the stereotypical Jew."

She swung around to look at the policeman, whose face might have been carved from dark wood. "Grendel was barking his head off in the backyard as I drove up. When I came out of the garage I could hear Katy shrieking. I found her in the hallway and picked her up; Grendel went out the open front door and managed to take the seat out of Dave's pants just before he got into his car."

She drew a deep breath and expelled it slowly as she returned to her chair. "Katy and I arrived at the police station to find Mr. Tucker and darling Davey there ahead of us. They intended to charge me with assault and have my dog destroyed. After Katy had told her story, and I'd mentioned that my friends the Solomons would represent

us in a damage suit, Mr. Tucker reconsidered." Gutierrez'
eyes widened; Isaac and Moishe Solomon, respectively a
lawyer and a forensic psychologist, were renowned in Los
Angeles and throughout the state for client satisfaction
and enormous settlements.

Pure bluff, she had known even as she'd said it. She
could never subject Katy to such a public ordeal, and the
Solomons were mere acquaintances, uncles of Sam Goldman.
But just their names had worked, their names and Katy's
obvious distress.

"They apologized," she told Gutierrez in a thin voice,
"both of them. Dave was a good Christian boy who'd
never been in trouble before; he desperately wanted to be
allowed to graduate and go on to college. He would
quietly, immediately transfer out of my class. He would
stay away from me, my daughter, my house. They promised he'd leave us alone. And I know I shouldn't have let
it go at that," she muttered. "But he hadn't actually touched
Katy, nor specifically threatened either of us."

"In your place, I'd have done the same." Gutierrez
brushed a hand over his face, yawned widely, and the
Aztec mask became simply the face of a tired, middle-
aged official. "I don't suppose Officer Nelson stayed to
witness your meeting? No," he sighed as she shook her
head, "he'd have run like a rabbit. Okay, I'll tell Tucker
that I've heard your side of things, and I'll let him know
that you have a better alibi for the murder than anyone
else so far." His smile was little more than a crinkling of
the skin at the edges of his eyes. "One last thing: have
you any idea what Dave might have been doing here
Saturday night?"

As her guardian inner self threw its hands up in dis-
may, Meg said, "Yes. He was leaving this in my mailbox."
She pulled the envelope from her pocket and dropped it
on the table before him. "I found it there this morning."

The paper Gutierrez teased from its envelope was
white with faint blue lines. He unfolded it gingerly and

stared at the words, written in tight, spiky letters with black ink.

Thou lovest all devouring words, O thou deceitful tongue. God shall likewise destroy thee for ever, he shall take thee away, and pluck thee out of thy dwelling place, and root thee out of the land of the living. Selah.

"That's from Psalms. I looked it up. Isn't it funny, I used to think of the Psalms as comforting: green pastures and still waters. I guess I should have paid more attention in Sunday school."

"Hey!" Gutierrez reached the length of the table to close his hand over her cold, entwined fingers. She blinked hard against the sudden glitter of tears and after a moment pulled her hands away.

"Okay. According to the Tucker family, and their minister, Dave was a devoted Baptist who rarely missed the Bible study classes. And he used to teach Sunday school." Gutierrez bent his head over the letter. "Is this his handwriting?"

"Not his usual handwriting. But that's exactly the aspect of the Bible Dave loved, never mind lost sheep and tender shepherds. This is the third letter. There was one in early April, about a month after our big confrontation, and another a few weeks later."

"Do you have the others?"

"Just a moment." She'd tucked them into her *Oxford Dictionary of Quotations,* in the dining-room bookcase.

"This," she said, handing him a folded sheet of lined yellow paper, "is a copy, reconstructed after I'd flushed the original down the toilet."

" 'Upon the wicked he shall rain snares, fire and brimstone, and an horrible tempest: this shall be the portion of their cup,' " he read aloud.

19

"Another Psalm," she told him. "But now a little varia-
tion; this is from Proverbs."

Gutierrez unfolded another sheet of white paper to
reveal the spiky script. " 'For the lips of a strange woman
drop as an honeycomb, and her mouth is smoother than
oil: But her end is bitter as wormwood, sharp as a twoedged
sword. Her feet go down to death; her steps take hold on
hell.' " His lower lip curled in distaste as he set the letters
to one side. "Did you tell anyone about these?"

"And to whom, sir, should I have reported that someone was dropping Bible verses into my mailbox?" she
demanded. "To the Port Silva police? Or maybe to my
principal? Burton professes to admire my work, but he's
not crazy about outlanders, particularly when they're female and four inches taller than he is!"

She threw herself back in her chair, aware that she was
giving a good imitation of a petulant child. So what. "I
was sure that Dave wrote those letters, but I had no proof,
nor had I energy to spare for another confrontation."
You were a coward, that's what, said her inner self coldly.
Stranger in a strange land, keeping your head down.
"Anyway, I thought the letters had ended with the school
year. I thought Dave had gotten his licks in, paid me back
for his humiliation, and then graduated and gone on with
his life."

"Um." His eyes were focused at some point behind her
left shoulder, while his pencil beat a slow tattoo on the
table.

Um to you too, she thought, and felt a wave of weariness engulf her as she pushed her chair back. "Will that
be all for now, Chief Gutierrez?"

"Oh, I think so, I think so. I'll just take these letters
along, if I may, for a few tests." Before she could protest,
he had come quickly up from his chair, settling himself
into his boots in a way that reminded her of something.
Yes, a desert neighbor's wolfhound, a grayish length of

dozing weary bones until a breeze wafted rabbit scent across his pointed nose.

"Mrs. Halloran . . . Margaret?"

"Meg," she replied automatically.

"Meg, I appreciate your cooperation. And I'm truly grateful for the information you've given me. Trying to get a handle on that kid has been like punching fog."

She nodded, managed a smile, and led the way to the entry hall. At the front door he paused, turning to face her. "Uh, there's something I've wanted to say to you for months; I kept hoping we'd run into each other but in different . . ." He faltered, shrugged, spread his hands wide. "My men were completely out of line on the drug sweep at the high school, and your protest was more than justified. They had no warrant for the locker search and absolutely no reason to roust that kid."

That morning in April was still clear in Meg's mind. She had watched in stunned disbelief as two shined-and-polished young policemen burst into her classroom, snatched a student from his chair, and cuffed his hands behind his back. As he was hustled to the door, the hulking, not-very-bright boy wailed that he never used dope, if there was marijuana in his locker someone else had ditched it there. Then he compounded his humiliation by bursting into blubbering tears.

"It was all so damned frustrating," she said now. "Burton refused to get involved, of course, and the counselors made the barest pretense of trying to locate Buddy's mother. I phoned the police station and got nothing, no one would talk to me. So when I went into the doughnut shop and found the chief of police himself right there at the counter, I'm afraid I lost my temper," she finished lamely, aware that her cheeks were glowing.

Gutierrez grinned. "JoAnne says her regulars took a vote later and decided we were more fun than the soaps." He pulled the door open and turned away from her to scan the street; his face in profile was hawklike, intent. "My men are probably on the street now, talking to your neighbors. They won't bother you."

"I wish them luck," she said, "and you, too."

"We'll need it," he replied grimly. "Port Silva is accustomed to murder on television, not on the local beach. Everyone is very, very edgy." He stepped through the door and paused to give her a nod. "I'll be in touch. Please let me know if anything else occurs to you, if you remember something more about Dave. And call me at once if you get another letter."

• 3 •

The big terra-cotta tiles they'd brought home from Mexico were smooth under her bare feet, and cool. Soon the heavy slab door, barrier against fierce late-day sun, would be flung open; Dan would drop his briefcase, lift her up in a rib-crunching hug, and wonder aloud what she'd been up to today.

"Hoo, boy." She bit down hard on the thumb she was worrying and blinked at oiled boards, a braided runner, a paneled door with a single small pane of beveled glass, set high. Strangers lived in the adobe house now. Daniel Halloran was gone, his generous spirit extinguished by the drunk driver who had forced him off a twisty mountain road in Arizona more than three years earlier. But she could picture the vivid blue of his gaze, a color that would deepen as he attempted to wrap his mathematician's mind around her latest dilemma.

They'd been a good team, Dan the thinker and Maggie the warrior. He'd be sad to know that she was now less than half, that time and events had quelled her spirit without, so far as she could tell, leaving her one whit the wiser. "You wouldn't even like me, Danny," she murmured.

The doorbell rang, and went on ringing, as if something had been propped against it. Meg flung her head up, unclenched her hands; she stalked to the door and yanked it open.

"Good morning, Mrs. Halloran." Eyes of a very pale blue squinted up from beneath a frizzy blond fringe. "You did ask me to use the doorbell next time, didn't you?"

"Did I? Yes, I suppose I did. I certainly hope you didn't break a fingernail on it. All right, Cyndi, come in. Katy's in the living room."

Cyndi Martin paused in the doorway to clip a ballpoint pen to the cover of a spiral notebook, conveying the impression that she'd been standing outside taking notes. Eloquent pauses were a specialty of Cyndi's, together with small exasperated sighs and shrugs of weary tolerance. Sly, bursting with curiosity, she was also intelligent and well-read, and according to Katy, sometimes really funny. Presently, with all Katy's local friends away on vacations, Cyndi was the only game in town.

Cyndi tucked the notebook into a bulging shoulder tote, lowered her head, and tromped in, a plump sausage of just-prepubescent female encased in the blue and white stripes of Oshkosh overalls. Poor Louise, thought Meg as she watched the pudgy figure disappear into the living room. Cyndi's mother was a potter, a free spirit who lived in the next block with her younger daughter, Flower; Cyndi's usual home was with her father in Oakland.

Murmurs of greeting, a giggle, a thud as something,

probably Cyndi's bag, hit the floor. Well, Katy spent far too much time being best buddy to her mother. A small dose of Cyndi's iconoclastic viewpoint would probably be good for her, might at least keep her from noticing Meg's frazzled state.

Move it, lady. The policeman had seemed disposed to be on her side, either because he believed her or because he resented Tucker's pushing. Meg yanked open the drawer of the telephone table and retrieved her keys. With luck, she'd find the receipts in the glove compartment of her van, a neat little alibi-packet.

The fog was gone, but the sunlight was lemony-pale, lacking force. The flagstones leading to the garage were still damp beneath Meg's bare feet, the concrete floor icy. She opened the passenger door of the dusty blue van and scrambled in.

The glove compartment was a jumble of travelers' odds and ends: maps, paper napkins, a cardboard cylinder spilling salt, several small packets of catsup, a pair of sunglasses missing one earpiece. A folded plastic garbage bag lay beneath the heap, and peeping from under it was the little notebook she used as the van's log.

There! Three flimsy receipts from her Shell credit card, dates and places pale but legible. Odometer readings for each purchase scrawled in the book, Dan had been a stickler for record keeping, and she'd continued his pattern. She leaned across the seat to look at the instruments, then worked a stubby pencil free of the notebook's spiral edge and recorded the present mileage.

Halfway there; now for the campground stubs. She began to empty the compartment, opening maps, shaking out napkins, but no small, stiffish pieces of pink paper came to view. Surely Katy had kept them, she always kept them.

Kneeling backwards on the seat, Meg surveyed the rear of the van: chilly, cavernous, and unpromising. A rapid search unearthed only a crumpled paper bag (empty), a dry, stiff scrap of orange peel (in the gloom, its color excited her for a moment), and a discarded paperback mystery.

Katy must have used them for bookmarks, or stuck them absently into a pocket. Meg clambered out of the van, reached back in for the log book, slammed the door and then opened it again to depress the lock button. "Paranoia," she muttered, but she circled the van nonetheless, to lock the other doors.

In the living room the perpetual Monopoly game was under way again. Questioning Katy now would involve Cyndi, a prospect Meg found intolerable. In her daughter's bedroom she ruffled pages, turned out pockets, flipped up pillows, pulled furniture away from the wall to peer behind it. Nothing, nothing pink at all except for a single old sock she found under the bed. Did Katy not like pink? How odd that she hadn't known that.

She twisted her fingers in her long tail of hair and yanked hard: think, stupid. It was afternoon, we were getting ready to leave ... Eyes squeezed shut, she pictured the campground, saw Katy sweeping out the van while she herself policed the campsite, stuffing debris into a plastic garbage bag. And they'd brought the bag home with them, because on their way out they'd found a big truck blocking the trash cans!

Her own garbage can sat in a narrow space between garage and fence. She tossed its lid aside, lifted out the opaque plastic bag and after a moment's fumbling simply upended it, shaking the contents out onto the driveway. A quick stir with one bare foot, and there they were, grease stained but intact. Three little pink stubs, with numbers and penciled-in dates; and under them, the map of the Red Bluff KOA campground, with site number 71 circled. She'd completely forgotten that they'd stayed in Red Bluff Saturday night, for showers and a pizza.

Hands on hips, Meg thrust out her lower lip and sent a

whoosh of held-in breath over her hot face; her heart was pounding as if she'd just run a mile. She shook her head, tucked her treasures into her back pocket and was sweeping up the mess in the driveway when she heard a car door slam on the street, caught the sound of voices before the roar of an engine blotted them out. Gutierrez' men?

Which of her neighbors had been so observant Saturday night? she wondered as she rinsed her hands at the backyard hose. And why had he or she waited until this morning to report observing Dave Tucker? And how did all those neighbors, who seemed to her a relatively ordinary lot, feel about being questioned by the police? Mildly euphoric at having secured her own alibi, Meg wiped her hands on her jeans, stepped into the rubber flip-flops she kept beside the back steps, and descended the steep driveway to the street.

The sun was picking up strength; it now carried warmth enough to bring out the peppery fragrance of the climbing roses on her front-gate trellis. But the sky was still a deep, resonant blue; in Tucson in July, the midday sun bleached the sky nearly white. Blue is nicer, Meg thought, shading her eyes with one hand.

Frank Wingate, Tom Emery, and Maria Mazzini stood before the Wingates' white picket fence, all of them watching a police car pull to the curb in the next block. Meg started across the street, her sandals slapping smartly against her bare heels; three heads swung in her direction, three expressionless faces, three pairs of unblinking eyes.

As her own polite smile congealed on her face, Meg found a fourth gaze, this one round and blue and friendly. "Hi, slugger," she said to the baby. "You're certainly getting to be a big boy."

Frank Wingate turned his bushy, bearded head owl-fashion and clicked his tongue at the baby on his back; nearly bald Frank Junior stretched pink lips wider, exposing six tiny teeth. "Yeah, old Square here is right off the charts, almost too big for his mama to lift and he's not even fat." Frank gave the taut canvas bottom of the baby carrier a loud swat, then cocked his head at Meg.

"So, how come the cops passed you by? You the one who saw the Tucker kid here and brought the fuzz down on your helpless neighbors?"

"No no, I've been out of town for a week; I got home only last night! And they didn't pass me by. That is, Chief Gutierrez talked to me. He's, um, an acquaintance of mine," she finished lamely.

Tom Emery, Meg's next-door neighbor, gave her a doleful smile. "Lucky you," he sighed. "Now *I* worked on my books Saturday night, down at the store, until after 2:00 A.M., but with the wife and kiddie off in La Jolla for six weeks, there's no one to vouch for me. Perhaps," he added, "you and I should arrange to keep an eye on each other, just in case."

"Mm," she replied, returning the smile but remaining out of reach. Little Tom Emery was the kind of man who would bring home a prescription for a sick neighbor, but he was also an inveterate fanny patter.

"The cop didn't go to old Proctor's house either, or to the Nordstroms'. I was out trimming the hedge, so I watched." Frank was intent on his original quest, the identity of the informant. "Before he got to me, he spent quite a while pounding on Miss Luoma's door. Is Felicity off on one of her trips?" he asked, fixing protuberant brown eyes on Meg.

Meg shook her head. "I have no idea. She comes and goes at all hours, and that Mercedes is very quiet. Katy might know." Felicity Luoma, Meg's next-door neighbor to the west, was an artist and local historian and the author of a popular series of children's books. Katy, who had read every volume of North Coast Children, was Miss Luoma's devoted admirer.

"Felicity was probably working and simply chose not to

respond." Maria Mazzini's face was so plump and unlined that Meg often forgot the woman had raised six children right here on Rose Street. "Eleanor was the one, I imagine."

The others gaped at her, and she gave her graying curls an impatient shake. "The officer said that a neighbor coming home from work at midnight saw the Tucker boy . . . on the sidewalk near your driveway, Margaret. Eleanor has a nighttime job; she waits tables at that truck stop when her husband is off with *his* truck."

"Well, it's too bad she didn't mind her own business! I've got better things to do than stand around all day talking to the cops." Wingate glared in the direction of the police car.

"Nonsense," replied Maria. "We should be happy to help the police; heaven knows we'll all sleep better when the murderer is caught. I didn't know the Tucker boy personally. He was two years younger than my Mikey, and of course the Tuckers are Baptists. Poor things," she added obscurely. "But the murder will probably turn out to have something to do with drugs; nearly everything does these days."

Meg glanced at Frank, then at Tom, but both faces were closed; if either had known Dave Tucker, he was not going to volunteer that fact. Suppose Dave had discovered that Frank, an assistant professor of forestry, was cultivating marijuana on one of the university's experimental plots. Or that Tom Emery's handling of controlled substances at his wife's family's pharmacy was less than ethical. She blinked and reined in her thoughts. As Dan Halloran had often reminded her, a vivid imagination was an untrustworthy substitute for a logical mind.

". . . makes me long for the days when Marion and Felicity and I belonged to that touring club," Maria was saying to Tom Emery. "My sweet little Honda bike *never* failed to start. But my miserable Seville is waiting for me again at Costello's Chevron, and I can't seem to locate Ben."

Ben Mazzini was a plumber/junk dealer, a short, burly man whose hands were nicked and notched with old scars, whose trouser-seat always hung a good six inches below his flat butt.

"Ol' Ben is probably hot on the trail of another claw-foot bathtub or galvanized horse trough," muttered Frank, who had built a tall fence between his yard and the Mazzinis'. "Or maybe he's sitting in a bar having a cool one, gettin' in position to feel up the barmaid. That's what I'm going to do when *I'm* an old fart."

Maria's round eyes narrowed. "Motherhood is confining, isn't it, Frank?" she remarked. "But you'd better go change poor little Frank Junior, or Anna will come home to a terrible case of diaper rash. Tom?"

Emery, muttering something about car keys, set off across the street with Maria at his side. "Interfering old . . ." Swallowing the end of his sentence, Frank reached around to touch the canvas supporting his son's bottom. "Yeah, okay," he sighed. "Hey, Meg, Anna will be glad you're back." With a nod he turned toward his own front door.

A testy lot they were today, and who could blame them? Meg suppressed a twinge of guilt and turned her mind instead to Eleanor Nordstrom, who had waited three days to call the police, who must have known Dave Tucker at least by sight or why would she have noticed him? Eleanor was not a jumpy sort; she was young and tough, and chatty. Perhaps she'd be willing to talk to a friendly neighbor. Meg had taken several steps in the direction of the Nordstrom house when she stopped short; Billy Nordstrom's red-white-and-blue Peterbilt tractor stood blocking his driveway. How on earth could she have missed seeing that gleaming monster?

The front door was closed, the front windows tightly curtained. This was not the time, Meg decided, to visit Eleanor. Billy Nordstrom was a hulking young man who glowered at the world from beneath the brim of an aged

Stetson; his grease-colored Levi's and grayish tee shirt usually failed to meet over a hairy bulge of belly. According to Eleanor, Billy's two loves in the world were his truck and his wife; what she'd actually said was, "Billy's two favorite things are trucking and fucking."

About to step into the street, Meg pulled back at the sound of an approaching engine. Marion Watson's little blue Mustang sounded fine now, with no sign of the hiccoughing and snorting that had dismayed its owner the previous week. When Meg diagnosed a simple case of fouled plugs, Marion had responded with profuse thanks and murmurs about "lunch one day."

Now Meg lifted a hand in greeting. With no movement except an upward thrust of chin, the sharp-nosed face under carefully sculptured hair stared straight ahead. The little car gave an accelerating scurry as it passed, spitting several pebbles from beneath rear tires.

The upraised hand felt huge and naked. Meg pulled it back and followed the car with narrowed eyes until it turned smartly into Marion's driveway, directly across from Louise Martin's house. The car door slammed, Marion disappeared through her own front door; and Meg clenched her teeth and locked her knees as a wave of heat washed over her. Dim little polyester bitch, who the *hell* did she think she was?

What Marion was, Meg remembered suddenly, was an employee of the First National Bank of Port Silva, William Tucker's bank. Meg took several deep breaths and set off for her own house, spine so stiff that her normally easy stride was almost a goose step.

• 4 •

Logic, she reminded herself. Marion Watson had just delivered a deliberate, unmistakable snub. Marion Watson was a ninny, and, of herself, unimportant; but Marion was not the woman to make a forceful public gesture all on her own. At the top of the driveway Meg caught one flip-flop on a broken bit of concrete and grabbed at the gate to catch herself. Had Banker Tucker called a staff meeting to announce the identity of his son's killer? posted a notice in the staff lounge? simply whispered the news to his secretary and asked her to pass it on?

And so we segue gently from logic to hysteria. She shut the gate behind her and hurried to the house, impelled by a sharp desire to see Katy, touch her; with some effort she restrained the impulse and merely put her head inside the back door to listen. Katy was still there, and Cyndi with her. Leave them alone.

Backing down the steps with exaggerated caution, she barked one shin, and it was through a shimmer of tears that she surveyed her backyard in search of a useful, mindless activity. The patchy grass was still too wet for mowing. She had not yet bought lumber to replace broken or missing boards in the high fence; and besides, that whole structure had an odd list, as if some of its supports might be rotting.

Never mind symbols and portents, find something to do. Katy's vegetable garden was freshly weeded but looked frowsy, with ragged leaves and chewed-off stems . . . Hah! There was an eminently suitable occupation.

Had Mr. Tucker publicly accused her of murder? she wondered as she carried a sloshing bucket of salt water to the side wall of the garage. And if he had, what could she do about it? She pushed aside trailing strands of ivy and exposed a cluster of snails, voracious little marauders who slid forth each night to ravage Katy's garden. "Mr. Tucker," Meg said, plucking a big snail from among his fellows, "I demand a retraction!" Plop. "A public retraction." Plop, and plop.

And then Mr. Tucker purses his lips, smooths his hair, and says, "Indeed? of what?" And where does that leave you? Plop, plop.

She moved the bucket, found a second huddle of brown shells. Perhaps she should tackle Marion Watson first, find out just what had been said. That for you, Marion. Plop. Or get a lawyer. Plop. Or simply cultivate her garden and wait for the whole thing to blow over, to disappear in the fog. Sure. There was a bubbling splash as she threw in a whole handful at once.

"Margaret?"

The voice from nowhere sent her tumbling back on her bottom. From atop the high board fence where it was balanced like a Halloween pumpkin, a head nodded, fluttering a broad-brimmed hat.

"Lovely day for gardening." Beneath the hat was a fine-skinned face untouched by the sun, almost unmarked by age. Pale-blue eyes were wide, with no hint of suspicion or condemnation.

"Hi, Miss Luoma. Yes, it's a nice day, I guess." She stood up, brushing wet grass from the seat of her jeans.

A tiny pucker of annoyance touched the older woman's brow. "Margaret, I've been wondering, could you perhaps do something about . . . that is, do you know anything about this disagreeable child who's been bothering me?"

Meg cast an involuntary glance in the direction of her own house, and Miss Luoma shook her head, making a gentle clucking noise as she rose higher to rest her arms along the top of the fence. Not levitation, Meg decided, but a ladder.

"No, no, not your Katy, she's quite lovely and never a bother. But for what seemed an hour yesterday, around noontime, this child kept ringing my doorbell. When I didn't answer, she went right around the house, rapped on the back door, and then on the studio door."

"A girl," said Meg, not making a question of it.

"Yes, I believe so. I sneaked a look past the curtains, but I didn't open the door; I was working and I didn't want to buy cookies or anything. Although she wasn't wearing a uniform, and the Brownies or Bluebirds or whatever aren't usually so persistent. No, this was a very . . . chubby girl, blond, in some kind of striped farmer's overall. And I went out to dinner," she continued, exasperation sweeping her voice high, "and when I came home, I think I saw her scurry out of my yard."

"Cyndi." Miss Luoma's eyebrows rose, and Meg added, "It sounds like Cyndi Martin, Louise's older daughter. She's visiting for the summer, and she seems unimpressed by the neighborhood rules."

"Neighborhood rules? How interesting, what are they?"

Meg grinned up at her. "Just a little list I worked up for Katy and her friends. We do not poke around all that interesting stuff in the Mazzinis' yard, we do not roller-skate on Mr. Proctor's sidewalk, and we do not call on Miss Luoma unless we see her out in her yard."

"How very thoughtful of you, Margaret; I'm most appreciative. Well, Louise Martin is an artist herself; I'm sure she'll understand if I ask her to . . . or perhaps you could do that for me, since you apparently know the child?" The tiny frown reappeared as Miss Luoma squinted down at Meg, who thought, Oh, shit.

"You see, I'm terribly busy. I've begun a new book, and I'm helping to prepare a special edition of the whole series, to come out on my sixtieth birthday. And the child was at it again today, I believe, ringing and then knocking, on and on. Really," she said with a long sigh, "I should have stayed at the farm, it was wonderfully peaceful there all weekend, but there's always something I need *here*, in my studio."

For all her sweet face and soft voice, Miss Luoma was relentlessly single-minded when working, probably capable of refusing to notice even a murder. But if she had been away . . .

"I'll speak to Louise, Miss Luoma, although I can't promise it will do any good. But I don't think it was Cyndi at your door today. I think it was a policeman."

"A policeman?"

"You may not have heard that a local boy was murdered Saturday night, a boy named David Tucker. The police learned only today that he was seen in this neighborhood late that evening."

"Good heavens!" Miss Luoma apparently took a step down the ladder; her chin settled to the fence top, to rest Kilroy-fashion between her hands. "I *should* have stayed in Covelo. David Tucker. What a shame, he was a very handsome young man. Although I suppose he may have been a nasty sort; his father certainly was. When William was a boy, he used to lurk outside the old Palace Theater and then rush off to his pastor with a list of the miscreants in his congregation. Those Baptists weren't allowed movies then, you know, especially on Sundays."

That sounded just like Banker Tucker. Perhaps, these days, he lurked outside topless bars. "Well, Chief Gutierrez has no suspects yet, and he says the town is very much on edge."

"Yes, I suppose . . . The farmers!" Miss Luoma said suddenly, triumphantly.

"I beg your pardon?"

"Those hippie farmers, the people who grow marijuana! Do you know, a few months ago I found that they were actually using some of my land? I had to call the

34

county sheriff! Suppose Dave was snooping like his father and came upon some of those people? I believe they're quite fierce; I certainly didn't stay around long after I made my report. I'll phone Vincent right now. I'm sure he'll be interested." The head sank slowly out of sight, and then the voice wafted back. "Oh, and Margaret? You won't forget to mention my little problem to Louise?"

"I won't forget."

"Good."

Meg stared at the old fence for a moment, caught between amusement and irritation. "High-handed old witch," she muttered, but very softly.

It occurred to her that speaking to Cyndi directly might be kinder than approaching her mother, perhaps even more effective. She had one hand on the back doorknob when a shriek split the air, followed by the unmistakable sound of a slap.

Meg was up the steps and through the service porch in what seemed one long leap, to find Katy and Cyndi facing each other in the kitchen. Katy was white faced and rigid; Cyndi, one hand nursing the other, turned at the sound of Meg's entry and quickly backed into the nearest corner.

"I didn't do anything! I was just telling her about this guy, my mom knew him and I've even seen him. And she hit me!"

"Katy?"

"I told her I didn't want to look, but she kept shoving it in my face."

The front page of the *Port Silva Sentinel* lay faceup on the floor. Prominently displayed on its top half was a picture of Dave Tucker, apparently his graduation portrait. Beneath the handsome face, the paper screamed FUNERAL OF MURDERED LOCAL YOUTH in large black letters before trailing off into regular type.

Meg glared at Cyndi, then turned to crouch before her daughter, taking a small fist in each hand. "Katy, I'm sorry. I heard about it only this morning, I haven't had a chance to tell you."

"It's okay, I don't care." Katy's chin came up; she took a step back, disengaging her hands. "That motherfucker, I don't care if he's dead, in fact I'm glad."

"Baby, I don't think . . ." Meg bit her words off short. Katy had suffered bouts of nightmares after Dave's intrusion into their house, had behaved for weeks with a wholly uncharacteristic timidity.

But Cyndi's voice came quickly, prim. "My grandmother says you shouldn't speak ill of the dead. And she certainly wouldn't permit that word."

"Just shut up, Cyndi." Meg spoke through clenched teeth. "People who quote grandmothers are boring. Out of the way, please." She snatched up the paper, twisted it tight, and thrust it into the garbage sack under the sink.

Cyndi, who had once again retreated several steps, now pushed her hands deep into her pockets and tipped her head. "What was so bad about him? Did he do something terrible to Katy? We had lectures at school about things like that, and you're supposed to talk about it if it happens; that's healthier."

Meg looked at the smug pink face which seemed to swell and bob before her eyes. It was eminently slappable, and her own hands itched to slap; they were twisting together like a pair of muscular animals. "That's quite enough, Cyndi," she said, surprised at the evenness of her voice. "Kathy and I are going to have lunch now; it's time for you to go home."

Cyndi cast a hopeful glance at Katy's cold face, then flushed. "Well, whatever else he did, he got murdered. And policemen were talking to everybody this morning but you had the chief of police; I know him because he's a good friend of my mother's. I'll bet he came here himself because he suspects . . . uh, somebody here."

Meg moved forward, but Katy was faster; a stiff-armed, two-handed push with all her weight behind it sent the larger child reeling. "So maybe he's right, so maybe you'd better get out of here!" Another push, then a slow, menacing stalk as she herded Cyndi into the hall. "Go home, go home, go home right now!" Grendel, who'd been watching with interest, uttered a soft growl; Cyndi gave a squeak, snatched the door open, and fled.

.   .   .

"Mommy?" Katy sucked a last crumb of tuna fish from her upper lip, then picked up her sweet pickle and took a delicate nibble. "Mommy, did that policeman really think you killed that . . . creep?"

Meg caught the up-and-down flash of blue, mute apology, and thought, well, at least we can skip the language lecture, aren't trivialities comforting. "Someone saw Dave Tucker near here Saturday night, Katy. And then his father reminded the police about our trouble with Dave, so Chief Gutierrez had to check."

"That's silly. You wouldn't kill anybody, and I'm not big enough." Katy took another bite of pickle and waited politely while her mother recovered from a too-hasty swallow of milk. "Besides, we were in the woods then." Her mouth tucked up in a grim little smile. "Did the policeman believe you, that we were in the woods? Because I can tell him, too, that makes two of us."

"I think he believed me, love. And after he left, I found the campground stubs."

"So okay then." Katy finished the pickle and licked each finger. "But there's one other thing I'd like to know."

"Ask away, little."

"If you're a Good Person"—her voice set capital letters firmly in place—"what are you supposed to do when a Bad Person bothers you?"

"Well, you can tell him you don't like what he's doing and ask him to please stop," Meg suggested. "Or you can try to stay out of his way. Or you can tell someone—your mother or a teacher."

"At vacation Bible school, two boys started having a fight," said Katy, who had decided to attend because her friend Joanna was going. "Then the teacher made them sit down, and she wrote this on the board and made us all copy it. It said—let's see—it said 'Whosoever shall smite thee on thy right cheek, turn to him the other also.' "

"Yes, I believe I've heard that."

"I told the teacher if that was the kind of dumb rule they had, I didn't want to be a Christian."

"Wonderful. And what did the teacher . . . ? No, never mind, I don't want to know." Meg rose, carried her plate to the sink, then turned to look her daughter squarely in the eye. "Sometimes you can slug it out, Katy, but that's not usually the smartest thing to do, because the chances are you'll get hurt. And right now, in this time and place . . . look at me, Katy . . . for now, let's be smart. If anyone gives you trouble I want to hear about it. Do you understand?"

"I guess." Meg drew herself taller, and Katy added quickly, "I understand."

"Fine, remember it. Now, I haven't seen Louise since we got back; I think I'll wander over and talk with her for a bit. Please clear things up in here, and stick around."

In the bedroom she unearthed a pair of sneakers from the closet and exchanged her sweatshirt for a short-sleeved cotton shirt. Before the mirror over the low dresser she unfastened her hair and shook it loose; as she reached for her brush, she noticed that the top drawer of the dresser, prone to sticking, was slightly, crookedly ajar.

Cyndi, the little wretch. Making a grim face at her reflection, Meg fastened her heavy mane tightly at the nape of her neck, then slammed the drawer shut. Anyone searching her bedroom for signs of interesting depravity was doomed to disappointment.

She had just pulled the front door shut behind her when she heard the telephone. By the time she had fished the key from her Levi's pocket and unlocked the door, the ringing had stopped. She leaned inside, listened for a moment.

"Katy? Katy, wasn't that the phone?"

"Yes," came Katy's voice from the kitchen.

"Who was it?"

"Nobody. Just a wrong number."

• 5 •

Big, forthright Louise . . . hard to understand how such a woman could have produced a Cyndi. As she descended her own steep front steps, Meg sketched an ironic salute in the direction of Felicity Luoma's house: Yes, ma'am. Equally hard to imagine Louise living the life she had described to Meg some months earlier: married to an orthodontist, living in Piedmont, and going to wine parties in girdle and high heels. Louise herself did not fret over past mistakes. Life, in Louise's view, should allow a general amnesty for anything you did before age thirty.

This segment of Rose Street, some two miles inland, had been part of the "nice" residential section of an earlier Port Silva. The stucco or clapboard houses, dating from the 1920s and '30s, had no claim to architectural distinction; but large lots with stately rose bushes and rhododendrons and huge old trees conveyed a sense of settled dignity. Louise's house, at the beginning of the next block, was barely visible behind a high fence— redwood-framed panels of flush, narrow boards topped by a miniature shingled roof.

Meg pushed the gate open, noted the closed door and blank windows of the house, and set off along the graveled path leading to a low, skylighted building at the rear of the lot. Here the door was open; she rapped on the frame, and Louise looked up sharply, then produced a weary smile.

"Hey, Meg, come on in." She dropped a wet cloth over a heap of clay, wiping her hands on the legs of her jeans. "It's okay, I'm just fooling around. My commissioned stuff is all ready for the kiln, but my friend Ursula can't get her things here until Saturday, and I hate to fire with less than a full load."

Louise's studio was sturdier and much more orderly than her house. The floor was vinyl over a slightly springy subsurface; the walls were lined with cupboards and with open display shelves deep enough for Louise's big stoneware platters and bowls. A worktable occupied the center of the room, directly under a bank of lights.

"Grab a chair," Louise instructed, "and have a cup of . . . no, let me get you a beer! Jesus, lady, I'm glad you're back, you and Katy. Cyndi's been driving me nuts the whole week."

"Thank you." Meg settled onto a stool and accepted a can of Coors; obviously today was a drinking day. "Ah, about Cyndi. I'm afraid . . ." Louise stiffened and turned slowly from the refrigerator. "Felicity Luoma says Cyndi has been pestering her, prowling around in her yard when she's not home, knocking on her door when she's there. Felicity asked me to ask you to talk to Cyndi. I'm sorry."

"Oh, shit." Louise opened a can of beer and propped her rear against the worktable. "Just shit, is all, this is turning out to be the longest summer of my life. I don't know what to do with that kid, never have." She brushed a hand over her face, leaving a smear of clay on one cheek. "Well, tell Felicity I'll talk, for whatever good it'll do. What about you? Has Cyndi been giving you any trouble?"

Meg hesitated for just a moment before shaking her

head. "Nothing I can't handle. It's an awful age for a girl; I hated myself the summer I was thirteen, and my whole family hated me, too."

Louise was nearly six feet tall, with a broad, fair face under a tousled mop of blond curls. Today the studio's strong lights picked out lines in the face, threads of gray in the curls; there was a slump to the broad shoulders, a sullen sag to the big breasts straining the buttons of the blue work shirt.

"Pick an age, any age, for Cyndi they've all been awful. She is completely screwing up my life. She criticizes my cooking and she criticizes my housekeeping, and I'm having to live like a goddamned nun, I'm so horny I can hardly get any work done. Christ, with Cyndi in the house I feel like I can't even pee without closing the bathroom door!" Louise's grin was shaky, and her eyes glimmered with tears.

"And poor Flower, Cyndi's driving her nuts, too. Can you believe it? that was the clincher when Chaz talked me into this; it would be nice for sisters to get to know each other. Hah! Cyndi's no more interested in Flower than Chaz ever was."

"Oh. Was Chaz . . . ?" Meg closed her mouth. None of her business at all, she'd simply assumed small, silent Flower had a different father.

"Oh, Flower is Chaz's kid," said Louise with a shrug. "God knows how it happened; I was hardly even getting a *look* at his cock by that time, much less any use of it. But poor Flower didn't turn out to be the *boy*, she was just a scrawny, sickly little girl-baby. She needed a full-time mother, and she needed a teat instead of a bottle, which totally messed up the Dr. Martins' busy social schedule and really freaked grandma; I don't know what the hell she thought these were for." Louise slapped the underside of one breast.

"Cyndi mentions her grandmother often," Meg remarked.

"Cyndi was her grandmother's girl right from the start,"

said Louise. "See them together and you'd believe in reincarnation, except I guess the old bitch would have to be dead for that. In fact, old lady Martin is the world's biggest snoop, so Cyndi's behavior around this neighborhood shouldn't surprise me."

"Like the Tuckers," said Meg without thinking.

"Huh?"

"Something Felicity Luoma said when I told her about the murder, Dave Tucker's murder. She said she didn't know Dave but he was probably a nasty sort, because his father certainly had been at that age."

"Dave Tucker was a prick." Louise's eyes, round and hard as pale-blue marbles, disappeared behind lowered lids.

"That's right, Cyndi said you knew him."

The corners of the other woman's mouth twitched downward, and she pointed with her chin to the shelf behind Meg. "That's Dave there, the runner."

The clay figure was perhaps eight inches high. The thrown-back head was smooth and nearly featureless, but neck tendons and chest muscles were sharp and specific, pushing and reaching legs beautifully modeled. Every line of the figure spoke of sweating, lung-bursting endeavor.

"It's beautiful," said Meg softly.

"Two things I'm good at, and clay is one of them. Well, maybe three, I'm a pretty good cook, too." A ghost of her big grin; then Louise picked the figure up, and turned it about in her hands. "I saw him on the high-school track one day; I run now and again, when I'm feeling fat. Anyway, I was kicking around the idea of doing some small bronzes, using clay to start with, and I asked him if he'd like to make a little money posing. He turned out to be a terrific model, one of those . . . who was that Greek guy who fell in love with his own looks?"

"Narcissus."

"Right. That kind of guy makes a hell of a model, he's

so pleased with his body that he'll hold the hardest pose, when an ordinary person would be falling into muscle spasms." She reached past Meg to set the piece back on the shelf.

"So what happened?" asked Meg.

"Huh?"

"How did you find out that Dave was a prick?"

"Want a cigarette?" Louise asked suddenly, picking up a pack of Trues from the worktable. Meg swallowed hard and shook her head; Louise spend some time extracting a cigarette and lighting it. "Three guesses," she muttered, spitting out smoke. "And you'd only need one. He turned down the money and asked for a free fuck instead." She took another deep drag on the cigarette. "In just about those words, like he thought I usually charged."

"Oh." Then perhaps her own judgment had after all been amiss, and the counselor's correct. Perhaps she had completely misinterpreted her classroom encounter with Dave, reading menace into what was merely the awkwardness of a painfully excited adolescent.

"In a saner world . . . or for a nicer kid . . . I might have said what the hell and taken him on," Louise said. "Poor little bastards, they watch TV and go to the movies, and what can they think except everybody else over age ten is getting more than he can handle?"

True. Perhaps those old Baptists were right about movies, Meg thought grimly. "So . . . what did you do to Dave, toss him out the window?"

"As I recall, I declined with thanks. You know, like 'that's a terrific temptation but I couldn't possibly.'" Louise reduced her cigarette to ash in one more long pull and dropped the butt into her empty beer can. "Hey, you must have known the kid, too; the high school isn't that big."

"Yes, I knew him." Meg took a slow moment to drink the rest of her beer. Louise would hear the story from Cyndi anyway. "I'd had serious trouble with Dave, so serious that the chief of police appeared on my doorstep this morning to tell me I was a suspect in his murder."

"A suspect? Jesus, what kind of trouble?"

"Not the kind you had . . . at least, I don't think so. He was failing in my class, and when I refused to change his grade, he got into my house when I wasn't home and frightened Katy."

"Like I said, the kid was a real prick. But you were out of town when he was killed. Tell Vince Gutierrez that I can testify to that."

"Thank you."

Louise sighed, lifted both hands over her head, and arched her back in a long stretch. "You know, it's too bad you met Vince Gutierrez under such lousy circumstances. He's a real sweetie." Her face creased into an eye-squinching grin, with a reminiscent edge that sent a flicker of turbulence along Meg's spine.

"That's hardly the term I'd choose," she snapped.

"Come on. Vince is a good-looking, straight, unmarried guy, probably about, oh, forty-five; it's hard to tell with Latino types. And nice besides. Don't come across many like that these days. Maybe a little serious, but nice."

"Louise, I am not in the market. Thank you."

"Well, you should be. Okay, okay. You don't need a man. But they're fun to have around. *I* think."

"I met Chief Gutierrez some months ago. It was not a pleasant experience; we yelled at each other."

"Sure you did. Vince is always looking for a good fight, just like you."

"I'm not . . . that's ridiculous," Meg said weakly.

"Some people get off on conflict, and some prefer comfort, that's me. Anyway, whether you like him or not, he's a good cop; he was with LAPD for years. He took early retirement and came back here because his mother got sick."

"That was filial of him." Louise blinked; Meg tossed her beer can into a nearby wastebasket and rose from the stool. "Do you know what time your neighbor Marion Watson gets home from the bank? She looked right through me this morning, although she'd been perfectly friendly before. She works for Dave Tucker's father, and I have a feeling he's spreading nasty tales about me and his son."

"She'll pull in around five, unless it's a church night. But I wouldn't pay any attention to Marion," said Louise with a wave of her hand. "You really have to feel sorry for her, poor silly bitch. What happened, about the time Marion couldn't manage to look nineteen any more—and she'd worked that for twenty years—her husband grew a beard and bought a Ferrari and took off with his secretary who *was* nineteen. Isn't that boring?

"In fact, that's something I've wondered about." Propping her elbows on the worktable behind her, Louise leaned back and gazed at the ceiling. "What would the world be like if it was men's gonads gave up around age forty-five, and women's went on? Would we boot the poor droopy old guy out and bring in a teenaged replacement?"

Meg ran a quick parade of students past her inner eye, hesitated over one or two, then shook her head. "Not me."

"Me neither. What a drag. It'd be wham-bang, about ten seconds' worth, with Sting or somebody on the stereo. And you wouldn't even get to lie back and enjoy a cigarette after; you'd have to get up and play volleyball."

The two women grinned at each other; then a sound from the house brought Louise to attention.

"Gotta go. That's Flower, just up from her nap, and Cyndi's off someplace." Louise glanced at her cloth-covered mound of clay, then moved to the doorway and turned off the bank of lights. "Tell Miss Luoma I'll talk to Cyndi good and hard. And besides, she's going home in five . . . no, Chaz and his new wifey are due back from Europe in *four* weeks, hallelujah! And hey, you take another good look at Vince Gutierrez, hear?"

• • •

At about seven that evening Meg followed Katy out the back door, viewed the thick fog, and decided that she'd still rather drive than cook. Besides, she'd promised her daughter Chinese food.

Backing the van down the steep, narrow driveway took concentration. As she finally eased across the sidewalk, Meg thought she caught a flash of movement beside the big rock marking the corner of their yard.

"Katy, was that Cyndi?"

Katy peered, shrugged. "I don't know. Probably."

"What on earth is she doing?"

"She watches."

"Watches? Watches what?"

"People. She's going to be a writer, and she says a writer has to find things out about people."

"She's going to find out that people don't like to find other people skulking about in their shrubbery. Katy . . . ?"

But Katy was staring out her window. "Look, Mommy, there's a police car."

Meg's head snapped around. A tan sedan bearing the Port Silva insignia sat before a house two blocks west of the Halloran home, a house owned by an elderly widow who rented rooms to university students. The car appeared empty, with no light flashing from the bar on its roof. In the drifting, thickening fog the tall old house looked isolated, a dwelling place for ghosts.

"Probably noisy motorcycles again," volunteered Katy. "Mrs. Ahonen says her 'guests' have lots of trouble about their motorcycles."

"Probably," agreed Meg absently. More likely Gutierrez or his men, trying to pick up Dave Tucker's trail.

• 6 •

Meg tossed her windbreaker at a hook on the back porch, toweled the dog's mist-dampened coat and scooped some food into his dish, wincing as the rattle of kibble against metal set off a harmonic echo inside her skull. She'd spent a night short in hours but endless in its succession of horrid dreams, with some subconscious guardian snatching her awake just before each fatal conclusion.

As she had requested, the *Sentinel* paperboy had left two days' papers; she scanned the previous day's issue as she waited for water to boil. The story under Dave Tucker's picture was eulogy and little more, statements from family members and local notables, conventional words along the line of "cut off in the flower of his youth." There followed a listing of Dave's interests: photography, gymnastics, cross-country running, Alpine skiing . . . solitary pursuits all, noted Meg. Then his expressed plans for the future: college, sports, and the ministry.

She snatched up the whistling kettle and poured the filter cone full, grimacing at the notion of Dave Tucker as a loving shepherd, guide, counselor. The story ended with a paragraph stating that the Port Silva police were hard at work on the murder, were following several leads but had as yet no actual suspects. Information from the public was requested.

On an inside page was another picture of Dave, erect and unsmiling next to a pommel horse. And a picture of the family at graveside: Mr. Tucker with pomposity show-

47

ing even through obvious grief, Mrs. Tucker simply a bent, fair head under a lacy scarf, and Dave's sister Jenny, a white face between slanting wings of long straight hair, eyes fixed blankly on something beyond the photographer.

Or on something beyond the world, thought Meg. The girl had been a shadowy, silent figure in Meg's last-period sophomore class, a creature of long, fragile limbs and huge eyes, who always sat near the door. The day after Dave transferred out, Jenny presented Meg with a transfer slip of her own, eyes downcast as she whispered something about an after-school job. Jenny's was a presence so tentative it barely stirred the air, hardly marked the ground; the death of a brother might have erased her completely.

Then again, when it was a brother like Dave . . . Meg wrapped her arms around herself and stared at the fog-misted window, trying to imagine a teenaged girl killing her brother, her older brother. Margaret and Neil Evans, Neil two years the elder, distant and impatient and sometimes unkind to the point of cruelty. Suppose Margaret had loaded one of Neil's guns, and . . . Her imagination balked, the images wouldn't form.

She poured a mug of coffee and took it to the table with today's paper. Nothing on the front page. She found it on page five: a quarter column of print, no pictures, mostly an amplified repetition of the final paragraph from Wednesday's story. On the facing page was an editorial about the rise of violent crime in small towns and rural areas. "We aren't safe anywhere" was the general message. The writer ended by urging the citizenry to increased vigilance . . . stopping just short, thought Meg, of suggesting that every right-thinking person should arm himself.

As she slapped the paper shut, she caught something she'd missed in her first scan: a small box, no head, one of those last-minute inclusions. And hastily written, Dave

Tucker's name appearing only near the end. Her spirits began an upward spiral as she read.

The police were interested in the whereabouts of a young man named John or Johnny Stein, who had come from Oakland in May to take classes at Port Silva's famed Art Institute. A boarder at 1720 Rose Street . . . Mrs. Ahonen's place? the number seemed right . . . he had not been seen there since the preceding Saturday night, his absence not noted until Monday when he failed to report to his part-time job at a local garage. In recent weeks Stein had been seen several times in the company of David Tucker; the police were eager to talk with him.

"Aha! like the English business of 'helping the police with their inquiries,'" said Meg aloud. A suspect, a real, believable suspect! A frequent companion, someone who might have fallen into violent disagreement with Dave over, well, over a girl, or cars, or even drugs, everybody's choice for cause-of-all-ills. Busy with her scenario, she started at the sound of the phone, then leaped to prevent its waking Katy.

"Hello?" she said softly.

"Filthy whore. Filthy, murdering whore." The voice was a slow, measured whisper. "You'll go to hell, you debaser of children, and your foulmouthed brat will go with you." Then a quiet click.

Meg dropped the receiver and lurched down the hall to the second bedroom, bracing one hand against the frame as she listened to the sound of quiet breathing from beyond the closed door. Foulmouthed? Like her peers, Katy could produce half-a-dozen rank terms, but she did so only under extreme provocation. Meg bit down hard on her lower lip as she remembered yesterday's "wrong number," but she withdrew her shaking hand before it turned the doorknob. Let her sleep, get yourself together first.

A metallic blatting hammered at her ears; she lunged

for the telephone, picked the receiver up in both hands, dropped it into its cradle. A notepad lay beside the instrument, and a pencil that proved slippery and awkward; debaser of children, what a peculiarly nasty phrase. She blotted her dripping forehead against a sweatshirt sleeve, blinked twice, and watched her numb right forefinger punch telephone buttons.

Chief Gutierrez' voice was crisp. "Yes, Mrs. Halloran? My sergeant says you asked to talk to me?"

"I've had an anonymous phone call, a filthy anonymous phone call!"

"Just a minute." A muffled clatter, the sound of a door closing. "All right, Meg. Please tell me just what the caller said."

She closed her eyes, swallowed hard against a bubble of nausea, and repeated the words.

"What can you tell me about the voice? Man or woman? Any accent or noticeable speech pattern?"

She tugged at her hair, closing her eyes again as she tried to hear the voice. "Perhaps a woman, although I don't know why I think so, it was just a whisper. No accent that I can recall, but I don't think ... I think whispering is like singing; accents don't show. She just said those few words very slowly and then hung up. I don't think she—it—was a young person, the words didn't sound young. But that's just another guess."

"Meg, I can quote you plenty of statistics about anonymous callers; that almost always they stop at that, just calling. And your caller didn't threaten any specific action. If he, or she, calls again, listen very carefully, let him talk as long as he will. Don't fight with him, just listen. If the calls continue we can put a recorder on your phone, try to get a trace. And you can always have the number changed."

"It had to be Mr. Tucker," she said suddenly.

"Did it sound like Mr. Tucker?"

She sighed. "Well, the words did."

"I'd be surprised if it were Tucker; he's a man for proper procedures and the letter of the law. Besides, he told me he was driving to San Francisco yesterday afternoon, to take his wife to relatives for a few days, and wasn't coming back until tomorrow or Saturday. But I'll call and check. Now," he went on, in brisk tones, "I've got this all down, and I'll tell Lieutenant Svoboda. You get in touch with him if it happens again."

"Svoboda? Why not . . . ?"

"I'm leaving for Oakland in a few minutes. But I'll be back this evening. If it's all right with you, I'll come by. If I can't make it, I'll call to let you know. Just try to stay loose, okay? And call Hank Svoboda if you need help."

Marion Watson! she thought suddenly, a moment later. She punched the first three digits of Gutierrez' number; then she paused, replaced the receiver quietly, and fished her keys from the drawer of the table. If she couldn't handle Marion herself, she should turn in her credential and get a job addressing envelopes. In the kitchen she set a yellow legal pad on the counter, scrawled a note: Katy, I'm paying a call on a neighbor. Back soon.

"Watch!" she whispered to Grendel, as she let herself quietly out the back door.

•   •   •

Fog swirled at her movement, a moist breath against her hot face. She reached the sidewalk and paused at the sound of an approaching vehicle: Ben Mazzini's truck, rattling like a tin can full of rocks, one headlight pointing down. That made it just after eight, and Marion usually left for work at 8:45. Regular dog walking had made Meg familiar with her neighbors' morning schedules.

The double doors of the Watson garage were still closed, but the newspaper was gone from the steps. The front door was a blank wooden panel, front windows heavily curtained with no light showing. Meg stepped onto the porch and heard distant sound, voices and then a familiar

51

snatch of tinny music: a radio. She put her thumb hard against the doorbell.

In the window beside the door a curtain flicked aside, fell back into place. Meg pushed the bell again and held it. Finally there was the click of a lock and the door was pulled open a few inches. The face that appeared in the gap was comically lopsided, one round eye fringed by darkened lashes while the other remained nakedly pale.

"Good morning, Marion," said Meg at once. "Glad I caught you. May I come in?"

"Um, Mrs. Halloran, I'm in the middle of . . ." Marion Watson was at least six inches shorter than her visitor, even in the fluffy high-heeled slippers that clattered now as she backed away.

"I've been thinking about your suggestion that we have lunch," said Meg in cheery tones, "and then when the phone rang just a few minutes ago, I thought perhaps it was you?"

"Your phone? Me?" Marion's face was blank, penciled eyebrows high. Well, scratch that idea, thought Meg. However, as long as I'm here . . .

"Is that coffee I smell?" she asked, moving down the hall toward the back of the house where the kitchen must lie. "If you have a cup to spare, perhaps we could arrange something about lunch."

"Mrs. Halloran. *Mrs. Halloran.* Please, I'm getting ready for work. And lunch, I don't think . . . I've just started on a diet; I'm not eating lunch at all." She paused in the doorway of her own kitchen, an aging Barbie doll in a short dark blue skirt and a shiny white blouse with ruffles cascading down the front.

"Mm," said Meg, distracted for a moment by the kitchen's array of reflecting surfaces. The stove gleamed, the teakettle twinkled, faucets dazzled, the sink was smoothly white. Even the grouting in the tile backsplash seemed to glow. A steaming Mr. Coffee machine, its pot half-full, looked messily out of place.

"And no breakfast either?" A stand like a miniature hat tree held an array of mugs; Meg took one and filled it. "Marion, you'll damage your health. Why don't we meet for lunch at Pure and Simple; they have wonderful salads." She took a sip of coffee and beamed at the other woman. Established less than a year ago by a pair of young faculty wives who missed Berkeley, the restaurant was the most popular breakfast and lunch place in town.

"Thank you, but I'm much too busy today. If I get hungry I'll send out for something."

"Tell you what," suggested Meg, leaning against the counter and crossing her ankles. "To save time I'll come by the bank for you, I'll just pull up out front and honk."

"No, don't do that! Mr. Tucker would . . ." Marion took a deep breath, sending a tremor along her ruffles. "I'm sorry, Mrs. Halloran, but it's nearly time for me to leave, I can't afford to be late."

And here we go. Meg took another sip of coffee, willing her body to retain its relaxed pose. "Mr. Tucker would what?"

"Mr. Tucker is a fine Christian man, a deacon in our church. He gave me a job when I was, um, alone, even though I hadn't worked since John Junior was born. And he and Reverend Kindelstadt worked out a new mortgage, so I could keep my house. He understands that woman is the . . . the weaker vessel and needs help." Brimming with tears and bitterness, the mismatched eyes were no longer funny.

"And after all," Marion went on, drawing herself up and blinking rapidly, "after all, I have a teenaged son of my own. Or I had, he's twenty now, and away at college. But if I'd ever heard that a teacher of his had tried to, well, uh . . ." Her voice trailed away.

"Had tried to *what?*" snapped Meg. She set the coffee mug down with exaggerated care and drew herself to her full height.

Two backward steps brought Marion hard against a

chair; she sat down abruptly. "I have nothing to do with this, you have no right to be here. Go away, Mrs. Halloran, or I'll . . ."

"You'll what? I'm between you and the door, you and the telephone. And I'm much bigger than you are, and much, *much* more angry."

Small hands fluttered in a warding-off gesture; Marion pulled them back and twisted them together in her lap.

"I'm alone, too," said Meg slowly through clenched teeth. "My husband was killed by a drunk driver. But he didn't think I was a weaker vessel, and he'd expect me to protect myself and my daughter from liars, and from cowards who make anonymous phone calls."

"But I'm not . . . I don't lie, I've never ever made an anonymous call." She ran both hands through her hair, causing a tinkling fallout of metal clips.

"But someone has, Marion," said Meg softly. "And yesterday you looked at me as if I were wearing a great big scarlet letter. Why?"

Marion sniffed, looking up at the electric clock over her sink. "I'll be late for work." It was complaint as a matter of form; she found her half-empty mug on the table and cast a timid eye in the direction of the pot. Meg snaked out a long arm, picked up the pot, and poured.

"Thank you." Marion straightened her spine and set her feet together. "Mr. Tucker was late yesterday, we hadn't expected the poor man to come in at all. When I went in with his coffee, he was on the phone; he had one hand over his eyes and didn't see me at first. I heard him say, 'That woman, that teacher, she's to blame; I should never have listened to her.'

"I didn't know who he was talking about," she added with a quick glance upward at her listener. "I gave him his coffee, and said something about how sorry we all were. He wiped his eyes, and thanked me. Then he said, 'Marion, if that boy of yours ever gets into trouble and needs you to believe in him, be sure you do it; don't let

liars and troublemakers blacken his name and break his
spirit.' "

After a moment, Meg said, "And that's all?"

"Well. Not quite." Marion sipped her coffee and then
cradled the mug in her lap. "When I went back to the
outer office, I guess I must have mentioned what Mr.
Tucker had said. And one of our new girls was there,
Jeanine Lester, and she said the teacher was Mrs. Halloran.
She said that the reason Dave dropped out of your class
was that you'd tried to, um, seduce him; Jeanine knew
Dave from the youth group at church."

"And that is a rank, outright lie!"

"Well, that's all, that's all I know." Marion set her coffee mug aside and prepared to rise. "Now if you don't
mind, I'd like to finish dressing; if I hurry, I won't be
more than a few minutes late."

"Certainly. But since you've been so helpful, let me
help *you* with a bit of advice."

"I don't believe I need your advice, Mrs. Halloran."
Marion stood up, squared her shoulders, and twitched
her skirt straight.

"But I believe you do," Meg said with a grim smile. "It
is illegal, as well as immoral, to accuse someone publicly
of a crime, unless you can prove your accusation. And it
is illegal to accuse a woman, at least, of being unchaste;
isn't that an archaic term?"

"But I didn't, at least not publicly, at least I don't think
I did." Once again Marion seemed very small, her face
damp and oily-gray above her white blouse.

"If that's true, you have nothing to worry about," Meg
told her. "Thank you for the coffee. I'll let myself out."

For a moment, as she trudged up the street, she felt
like someone who'd gone mouse hunting with a .30-06.
Then she lifted her head to see her small brown house
shouldering aside remnants of fog, giving off a few steamy
breaths of its own as vagrant rays of sunlight touched its
damp roof. Men like to make rules, her husband had

remarked one day, for wars as well as for games. Woman are guerrilla fighters; what they care about is getting the job done. Right, Danny.

.   .   .

Katy was fixing herself breakfast. Meg watched as she set a plastic mug of milk on the table, then slid a cheese-covered flour tortilla from griddle to plate. "Mommy, are you sure you don't want one?"

Meg shook her head. "I told you I'm not hungry, sit down and eat. Katy, yesterday . . . ?"

Katy settled into her chair, flicking her gaze across the littered sink counter before turning it on her mother. "I guess you don't feel good. I guess you drank a lot of wine last night."

"I stayed up late reading, I drank a lot of wine. I will probably do the same tonight. Look, sweetie, let's just keep in mind who's the mommy and who's the kid around here. Okay?"

"Okay." Katy's shoulders twitched in the beginning of a shrug; she caught her mother's expression and thought better of the gesture. "Okay. But I can say what I think, can't I?"

"You may, so long as you say it politely. But you may not nag. Katy, what did that wrong-number caller say yesterday?"

A quick flash of icy blue; then Katy turned her eyes to her plate. "Oh, nothing. I don't remember."

Meg pulled a folded slip of paper from her pocket and reached across to lay it beside Katy's plate. "Was it something like this?"

Face tight, Katy inspected the scrawled words. "Pretty much, except he said, 'Your mother is a whore,' and . . . Mommy, what does 'debaser' mean?"

"Damager, spoiler. Katy, what did you say?"

"I told him to fuck off. I know I'm not supposed to say that word, but . . ." A real shrug this time, and then a wide-eyed, beseeching look. "Mommy, are you sure he's dead? Because that's the way he talked to me before."

"I promise you, baby, Dave Tucker is dead. The chief of police told me he's dead, and I saw a picture of his funeral in the paper. It was not Dave Tucker on the telephone. Katy?" Meg stretched her hand across the table, palm up, and Katy gripped it. "Katy, when someone is nasty to you, you have a perfect right to be nasty in return. But you have to tell me about things like that; you must never lie to me."

"I didn't lie." She pulled her hand away and sat back, picking up the last wedge of cheesy tortilla. "Anyway, I didn't mean it to be a lie, I just didn't want to talk about it. And you were worried enough already."

"Damn it, Katy, it *adds* to my worry to find you keeping things from me, important things. You play it straight, little kid, or I'll ship you off to your grandmother before you can even blink; at least then I'll know you're safe."

"Oh, Mom." Katy swallowed her last bite, licked her fingers, then took a paper napkin from the basket Meg pushed across the table. "Mommy, did you know Eleanor was going to have a baby?"

"I don't remember hearing that. Who told you?"

"Eleanor did; she said she'll hire me to baby-sit. Too bad it's going to be a boy."

Meg raised her eyebrows, and Katy went on. "She says it's sure to be a boy, because the Nordstroms always have boys, never any girls, just lots and lots of boys."

"Wonderful," said Meg, picturing a neighborhood awash with tiny Billy Nordstroms propelling tiny trucks along the sidewalk. They'd probably be born in tiny tee shirts with a miniature cigarette pack rolled up in each right sleeve.

"But I don't know if I want to baby-sit. I think Eleanor's kind of dumb. She talks dirty even when she's not mad."

I can just imagine, thought Meg, and blinked as Katy said, "Mommy, do we have a gun?"

"No, we certainly don't have a gun. Your father and I don't—didn't believe in owning guns, Katy. Except for hunting, of course, if that's something you like to do."

"Eleanor says people should have guns to protect themselves, Billy brought her one. She showed it to me."

No baby-sitting. "Katy, I think it would be better for you to stay away from Eleanor's, please."

"Oh, it was okay. It was like a cowboy gun, with a long skinny front and this fat piece in the middle that goes around. That part pushes out sideways and you can see for sure that all the little bullet places are empty. She let me—"

The sound of the phone lifted them both out of their chairs; Meg waved Katy back and ran for the hall. But it was only Cyndi.

"Just remember what I said, kid," she murmured as she handed her daughter the phone. "Truth, or exile to Tucson. Get it?"

"I get it, I get it."

She poked her head into the kitchen moments later. "Mommy, Cyndi wants me to come over. Her mother is working and she's supposed to baby-sit Flower."

"Um. Okay, love, but take your key. I haven't shopped for groceries since we got back to town; I think I'll venture out to stock the larder." Venture out was about it, or perhaps sally forth, she thought as she listened to the front door close behind Katy. Sally forth to find out how fast, how widely, villainous rumor spread in Port Silva.

• 7 •

Safeway, Meg thought suddenly. In the big, newish shopping center down at the south end of town, where two highways met. There wouldn't be a local in the place; she could buy her groceries in peace. She backed down to the sidewalk, paused to peer around her like a rabbit about to leave its burrow, and killed the engine. Another fumbling start, the acrid stink of gasoline; the flooded engine would need time to settle. Hands on the wheel, she sat staring straight ahead, sweat trickling down her temples and along her spine. She was seriously disappointed in her own character.

Now. Stupid. Start your car and drive away. Do not look back, do not for God's sake run over that cat. There's a policeman just getting out of his car at Mrs. Ahonen's; don't duck your head, you silly bitch, you haven't done anything wrong. Safeway indeed, what would Dan say? What would your father say?

He'd say, Maggie, never start the fight, but make sure you finish it. He'd say, Come home with your shield or on it. Meg turned north on Main Street and headed for the center of town and Silveiras' General Store. "He'd say 'Fuck 'em all!' " she said aloud, and then thought, no, probably her seventy-five-year-old father wouldn't say that.

She pulled into the parking lot behind the sprawling, tacked-together wooden building. The Silveira family had started out before the turn of the century with a tiny grocery store, had worked and added on and employed the entire family in the business until the store was a supermarket in all but name. Meg had heard that the Silveiras actually owned the block: the Mazzinis' hardware-plumbing store, Tom Emery's small pharmacy, and the bakery and coffee shop run by the Arminos.

Okay, lady, chin up. Your strength is as the strength of ten because your heart is pure. More or less.

Dim and low of ceiling, with an occasional, startling slant or half-step as the floor changed levels, the place looked and felt like a small country store until the looker calculated the extent of the space, the variety of goods offered. Meg pushed her cart up and down aisles, forcing herself to meet the eyes of each person she encountered. Familiar face, giving her a nod and half-smile; complete stranger, distant nod; familiar face, no reaction. Big smile from Mr. Maher the butcher, who conveyed best regards from his son the football player . . . with no undertones Meg could detect.

"Mrs. Halloran, good to see you!" Mr. Silveira himself manned the first checkout counter, looking like a silver-maned pirate; Meg always wondered whether he dyed the black brows and mustache. "And how's my best little girlfriend?"

"Katy is fine, thank you, Mr. Silveira." Mr. Silveira's granddaughter Kimmie was Katy's dearest friend.

"Good." He whisked items from the cart and played the silent buttons on his modern cash register. "You tell her I haven't forgotten; before school starts we'll get that tree house finished, the three of us."

Weather, baseball, fishing, his grandchildren . . . he kept up a steady, low-toned chatter that had a distinctly soothing effect on Meg. Mr. Silveira was a former city councilman, he was on the board of the Art Institute, he rode his gray Arabian mare with the sheriff's posse in Port Silva parades. If rumors were widespread, they'd surely have reached him.

He peered at his machine, read off the total. "Family

ganged up and made me install the computer stuff," he said with a sigh, "but the damned little red numbers are hell on old eyes. Charlie!" he bawled as he set the final bag in the cart, "get it in gear, boy; take Mrs. Halloran's stuff to her car."

"Charlie, when did you get back?" Meg asked as she surrendered the cart to a slim youth of medium height. "Kim told Katy it would probably be the end of the month, and we've been counting the days."

"Oh, the rest of them aren't back yet. Well, they're back from Hawaii," said Charlie Silveira, Kimmie's older brother, "but now they're off camping. You want these in the back here?" He slid the side door open and began to stash the bags neatly. "Hawaii was okay, terrific in fact," he went on, "but I've done that family camping scene too many times. Marshmallows make my teeth ache, and no matter where I sit, smoke blows in my face. Besides, Grandpa needed help at the store, not many kids around this summer. There you go." He slammed the door.

It occurred to Meg that Charlie was the first student she'd come across since hearing about Dave. He was younger than Dave, would be only a junior this year, but he had lived in Port Silva all his life. "Charlie, did you know Dave Tucker?"

Charlie straightened, and for just a moment a frown disturbed his smooth brow. A low-keyed boy whose mother was Japanese-American, he had a face much less mobile than that of his ebullient grandfather. "I guess everybody knew Dave."

Meg leaned against the van and looked directly at him, counting on his good manners and her status as his teacher to keep him in place.

"Did you like him?"

The boy shrugged, his eyes sliding past her face.

"*I* didn't like him," Meg said, "for good reason. Now his father is suggesting that I was somehow involved in his murder."

Charlie jammed his hands in his hip pockets. "That's pretty dumb, people won't pay any attention to that."

"Someone is paying attention. Katy and I are getting anonymous phone calls."

"I'm really sorry, Mrs. Halloran." Charlie straightened, shook his hair back. "I wish I knew something to help. Look, I gotta go, Grandpa'll be needing me."

Meg drew her mouth tight as she watched his departing back. He was walking so fast that he had to execute a fast side step to avoid running head-on into Val Armino, who had just stepped out the back door of her bakery with a coffee cup in her hand.

"Hello, Val," said Meg absently, still frowning after Charlie. "How's Dom Junior? Getting ready to pack for Stanford?" Dom Junior was Armino number three (of nine), a handsome, affable boy whose excellent mind was often overwhelmed by his glands.

Val Armino had a trim figure, flowing dark hair, and a classically oval face. As she met Meg's eyes, her own eyes narrowed, her lips thinned, and she flushed an ugly, mottled red. "Dom Junior will be going to Holy Names," she snapped.

"But he was so proud he'd been accepted at Stanford," breathed Meg. "You know, there is financial aid available, and the fact that Dom is from such a large family would probably make him eligible . . ."

"We could afford Stanford!" Val spit the words out. "What we can't afford is any more risk to our children's immortal souls!"

"I beg your pardon?"

"Big Dom kept saying parochial schools, but I thought in a small town, where I went to public school myself . . ." Val looked at the cup in her hand, grimaced, and poured the dark fluid into a nearby trash can. "But that was when it *was* a small town, when our teachers were decent local people. The rest of my boys will go to the brothers at Saint Mary's, believe me." She spun on her heel and stalked to the bakery door.

"Mrs. Halloran, don't . . . don't let her bother you." Charlie materialized at Meg's elbow. "See, Mary Beth Healey's gonna have a baby, and she says Dom is maybe the father. So everybody's mad at Dom."

"If Val Armino thinks it was my indecent foreign influence that set Dom off, I'd say she hasn't been paying attention for two or three years." Meg's voice shook, and she widened her eyes against the threat of tears. Val served on every possible school committee, library committee, interfaith committee; she was ideally placed to receive and amplify nasty stories.

"Hey, Mrs. Halloran . . . look, you don't want to pay attention to stupid talk." Charlie was all Silveira now, chivalrous male intent on soothing distressed female. "See, I don't really know much about Dave Tucker, but I'll tell you what there is. Mainly kids didn't like him, because he was never easy, you know? He thought he was better than everybody. Sometimes he got guys to hang out with him because he always had money and a car, but nobody really liked him."

"Dave's father told the police that his son had no enemies, no problems, had never had any trouble except with me."

Charlie concentrated on the toes of his boots. "Like I said, I never had anything to do with him, and I didn't hang out much with seniors." He sighed and lifted his glance, black eyes unreadable. "But I know that sometime last fall a bunch of guys beat Dave Tucker up, bad enough so he didn't go anyplace for a few days. I don't know who they were or why they did it. I really gotta go now, Mrs. Halloran. Tell Katy that Kimmie really misses her and she'll be home the end of next week." He swung around and set off at a trot toward the store.

Meg climbed into her van and drove home on the

strength of well-trained reflexes. It was a very peculiar story Charlie had told her. In Tucson, say, or in San Francisco, getting beaten up might be accounted part of the adolescent male's daily risk, hardly worthy of comment. But in a town the size of Port Silva, surely the banker would expect his pampered son to be safe from such hazards. Why hadn't daddy called out the National Guard? Why had Gutierrez failed to mention such a beating?

"Shit," she muttered as she realized she had just driven past her own house. She made a wide, defiant U-turn at the next intersection. Recently her life seemed populated by liars and manipulators. Except for Charlie; she did believe Charlie.

◆ 8 ◆

"But the program isn't over until late, Mommy, like maybe ten-thirty."

"All right, Katy, but I don't want you out alone at that time of night." The telephone bell broke in; Meg reached for the receiver. "If Louise isn't free when you're ready to come home, you call me. Yes, hello."

Gutierrez' voice in her ear was harried, weary. He had just returned to town, had some business yet to accomplish; but he would like to talk with her and tomorrow looked tight. Ten o'clock tonight, perhaps, if he promised not to keep her long?

At nine-thirty Meg set aside the last of several novels she'd been trying to read, gave a jaw-cracking yawn, and focused print-blurred eyes on her outstretched body. Faded sweatshirt, jeans grass stained at the knees: hardly appropriate attire for receiving the chief of police, either officially or socially.

She pawed through her closet in mounting irritation. Shirtwaists seemed too schoolteacherish, Levi's too casual, a favorite tunic too low cut. And damn and blast Louise Martin. She finally unearthed an old caftan with a mandarin collar and a discreetly slit neck. Flowing, not clinging, made of soft cotton in stripes of silvery blue and gray and cream, it was just the sort of thing a dignified middle-aged lady might wear of an evening in her own home.

"Goddamned game playing," she snarled at her flushed reflection as she brushed her hair into submission. She plucked a tortoiseshell clip from her jewel box and fastened her hair back; reaching out to close the box, she saw her old high-school class ring and thought, Well, of course!

It wasn't just Louise's suggestions, nor some random, time-triggered lust of her own. Vince Gutierrez took her back twenty-five years to the "Mexican" boys, gloriously male and absolutely forbidden to Tucson's nice "white" girls. The doorbell rang; she started and grinned at herself. Not that any of them had been interested in Margaret Evans, who was not only a Protestant gringa but much too tall.

She opened the door, surveyed her visitor, and nodded; got it, nice to have one answer at least. And she was no longer too tall.

"Uh, am I late?" Gutierrez blinked against the light. "I stopped by the station for a shower; maybe I let the time get away." He moved past her and set a paper bag on the telephone table, eying the silent instrument as he pulled off his windbreaker. "Any more calls?"

She shook her head. "Not yet. But the one I reported was the second. Katy took one yesterday, same sort of thing. She hadn't told me because she didn't want me to worry."

His mouth drew down in a grimace of distaste. "If it rings while I'm here, I'll get it; I left your number with Svoboda. Oh—I brought a bottle of wine," he added, lifting the bag. "Long day, last stop. I hoped you wouldn't mind."

"Lovely idea," she murmured as she led the way to the kitchen. Good thing she'd taken the trouble to change. Gutierrez wore a trim plaid shirt, clean, pressed Levi's, polished saddle-colored boots. Neat but not gaudy; friendly. "No big breaks yet, I take it?" she asked, handing him a cork-puller and then taking a pair of stemmed glasses from the cupboard.

He shook his head glumly. "We're working one good lead, but I figure we've got a fifteen-day deadline, or actually less by now."

"Deadline? Whose?"

"The town's." There was a subdued pop as he drew the cork from the bottle of white zinfandel. "We're up to our . . . we're buried in reports of handgun purchases. Most of the old-timers have long guns of one kind or another; as soon as the fifteen-day waiting period is past, many of our more recent citizens will be armed with handguns. Bang bang."

Meg hugged her elbows, watching him pour the wine. "Eleanor Nordstrom showed Katy a gun Billy got for her. Katy says it's a cowboy gun, a long-barreled revolver."

"That's very interesting; I don't believe I've seen any paper on that one," he replied grimly.

"Oh, wait. Speaking of paper, I have something for you." She pulled open a drawer beside the sink, retrieved her little alibi-packet, and spread it out on the counter.

He bent to peer at the display. "Receipts, dated, and . . . odometer readings? Great. Look, here's what you do. Take those downtown tomorrow and photocopy them, then put the originals away somewhere safe. Drop the photocopy at my office."

There was a clatter of feet on the front steps, the sound

of the door hitting the wall. "Mommy? Why is there a police car here?" Katy lurched to a stop in the kitchen doorway, planted her feet. "My mother didn't kill anybody."

"Hello, Katy. I know she didn't."

"Then why are you here?" she demanded. "Why aren't you out catching the murderer, or that creep who keeps bothering us on the telephone?"

"Kathleen Elizabeth Halloran . . ." intoned Meg, but Gutierrez broke in.

"We're trying, Katy, I promise you. I have thirty-five men working for me, and we're all trying hard."

"Katy?" said Meg in ominous tones.

"Okay then, I'm sorry I was rude. But I wish it would get over with, it makes me tired." Her voice wobbled, and Meg came to give her a kiss.

"So go to bed, baby, and sleep tight. I'll try to think of something interesting for us to do tomorrow."

As the bedroom door closed, Meg picked up the glasses and led the way into the living room. "I intend to see Mr. Tucker tomorrow," she said as she settled onto the couch, tucking her feet under her.

Gutierrez set the wine bottle on the hearth and stood looking around. "Nice room," he remarked, "sort of a lived-in library." The room was large and well proportioned, with white walls and dark oiled floors. Facing the street was a big bay window draped in deep red; a stone fireplace dominated the outer wall, flanked by a pair of small, high windows. And books: filling the shelves beside the fireplace, stacked on the mantel, spilling across the window seat.

"Well, yes, I've been trying to work, and . . ."

But Gutierrez wasn't listening. "Why don't you let me deal with Tucker?" he suggested as he sat down in the wing chair beside the couch. "The man was in bad shape the last time I saw him, balanced on a very thin edge." Meg's right hand cut the air in a sweeping, vicious chop, and he sat back, startled.

"Don't talk to me about poor Mr. Tucker," she said through her teeth. "He's telling people that I lied about his son and ruined the boy's life. And his employees are passing around the story about my making passes at Dave; I browbeat *that* tasty item out of Marion Watson today. Then," she hurried on, waving off Gutierrez' attempt at speech, "I saw Val Armino in town, and she virtually accused me of introducing her son to sex. Dom Junior, if you can imagine it! That kid was getting so much action he sat through every class with half-closed eyes and a satisfied smile."

Gutierrez' expression wavered between sympathy and amusement. "Yeah, the Arminos and the Paolis. Val was a Paoli, and she's probably having guilty memories. My baby brother graduated with Val; he says she left a whole trail of satisfied smiles."

Meg looked up from her wine glass with a snort of disdain. "I don't give a damn about Val Armino's sexual history. I'm interested in my reputation and my job."

He rose to refill her glass, touching her shoulder lightly with his free hand as he poured. "Sorry, I know none of this is funny. And I'm not making a case for Tucker, just trying to look at your best options." He sat down, propping a booted ankle on a bent knee. "Personally the guy is a pious jerk, but he *is* a successful businessman; he has a lot of friends, and his bank holds a lot of mortgages and business loans. And a slander suit is a tricky thing; people tend to hear the accusations and forget the results.

"What I'm trying to say is, you could be making a big mistake by going in there for a public showdown." He raised his eyebrows, lifted his shoulders in a half-shrug. "If I were you, I'd sit tight, or hire a lawyer and send him in. Tucker will call me the minute he gets back to town, and I'll tell him a few things about slander. I can also tell him we found Dave's prints on the envelope of that letter."

"Ha!" She sat straighter, then frowned. "Just the envelope?"

"Yeah, the letter had no clear prints, just smears. Nothing on the mailbox, either; I had a man check it this afternoon. You weren't here, but I didn't think you'd mind."

"Feel free, everyone else does."

"Anyway, it is significant but not conclusive. Can you be sure the letter was put there Saturday? By the other mail?"

She shook her head. "I had my mail held at the post office."

"Well. No one else on the street has any connection to the boy, so far as we can tell."

"How sensible of them all," said Meg tartly. "And have you learned anything about the missing Johnny Stein?"

He stared at her a moment, then took a sip of wine and sat back with a wry grin. "Well, hell, none of it's really privileged information. Stein's parents split up years ago. Daddy is a businessman in Chicago, sends a chunk of money when it occurs to him. Mommy travels; last card the kid had was from someplace in Alaska. The mother grew up in Port Silva; the kid's aunt thinks that's why he came here. The aunt is a single lady, the father's older sister, and Johnny lived with her in Oakland, off and on anyway."

"Has she heard from him?"

"Nope. Says he'll probably turn up on the doorstep one day, she's not going to worry about it."

"That all sounds very . . . sad."

"I guess it is. He's just a kind of blank. Everybody had to think a minute to remember who Johnny Stein was. Finished high school but just barely; no trouble, just poor attendance and lack of effort. I didn't locate any real friends. Had a minor police record: drunk in a public park once, couple of marijuana busts, picked up on suspicion of holding something bigger but that was dismissed. Only unusual things about the kid were his big Kawasaki cycle and some expensive photographic gear; that's the way he spent his dad's money."

"The newspaper article said Dave was interested in photography," Meg said, remembering.

"Right. In fact, he and Stein apparently met in a photography course at the Art Institute this summer. But the teacher says Stein was the one with the serious interest, Dave was just fooling around. We figure it was the bike that attracted Dave; that was the one thing his parents refused to let him have." He looked with surprise at his empty glass and rose to fill it, then remained standing, leaning against the mantel.

"So that's it for Stein, all I know so far."

"Well." Meg cleared her throat. "More or less by accident, I came across a few bits of information."

He raised his eyebrows.

"I learned that Dave Tucker made . . . Louise Martin told me that Dave Tucker made a pass at her."

"When?"

"Sometime in the spring. She hired him to model, and she said he didn't want money, he wanted sex." Meg frowned at her wine glass, swirling the pinkish liquid. She still had trouble with that story, with such a direct approach on the part of that peculiar boy. And why had easy-going Louise been so irritated? "Louise said that if he'd been a nicer kid she might have taken him on."

Gutierrez threw his head back for a bark of laughter. "That's Louise, always right to the point. You know, we haven't turned up any sign of a girlfriend his own age. And Louise says this was in the spring." He turned a speculative gaze on Meg. "Maybe the kid was determined to work something up with an older woman . . . first you, then Louise, then . . . who?"

To her astonishment, Meg was offended at this neat bracketing of herself with Louise Martin. "I can only say that, to me, Dave Tucker's motives remain a mystery," she said, biting off each word. "But perhaps I should defer to Louise and her wider experience."

Gutierrez turned to face her fully, his eyes cold. "Casting Louise as the town whore? That's the kind of crap I'd expect from the Tuckers." His voice was harsh, and his boot heels scraped on the bricks of the hearth as he drew himself up stiff backed and foursquare. Grendel, lying in the entry hall, lifted his head from his paws and gave a soft whine; the big shoulders hunched as he prepared to rise, his eyes on Gutierrez.

"Grendel, no!" snapped Meg. "Down, you idiot." The dog let his legs slide forward, dropped his head, and gave one sad thump of his tail.

"Jesus!" Gutierrez bent very slowly to lift the wine bottle. "Will he mind if I have a drink?"

"He won't mind at all, poor thing. He's embarrassed, just look at him. I'm embarrassed. Apologies from both of us."

"And from me." They exchanged polite smiles, mutual flags of truce.

"Okay, so what else? You said you found out 'a few things,' " Gutierrez added as he returned to his chair.

"Oh. Well, first of all, it appears that David always had money, so kids would sometimes spend time with him even though they didn't like him."

"We turned that up, too. But it looks like all of it came from his parents; that kid got an allowance of $500 a month plus the use of the family credit cards. Can you imagine it? My mother used to feed a whole family on less than $500 a month."

"Um. All right, one more thing. Let me be sure I get this right, just the way I heard it," said Meg, narrowed eyes on her wine glass as if she were seeing pictures in the fluid. "Sometime last winter 'a bunch of guys' beat Dave up, beat him badly enough so that he stayed home for several days."

"Goddammit to hell!" Gutierrez spoke through clenched teeth as he fished his small notebook from his shirt pocket. "It sure as shit wasn't reported, and Tucker's said nothing about it in all the time I've— Where did you hear this?" He waited a moment, then said softly, "This is a murder investigation, remember? Now I promise you I don't get off on pushing people around and I don't reveal private information unless I have to. But I need to know who you talked to."

Meg looked at him. Poised on the edge of his chair, he looked like a powerful and very hungry hawk who'd just spotted a fieldmouse. Poor Charlie, what a way to repay his kindness. "All right, but . . . all right. Charlie Silveira told me, reluctantly. But he said he didn't know who the guys were, nor why they did it." About to add that she believed him, she closed her mouth. It was an arcane world teenagers inhabited, hedged about with rules and laws that changed frequently in everything but their exclusiveness. Charlie had probably told her just as much truth as he felt she was entitled to.

"I know Charlie, and I'd be surprised if he's in any trouble. But," said Gutierrez as he rose, "I'm going to call him right now."

Devoutly wishing herself elsewhere, Meg in fact heard only murmurs; but Gutierrez was back almost at once. "Charlie is not available," he told her, picking up the wine bottle. "Shall we finish this off? Charlie, it seems, has gone camping."

"Camping?" Meg frowned as she held out her glass. "Thanks. Gutierrez, I saw that kid at what, 11:00 A.M., and he told me quite specifically that he hated camping, he had come home to help his grandfather in preference to going camping with his family."

"Perhaps something better than a family camping trip turned up," said Gutierrez mildly. "Funny thing, the high-school kids seem to be very thin on the ground right now, especially the older ones. At any rate, Mrs. Halloran ma'am," he said, raising his glass to her, "my sincere thanks for your help. That is the very first breach in the brick wall; *I've* gotten zilch from every kid I've talked to."

"The kids are more likely to talk to me," Meg said.

"Except I suppose they won't be any longer, not after you get hold of Charlie."

"Don't worry. Charlie Silveira gave you information because he chose to. He's a smart boy, he had to know it wouldn't stop there. You go ahead and make discreet inquiries among your students. Just remember to back off at the first hint of trouble, and call me." He set his wine glass on the mantel, looked at his watch, and tried to stifle a yawn.

"Getting late. I'm tied up tomorrow with the DA, and probably Saturday, too; but I promise I will find time to talk to Tucker tomorrow, explain to him about slander. Also about concealing pertinent facts from the police." Meg followed him into the entry hall and retrieved his windbreaker from the closet.

"Still foggy out," he remarked, peering through the small window in the door. "Probably no one but Katy has noticed that there's a police car parked in front of your house." He grinned at her involuntary grimace.

"Still, just in case, let me take you to dinner Saturday night. That way the town will know this is basically a social relationship."

"Tricky for you if it should turn out I did it," she muttered. "No, I really can't, Katy . . ."

"Please. There's a good Italian place up-coast a ways. I think you'd like it. By then we may even have Stein, and something to celebrate. And I have a number of nieces and nephews who baby-sit; I'll corral one. Does sex matter?"

"I beg your pardon?"

A flash of white teeth. "Would you prefer a niece or a nephew?"

"I haven't said . . . no, in this instance sex does not matter."

"Fine. Let's say seven, unless something comes up, in which case I'll call. That's a nice dress." He had his hand on the doorknob when the telephone bell sounded.

"Go ahead," she said in response to his questioning look.

She heard "Gutierrez here," and then, "Shit! Where? How long ago? All right, I'll meet them there."

His face was grim when he returned. "A nervous house-wife on Juniper heard noises in her backyard. So she got her husband's shotgun, pointed it out the back door, and fired both barrels. She thinks she hit something, but she can't see in the fog and she's afraid to go out."

"She just . . . opened the door and pulled the trigger?"

"That's the story at this point. Talk to you later—or Saturday night." He was out and down the steps into the fog before she could reply.

◊ 9 ◊

They've done it, they've caught him! Meg ran up the steps holding the plastic-shrouded Saturday *Sentinel* before her like a trophy.

In her living room she spread the paper out on the coffee table and felt her spirits plummet. The two-column picture on page one, the name "Johnny Stein" beneath it in boldface, appeared at the behest of Lieutenant Henry "Hank" Svoboda of the Port Silva Police. Lieutenant Svoboda asked that Port Silvans (a) report at once the sighting of anyone resembling the boy in the picture, and (b) exercise caution in the event of such a sighting, under no circumstances attempting to approach the person.

"Read 'May be armed and dangerous,' " Meg muttered, inspecting the picture more closely. Poor little rat, he didn't look the least bit dangerous. He looked like some-one who knew that a vague resemblance to Elvis Presley was his sole distinction. He looked like a spaniel wagging a hopeful tail even as he prepared to cower. "You'd better give yourself up, boyo," she told the picture, "before some citizen blasts you with a deer rifle and tosses you in the back of his pickup."

She sat on the floor to page through the rest of the paper and then read the police calls. A housewife on Juniper Street had fired at what she thought was a prowler and had killed a large raccoon. Houses on Sierra Street, Mountain Avenue, Santa Clara Street, and Sequoia Way had suffered burglaries on either Thursday or Friday night; police urged householders to be careful about locking up during this season of heavy fog. A 1965 Ford Mustang and a 1978 Chevy Camaro had been stolen Friday, the Chevy later found abandoned; teenagers were suspected. Four local youths, names withheld, had been arrested for playing late-night games of chicken-in-the-fog on a curvy stretch of coast highway just north of town.

"Teenagers have all the fun," she remarked aloud as she folded the paper; then her eyes met the Stein boy's sad gaze once again, and she regretted her flippancy. He didn't look as though there'd been much joy in his life. Whatever Dave Tucker had been up to, *he* certainly never gave any appearance of enjoying himself. And the two kids on her list . . .

She set the paper aside, uncovering a yellow legal pad bearing a few penciled notes. Talk to the kids, Gutierrez had suggested, probably a facile suggestion intended mainly to soothe and occupy her. But late last night, unable to get to sleep, she had probed her reluctant memory (what teachers dislike most of all during summer vacation is thinking about students) and had dredged up, finally, two potentially useful names, two just-graduated seniors who had behaved . . . oddly was the best term she could apply . . . in Dave Tucker's presence. And both of them had summer jobs here in town.

Gutierrez! she thought as the phone shrilled, and then,

for the second time that morning, They've got him! "And about time, too, what are we paying taxes for?" She scrambled to her feet, wincing as her jeans rubbed several patches of sunburn. She and Katy and the Martins had spent the previous day at a lake some miles inland, and last year's bikini had not quite matched this year's tan.

"Hello?"

"It won't be long now."

Gutierrez had a truly awful cold, poor man.

"Soon now all the God-fearing citizens will know you for the murdering harlot you are, and drive you out."

"What? You! Listen here, you vile old . . ."

But the voice went on, a hissing, spitty whisper out of a bad horror movie. " 'But it shall not be well with the wicked, neither shall he prolong his days, which are as a shadow; because he feareth not before God.' " Silence, and then a click.

Rage coursed through Meg like electricity. She banged the receiver into its cradle, then pinched out the small plastic clip connecting line to instrument. The line slithered to the floor like a slim silver snake and lay there, inviting boot heels.

Yes indeed, and then you can go buy a new one. Breathe deeply. Count backwards from a hundred—no, that's for anesthesia.

She swung around and walked stiff legged into the living room. Resisting the urge to pull all curtains against prying eyes, she dropped to the floor again, her back against the couch, and reached for a pencil; then she muttered "Oh, what the hell!" The words themselves didn't matter, were only more of the same.

Well, not quite. Never mind the bit from the Bible, it's those God-fearing citizens you'd better think about. Murdering harlot?

"Mommy?"

She clenched her body against a shudder, then looked up at Katy and managed to produce a smile.

"Mommy, I heard the phone. Was it the creep again?"

" 'Fraid so, baby. I guess we'd better have our number changed."

"No, let's just blast him." Katy reached a garden-stained hand into the neck of her sweatshirt and fished out a large silver whistle, the kind used by coaches and referees. "Cyndi gave me this. She says you blow it really hard into the telephone and pow! like punching the creep right in the ear."

"That's a wonderful idea," Meg admitted, "but let's save it for last resort." She got to her feet and found herself blinking in a sudden wash of warm, yellow light: the sun had defeated the fog once more. Good sign, grab it and run. "Sweetie, I have a few errands downtown," she said, reaching out to tousle Katy's hair. "It's such a pretty day, I think I'll walk."

"Please take Grendel, *please.*"

"Oh, dear. Is he digging again?"

"He doesn't have to dig, he just *steps* on the poor baby plants."

"I thought Cyndi was coming over," Meg said a short time later as she settled a tote bag over her shoulder.

"She is, pretty soon. Don't *worry,* Mom. Miss Luoma's home, she was talking to me over the fence. And Mr. Emery's in his backyard; he's building a playhouse for when Mrs. Emery gets back. It's for Eddie, silly," she said in response to Meg's raised eyebrows.

"Well. All right, but you stay right here."

Katy rolled her eyes. "Mommy, I *said.*"

On her way to the door Meg paused, eyed the telephone, then reconnected it. It would be stupid to let that Bible-quoting cretin deprive them of communication. "But you're on my list, old lady," she said softly, flicking a fingernail against the tan plastic, "and I will get to you eventually. Katy," she called over her shoulder, "answer the phone if it rings, but please just hang up if it's the creep."

. . .

Under a sky of brilliant blue, fog-damp roofs steamed gently. Nearly every yard had a worker, someone digging or weeding or pruning or simply puttering; North Coasters knew better than to waste a sunny day. Keeping an absent eye on the dog ranging ahead, Meg strode westward. Dark glasses gave her the illusion of invisibility, and a brisk two-mile walk should settle her mind as well as her muscles, prepare her to elicit information without ruffling feathers.

Hilly, curving Rose Street leveled and straightened, irregular lots and tree-sheltered houses giving way to smaller dwellings set primly behind chain-link or picket fences. Neat gardens, carefully pruned hedges, houses whose window-door-window fronts resembled austere faces. Suddenly, a two-story version of the same house, at a corner; projecting from its roof was a sign with blue-neon pages turning endlessly: Pentecostal Bible Church, Come and Be Saved.

Flip-flicker, flip-flicker, flip-flicker went the pages, their rhythm nearly that of a heartbeat. She watched for a moment in grim fascination, wondering whether the pulse effect could have been intentional. The building was freshly painted, with scaffolding still slung from one side; a litter of pipes and rows of shallow trenches indicated that a sprinkler system was being installed. Business must be good, she thought, and shivered as a trickle of sweat rolled down her spine. Skeptical by nature, raised by a father who regarded the Bible as one of the better mythologies, she found Evangelical Christianity disquieting.

Broader, smoother sidewalks, planter boxes full of petunias, small businesses aswarm with tourists. With Grendel on lead now she moved past ambling groups of strangers, none of them paying her the slightest attention. Directly ahead, across Main Street, lay the city park, its long grasses and tall wildflowers sweeping to the bluff above the ocean.

An old, narrow road ran the length of the park; ranged along it were Port Silva's post office, exhibition hall, and library. Chrissie Maldonado worked in the library.

Meg let Grendel pull her to the edge of the bluff, where he planted his feet and barked happily at soaring gulls. Below the bluff were a strip of sand, a huddle of tall black rocks, and a limitless expanse of wind-whipped blue water. Just beyond the small harbor a sailor sported with the wind, tipping his bright-sailed catamaran high on one hull as he hiked out on an invisible line.

That looked like fun—nerve and muscle with no demands on the intellect or emotions. Something Chrissie might enjoy. Chrissie Maldonado was tall, athletic, inarticulate . . . an A student in math and science who had made B's in English by dint of very hard work, hers and her teacher's. Searching her memory last night, Meg had come upon a picture of Chrissie as Dave Tucker approached the girl's desk: face blank, eyes down, shoulder shrinking from Dave's reaching hand. An awkward approach, and an abnormally shy response, Meg had thought then; in retrospect, the scene had a cat-and-mouse quality.

. . .

The Port Silva library was housed in an 1880s private residence that had been moved from its original site. Now the two-story bay window and the broad columned porch faced town rather than sea, and dove gray paint with white trim muted the building's architectural exuberance.

Meg peered through vines and leaves etched in thick, beveled glass, then pushed open the heavy door and stepped inside. A red-haired girl of perhaps fifteen was posting notices on the bulletin board to the left of the door; a tall, skinny boy pushed a loaded book cart toward a between-stacks aisle. No sign of Chrissie. But behind the high counter on the right, blond head inclined deferentially toward a group of mostly gray-haired women,

79

was Meg's neighbor and friendly acquaintance, Anna
Wingate. Anna would know where to find Chrissie.

Meg's sneakers were silent on the polished wood floor,
and the speaker did not pause. ". . . so I'm sure you'll see
that an exception must be made in this case, since we're
trying to do a real important work here, the Lord's work."

She must have made some noise, a groan or perhaps
only a sigh, and the woman's head snapped around. Cold
eyes swept assessingly over Meg's worn sneakers, her jeans
and her loose shirt, paused on her face as if committing it
to memory. Then the woman turned back to Anna, body
angled forward slightly from the hips, chin out.

Anna had been rolling a long yellow pencil between
her fingers. Now she laid it aside and folded her hands.
"I'm sorry, Mrs. Denton, but the main reading room is
simply not available before 9:00 P.M. except on Sunday
nights. One of the smaller upstairs rooms will have to do."

"But I'm just trying to tell you, we'll have too big a
turnout for the upstairs rooms. And Sunday night is out,
all our folks go to evening services."

"I'm sorry," Anna repeated. "Perhaps one of the
churches could accommodate you on a weeknight."

Mrs. Denton gave an exasperated sigh, wheeled about
and marched off, the rest of her group behind her. Meg
watched them for a moment; then she blinked hard and
shook her head. How quickly a sense of persecution could
swell to bigotry. Besides, that woman wouldn't make anonymous calls; she'd walk right up and ring the doorbell.

"Meg?"

And she herself was not the only person with troubles.
"Hello, Anna. I'm sorry to see that Port Silva's head
librarianship is not necessarily a peaceful position."

Anna took a slow, quivering breath as she stroked
smoothing palms over tightly bound pale hair; then she
moved her long gray eyes over Meg's face, past her,
around the room. "Still only acting head. And no, it's not
peaceful."

"Mrs. Wingate?" One of the group, a tall, solid woman in a flowered print dress. "You did say that you had not purchased, um, *How to Have Terrific Sex?*" She pushed the words past her teeth, as if to keep them from touching her lips.

"That's true, Mrs. Bishop. Our budget was exhausted before that came up for consideration."

"But I saw the title on that list over there." She gave a stiff wave in the direction of the bulletin board. "Anyone walking in the door could just glance right over and see it!"

"Mrs. Bishop, that is the best-seller list from *The New York Times.*" Anna's voice was higher.

"Oh. Really? Well, I suppose . . . Anyway, I was assigned to check the card catalog, and I was pleased to ₁d no Rosemary Rodgers, no Patricia Mathews, and no Marigolde Meadowes. I'd have to say you're doing pretty well."

Anna turned a gasp into a cough, and a flush swept her face from chin to forehead as she fixed pleading eyes on Meg. Under the name Marigolde Meadowes, Anna wrote what she described as "*good* historical romances, with just enough steamy sex to make them sell." Now Meg shook her head slightly; and Anna pressed her shoulders against the back of her tall chair as she watched Mrs. Bishop move away.

"You have just seen a new local phenomenon: the Port Silva Volunteer Library Advisory Committee," she murmured. "I suppose they will eventually learn that we don't catalog paperbacks. But if they ever find out about Marigolde, I am well and truly screwed." Behind the counter she pounded one fisted hand against the other. "I fooled them this morning, though; I got in early and removed every single Judy Blume title from the children's room."

Meg took the quaver in the other woman's voice for a repressed giggle, until a tear splattered on the counter.

"Anna, I'm sorry. Can I get you a cup of coffee? Or proclaim closing time and send everybody home?"

"Just stand in front of me for a moment longer, please." Anna wiped her eyes, sniffed once, then lifted her chin. "Thanks. Now what may I do for you?"

"Oh. Yes, if it won't upset operations here, I'd like to talk with Chrissie Maldonado for just a few minutes."

"Chrissie?" Anna glanced around the big room. "She's probably in the lounge. She's spent a lot of time there lately." She looked around again, then leaned across the counter and spoke more softly. "I think the poor child has just realized that she's actually going to Vassar in the fall. She's behaving like someone with an incipient ulcer, or perhaps a clandestine pregnancy."

"Vassar?" Meg flinched at the ring of her voice in the quiet room. "Vassar will be very—strenuous for Chrissie," she finished lamely.

Anna's long face grew longer. "Her mother is a Vassar graduate, and I believe her maternal grandmother as well, so . . . Well, it's none of my business, and of course you may see her; the staff lounge is just beyond the office. Meg?"

Meg, who had turned to leave, turned back.

"After you've seen Chrissie, why don't you . . ." Anna tipped her head back, blinked rapidly. "No. I'll be home not long after six. Come over for a glass of wine, if you can spare the time. I've had—that is, the library has had—a phone call I think you're entitled to know about."

As Meg stared wordlessly, the telephone behind Anna rang, a woman herding two smallish children approached the counter, and the front door opened to admit a gaggle of camera-bearing tourists. "After six," Anna repeated.

Reluctantly Meg turned away, catching one sneaker on the extended leg of a free-standing bulletin board to the right of the counter. Black edges on the board, in its center an enlarged group portrait of Port Silva's latest graduating class, one face ringed in black. Black letters blurred as she swung about and set off down the hall. No wonder Chrissie preferred the lounge.

Rest rooms, then the office; and at the end of the hall a double swinging door with Employees on the frosted glass of the left half, Lounge on the right. Meg took a deep breath, pushed the right-hand door open, and stepped in.

The room was shabbily comfortable, with big, low windows pouring light over a wooden floor, two spavined couches, several porch-style wicker chairs with faded cushions. A table along the right wall bore a coffee urn, a tray of mugs, spoons, and jars; Chrissie was slouched in the chair nearest the table, hands cradling a steaming mug.

"Hello, Chrissie; Anna told me you might be here. Is there any coffee left?" Without waiting for a reply, Meg picked up a mug and set it under the spigot. "And she told me you're going to Vassar, so I guess our hours and hours of work paid off."

Still no sound from the girl. Meg turned her gaze on the bent dark head and waited; and slowly the head came up and back. Framed by once glossy black hair now limp and lifeless, the girl's face was a mask of misery. Meg recalled Anna's remark about a pregnancy, and wondered.

"Chrissie, I'm sorry. It's . . . in a small high school like ours, the death of a classmate is particularly sad, and Dave was . . ." As Meg reached for her, the girl flung herself up and out of her chair; her mug hit the floor and bounced, spewing brown liquid. "Eeeee-eh!" wailed Chrissie, and in an angular flurry of arms and legs she stumbled toward the back of the room, to disappear through a single swinging door.

"Chrissie, for heaven's sake!" It was a small bathroom: tile floor, a sink and mirror, two toilet stalls. The door of the stall on the right was still quivering; behind it was the noise of a scramble, then only harsh, ragged breathing.

"Please, Chrissie." Meg pushed the door and found it locked. "Please come out, Chrissie, maybe I can help." There was a muffled wail, and the breathing roughened to the edge of sobs. Meg stepped back and found that she could see no feet under the door; the girl must have scrunched her whole long body up onto the toilet seat.

"Chrissie, are you ill?" Meg kept her voice low. "Can I get someone for you? Anna? Your mother? A doctor? Chrissie!"

"No!" A loud sniff, and then thick silence. Would she hold her breath until she fainted and toppled off her perch? "All right, Chrissie, I'm leaving. I'm sorry."

. . .

"One thing," Meg told Grendel as she bent to untie his leash from the bicycle rack. "Every dog owner has at least one friend." And Chrissie Maldonado, whatever her trouble, had family to help her, mother and father and big brothers as well. Perhaps the girl was simply worried about her future. Perhaps she was on something, some obscure but newly popular drug that induced paranoia. More likely, she had heard the stories being spread about her former English teacher and feared, reasonably enough, that such pariah-hood might be catching.

Meg sighed, and paused for a moment to massage her taut shoulder muscles. If she couldn't win cooperation from a biddable girl like Chrissie, what kind of response could she expect from the mountainous man-child who was next on her list? Was, in fact, all that remained of her list.

· 10 ·

Tiny Olsen's white-blond curls towered above any group, his massive shoulders filled any doorway. Meg had found him awkwardly chivalrous with females, treating them as a foreign and fragile species; with the high-school boys, inferior examples of his own kind, he was usually good-tempered.

But not with Dave Tucker. Whenever the two of them crossed paths in Meg's classroom, Dave had seemed to shrink and scuttle, Tiny to swell even larger, big pink lips curling.

"Let's see if we can find out what that was all about," Meg suggested to Grendel as they crossed Main Street and headed for Olsen's Auto Supply. It was comforting to have him with her—an Olsen-sized dog.

The shop was empty except for Tiny, who hunched over the back counter writing laboriously. At the sound of the door's bell he looked up. "What can I do for . . . Oh, hi, Mrs. Halloran, how's it goin'? Hey, that's some big dog, he'd make at least two of my dad's pit bull. Probably not as tough, though." Small blue eyes inspected Grendel thoughtfully, as if probing for muscle.

"I think he's tough enough," said Meg, shortening the dog's leash. "But he doesn't fight for fun. He's a guard dog, a protector for me and my daughter."

"Yeah, a dog that big, he wouldn't hardly need to fight." Tiny gave a grin of fellow-feeling and straightened to his full height, some six and a half feet. "What can I do for you, Mrs. Halloran? Looking for a good mechanic? I'm off Mondays and Tuesdays."

"Thanks, Tiny, but not yet; I'll keep you in mind. I need a set of plugs, and I guess wires too, for a '78 Chevy van, 350 engine. Oh, and a plug wrench, I seem to have lost mine."

"You do that sort of thing yourself?" He peered down at her in astonishment, and she thought, Oops, wrong image.

"Oh, I can just about manage it, so long as I take my time and follow the manual. And right now I need something to occupy my mind until the police find Dave Tucker's murderer," she told him with a palms-up gesture of helplessness.

"Huh?"

"Dave's father is telling people I was his son's only enemy."

"What . . . ? Oh, yeah." Tiny's knotted brow smoothed. "That's right, I heard you and him had some trouble. Don't you worry, Mrs. Halloran, cops are dumb but not that dumb. What I think is"—he leaned over the counter in conspiratorial fashion—"I think it finally occurred to ol' Dave that everybody knew him for the real prick he was—uh, 'scuse it, ma'am. Anyway, everybody knew, so he just went down to the beach and offed himself, end of story."

"I don't really think so, Tiny. No gun was found near the body," she explained.

"Well, maybe the tide washed it out. Maybe a sea gull took it. Who knows?" He gave a shrug that said clearly, Who cares.

That was more imagination than had ever appeared in his schoolwork. "At the moment, I believe the police are curious about a beating Dave suffered some months ago."

"Beating?" The big head went back and high; Meg had a sense of breath blown hard through flared nostrils, of enormous feathered hooves shifting uneasily.

"Apparently someone beat him up. And apparently his parents didn't know about it, which is odd. Perhaps he was too frightened of his assailant to tell anyone." As she spoke, Meg's eyes were on the counter, on Tiny's huge, spread-out hands.

"Oh no, no ma'am!" Tiny crossed his arms over his chest, tucking hands into armpits. "Not me. My daddy says Olsens're too big to go getting in fights. And he's still bigger than any of us, and a whole lot meaner. Any of us boys cross him, he's on our butts with a two-by-four."

"All right, you didn't fight with Dave. So who did? Come on," she pleaded, "the truth can't hurt; no one's going to get in trouble over a fight that happened months ago." And you should cross your fingers, she told herself.

"It wasn't a beating. More like self-defense."

"Against whom?"

"Dave." He leaned forward. "He started hanging around the team, see, we thought at first he was just another jock sniffer . . . 'scuse it. Just one of those guys like to hang out with the team. We finally got real tired of finding him in every corner, behind every door. And he was a Christer, too, always preaching. So we . . . kind of set him up, see."

"How?"

"Some of the guys had had a few beers, and they started fixing his Coke—he wouldn't drink nothing but Coke—with grain alcohol. Several Cokes."

"And he got sick?"

"No ma'am, he passed out. So . . ." Tiny's face grew several shades pinker. "So we, they, stripped Tucker down to his underpants, and then they, uh, a couple of them got their girlfriends to go topless, like. And we had this old Polaroid camera."

"Oh my," said Meg faintly.

"Yes ma'am. Anyway, when he come to and we showed him the pictures, he just went crazy, picked up a heavy pool cue and did a whole lot of damage before we got him stopped. He even hit one of the girls."

And why not, thought Meg. "Then what?"

"Oh, well, we gave him the pictures. And he kind of limped off. Then we left." Tiny shrugged. "Never heard any more about it; guess he found somebody else to preach at."

. . .

She paused just outside the shop door to tuck her purchases into her tote bag and adjust the straps that made the thing a backpack. Tiny's fascinating if unsavory little tale probably had nothing to do with murder, simply providing another piece to the puzzle that was Dave Tucker.

Tiny had been, however, remarkably forthcoming, even indiscreet, or so it might appear to the other members of . . . it must have been the football team. She knew he had played football but couldn't imagine him at baseball, basketball. Or track, certainly not track. So, football. How would the entire football team feel knowing that she was in on their secret? And if—no, when, when!—she sicced Gutierrez on them . . . no, when she *told* Gutierrez about all this . . . She wished she could remember more about the team, exactly who was on the team. Football was not a sport she paid much attention to.

Grendel pushed against her with his shoulder, uttering the squeaky little yip that proclaimed boredom.

"Yes, all right. Let's move out smartly, friend." With the dog tight at heel, she reached the corner, turned left, lengthened her stride. The shoppers and tourists around her seemed sullen faced, balky, inclined to sudden pauses or erratic lines of movement. For a block or two an odd tightness gripped her shoulders, as if a crowd were forming behind her, honing itself for pursuit; but she did not let herself look back.

. . .

Gardeners, an occasional sunbather, basking cats that tucked tight or fled at the sight of Grendel. A compelling rustle in the tall grass around the abandoned water tower, caused by a snake that easily eluded the dog's pounce. Mechanics in the yard at the boardinghouse, shirtless bodies leaning under raised hoods or squatting beside motorcycles; no police car there at the moment . . .

Meg stopped at the corner of her own block and rested an arm atop Miss Luoma's fence; her face was hot and damp, her leg muscles quivering slightly. Before her lay a magazine picture of a peaceful summer day: Miss Luoma flinging grass cuttings into a two-wheeled garden cart, Katy and Cyndi sitting halfway down Meg's front steps with open books on their knees. Although Cyndi's pose might be counted less than neighborly, Meg noted with mild amusement. The girl had her chubby back firmly turned in Miss Luoma's direction; according to Katy, Cyndi didn't like reprimands any more than Felicity Luoma liked prowlers.

And there was Frank Wingate, hedge clippers . . . Anna! she thought suddenly. She'd forgotten Anna, who'd had a phone call. No. Quite specifically, the library had had a call. About Meg, obviously. Why on earth the library? Was Mr. Tucker or whoever seeking help with quotations?

Anna. After six. She blinked harder and returned to the scene around her. Billy Nordstrom's truck gleamed mightily in the sun, and a vaguely familiar child, a skinny little girl with white-blond hair, stood in the street and stared in awe at the enormous multicolored machine. Flower, of course, Louise's Flower. Ridiculous name.

"Margaret?" Miss Luoma tossed her gloves atop the heap of green in the cart, pulling off her floppy hat as she strode toward the fence. Her square-shouldered body was short and solid, her long arms and legs freckled and corded with stringy muscle. In blue work shirt and denim skirt, Felicity Luoma looked less the writer she was than the countrywoman she had been. Still was, Meg remembered, since she still ran a few head of cattle at her Covelo farm. In her most recent book, the scenes of roundup, of branding and castrating and dehorning, had stood out with compelling force from what was otherwise a fairly wooden effort.

"Margaret, I wanted to tell you what a nice talk I had with Katy today. She is a delightful child, and she's going to be a fine gardener, too."

"Thank you." Meg snatched another look at Katy-in-the-sun, waved. Shouldn't have left her at home alone, she thought, and then, Don't hover.

Miss Luoma's voice broke in. "I'm terribly curious about the murder investigation. Have you heard anything further? Have the police any—what are they called—leads?" Clasping her hands beneath her chin, she fixed a round-eyed gaze on Meg's face.

Who appointed me police liaison, thought Meg sourly. "I haven't heard anything new, Miss Luoma." When the other woman continued to regard her hopefully, silently, Meg said, "I, um, I do expect to see Chief Gutierrez tonight. For dinner, that is," she added, feeling a wave of heat sweeping her face. "I imagine he'll tell—"

"Oh, that's good. How nice that you know Vincent personally. He's a fine man, I believe, a real support to his dear mother. And she's a wonderful woman, raised all seven of those children almost single-handedly; her husband was often away."

Not often enough. Meg clamped her lips shut, hoping she hadn't spoken.

"A wonderful woman," repeated Miss Luoma, "I'm sure you'll enjoy meeting her." A girlish giggle, while Meg quailed, envisioning a long dinner table, an imperious ancient all in black at its head, white hair over a delicate hawk's profile, sharp black eyes assessing a newcomer.

". . . absolutely a pillar of the Port Silva Historical Society," Miss Luoma rattled on, "and very active in local affairs. New Englanders do seem to have a wonderful sense of civic responsibility."

New Englanders? Meg drew a deep breath. Fear, or

perhaps oxygen starvation; her mind was a balloon on a string, tugging against reality. "Miss Luoma, you'll have to excuse me, I need to talk to Katy." Squealing tires and the roar of a laboring engine drowned her words.

A battered pickup truck swung wide around the corner, swerved, and seemed to collect itself as the driver, invisible behind a sunstruck windshield, shifted gears. In the center of the street Flower Martin stood, transfixed. Meg heard Katy's scream and her own shout as she lunged away from the fence, knowing she'd be too late.

Grendel shot in front of the pickup like a pale, hairy arrow. Meg saw him hit Flower with head or shoulder, she couldn't tell which. Then the whine of brakes, a howl from child or dog, grinding gears, and the truck careened on.

The little girl lay sprawled against the opposite curb, tears making tracks on her cheeks as she gulped and gasped, struggling to regain knocked-out breath. Grendel stood sentinel over her, head lowered, upper lip wrinkled back. At Meg's approach he moved aside, yipping once as he put weight on his right hind leg.

"Never mind, it's all right, you're just fine," Meg said softly, more or less to child and dog both. As a portion of her mind noted that the dog was unbloodied and alert, she knelt to pass gentle, assessing hands over Flower. Scrapes from the road, but no real bleeding, no obvious broken bones.

"You're fine," she repeated, "nothing hit you but dog. Just stay there and we'll find your mother."

Flower sniffled, gulped once more, and then lurched upright to launch herself at Meg.

So much for the rules of first aid, but at least the arms and legs worked. Meg got to her feet, the child wrapped around her like a monkey. She stroked the pale hair, drawing several slow, deliberate breaths; as the tingling chill of near-disaster faded, rage seemed to flow hot to her very fingertips.

The slow-motion world resumed normal speed. Wingate had dropped his clippers and begun to move toward the street, and Miss Luoma's gate flew open, but Katy was closest, Cyndi was just behind her.

"Here, love, you take her." Meg peeled Flower loose and thrust the little girl at her own wide-eyed daughter. "No, Grendel, stay! Stay with Katy!" She watched the small body settle against Katy, saw Katy's hand cup Flower's head and nestle it against her own.

"I think she's all right." She tossed the words over her shoulder, and then gave herself up to a wave of pent-up fury and frustration that sent her headlong after this latest, and finally visible, enemy.

The truck was canted over the curb at the end of the block, in front of the house owned by Marcia Dietz and Mark Haywood. As Meg neared, the driver's door swung open and a young woman tumbled out, long hair obscuring her face. A man's tee shirt clung to her thin torso; her legs and dirty feet were bare beneath a gathered skirt whose print had faded to pale smears.

The woman stumbled, righted herself, and climbed back into the truck to lift a double-barreled shotgun from its rack. She slid out backwards, took an awkward step away from the vehicle. Exhaling a wordless grunt of rage, Meg lunged between woman and truck and yanked the weapon away.

"Just what the hell do you think you're doing?" She swung around and planted her feet wide, breaking the gun open. "Stay where you are, you silly bitch, or I'll wrap this around your head! Do you know that you nearly killed a child back there? Not to mention a dog!"

"Marcia, I have to see Marcia!" Pale eyes flashed in the dirt-streaked face; she teetered as if she might throw herself at Meg, then leaped sideways to seize the arm of the big red-haired man who had appeared beside them.

"Marcia, where's Marcia? The cops came, and they're going to take it all and burn it, and there were guns, somebody maybe got shot! It'll all be gone, all our work, and what'll happen to Jerry if he shot a cop? Marcia!" she wailed.

Mark Haywood clasped the woman tight for a moment, patting a shaking shoulder. "Just settle down, now, Cassie, we'll work it out. Marcia's downtown. You go on in the house. I'll be there in a minute, and we'll call Marcia."

The woman stumbled up the path to the house, climbed the porch steps and sat there, long legs trailing, eyes glued to Mark.

"Hey, Meg, I'm sorry." Mark ran a big, freckled hand over russet curls. "I don't know how she got this address; we try to keep our business at the office where it belongs. Cassie and her old man and some friends have a little, um, farm out in the woods, and it looks like they put in a year's work for nothing." He shrugged. "Kind of early for a raid, I guess they weren't prepared."

"That certainly is a gut-wrencher, Mark. A real old down-home sob story." Mark took a quick step back, his face wary; Meg toyed with the notion of closing the gun and loosing both barrels skyward. "Poor Cassie's tale of woe will surely touch Louise Martin," she went on. "It was Louise's daughter Flower she almost killed. Probably the vet will give me a rebate when I explain that my dog got hit by a beleaguered small-business person."

"Jesus!" he breathed, casting a glance over his shoulder. "Look, Meg, I really am sorry. After I get hold of Marcia I'll go and apologize to Louise; I'll see that Cassie apologizes. But these raids are simply a waste of time and money by a lazy D.A. with an election coming up. The fact is that the North Coast is a depressed area, and marijuana is an important element in the local economy."

The D.A. Gutierrez had told her that he expected to be tied up with the D.A. on Friday and Saturday. Did local forces back up county personnel on drug busts? "Apparently a cop got shot this time," she said, her voice shaking.

Mark's freckles took on a greenish tinge. "Jesus, that's

right, she said . . . but she said maybe, and she's hysterical. I've gotta call Marcia. Here, give me the gun, and I'll try to get things straightened out."

Slippery bastard. Hands tightening on her trophy, Meg stepped out of reach. "Not just yet. You tell Mountain Laurel, there, that she can have it back when she apologizes. Unless, of course, it turns out to be evidence of some kind."

She draped the shotgun over her shoulder and marched smartly homeward. Acquainted with only two lawyers in town, she had just affronted one of them, and the other was his wife. Her policeman-ally might have carelessly permitted himself to be shot. Her faithful guard dog had been hit by a car. "I bloody well need the damned gun," she muttered as she trudged up her front steps.

• 11 •

"The place is a mess, but the wine is good." Anna Wingate lifted her glass to the light as she settled onto a hassock, the skirts of her caftan a vivid swirl around her bare feet.

"Mm." As Meg took a mouthful of the chilled, straw-colored liquid, she surreptitiously explored the chair seat behind her.

"What's the . . . oh, that's where the engine got to. Little Frank is walking now, which means he carries things around and hides them in the oddest places, you wouldn't believe where I found . . ."

"Oh yes I would." Meg had hovered near the clock all afternoon, a hungry cat awaiting a six-o'clock mouse.

"Anna, I really need—I'd be most appreciative if you'd tell me about the telephone call."

"Yes, of course." Anna set her feet together and arranged her body in straight lines and right angles. "I'm always the first person in. The baby is a 6:00 A.M. alarm clock, and if I get right up and feed him, Frank does the rest and I go off to work."

"And this morning you got a phone call about me," Meg prodded.

Anne sighed. "Yes. Or rather, not quite. It was on the answering machine, after several reference questions and a message for one of the assistant librarians and an obscene call. There was this salesman's let-me-leave-you-my-card voice asking if I'd like to have my pussy licked, and while I was still trying to decide, some whisperer started a nasty spiel about Margaret Halloran."

Meg released held-in breath.

"Nobody heard it but me, at least I don't think so," Anna told her.

"A quotation from the Bible, no doubt."

Anna blinked, nodded slowly. "From Proverbs, about 'a woman with the attire of an harlot, and subtil of heart.' Drawing young men to her 'straightway, as an ox goeth to the slaughter.' The idea was that you definitely did not belong in the schools with our young innocents. And so on and so forth. I'm a librarian, so the quotes stuck; but the rest I remember only as mindless vituperation."

"Anna, what did you do with the tape?"

"I erased it, scrunch, like stepping on a bug."

"What kind of voice was it?"

"Nasty. Meg, I don't know." Anna gestured at Meg's glass, then filled her own as Meg shook her head. "Maybe female, at least it made me think right away of the good Christian ladies who are presently making *my* life hell. Someone is certainly out to get you; are you leading an interesting secret life?"

"No, and I haven't written any dirty books, either!" snapped Meg.

Anna cast a look toward the back of the house; Meg said, "Sorry. Doesn't Frank know about Marigolde?"

"Oh, Frank knows, he's my resource person. Marigolde's sex scenes are very thoroughly researched." A catlike smile, which faded quickly. "And God knows we need the money; we're always broke. But he doesn't want anyone else to know, especially his family."

Meg snorted. "You may assure him that my lips are sealed. Why do you suppose my anonymous enemy picked the library?"

"It was probably meant for Miss Hurlbutt. She's the librarian who had a stroke, the one I replaced six months ago. Not a bad old girl, but she took herself and her quote position unquote very seriously."

"Her position. Of course." Meg gulped the last of her wine. Library, chamber of commerce, planning commission, school board ... "I'm probably on answering machines all over town."

"Oh, dear. But sensible people don't pay attention to anonymous calls." Anna's expression was more hopeful than confident.

"Hey, Anna!" A slamming door, a clatter from the back of the house, and Frank appeared in the doorway. "Anna, when I walk in the kitchen my shoes stick to the floor."

"I know, dear." Anna rose from her hassock to give her husband a kiss. "That's one reason I try not to go out there."

Wingate gave Anna's bottom a resounding slap. "Damn good thing you have other talents. Hey, did Meg tell you about her heroics today?"

With no sign of embarrassment, Anna captured her husband's still-groping hand. "No, what happened?"

After Frank had told the tale, Meg said, "It was Grendel, all on his own. And Louise is awash in guilt, so please, let it go."

"But you ought to call the *Sentinel*, it'd make a great story."

"No." Louise's ashen face, and the yearning arch of her body as she cradled the child, were etched in Meg's brain. "Sorry, Frank, but flashbulbs upset my dog, he'd probably eat the reporter. Anna, thanks for the wine. I'm expecting company, so I'd better be on my way."

. . .

Answering machines all over town: her own words stayed with her even under the hot pounding of her shower. Not all city offices were open on Saturday, of course, but what a treat Monday promised. William Tucker was still her villain of choice, never mind what Gutierrez thought; it was easy enough to dial direct from San Francisco or wherever he was. Or if he didn't want to make the calls in person, he had a whole bankful of humble servants.

"But I was told he'd be back by now," she said a few minutes later. The mealymouthed slandering son-of-a-bitch! she added, but silently, as she pressed the receiver hard against her ear.

"Not till late Sunday night or real early Monday. Can I take a message?" Jenny Tucker's voice was thin and mechanical, with no inflection except for the slight question-rise.

"Just tell your father that I called, and will call back. Or perhaps you can help, Jenny. Someone has been making anonymous phone calls to me and about me, and I think the calls must be connected with . . ."

"I'm not supposed to talk to anyone. I'll leave your name, Mrs. Halloran." Fade-out and click.

Meg punched the numbers again, but hung up before the first ring. She had no right to harass a grieving sixteen-year-old, especially one who appeared to have been abandoned by her parents. The dining-room clock bonged gently; she hitched up her damp towel and dashed for the bedroom. Gutierrez was due in fifteen minutes . . . unless he'd been shot, of course.

Navy blue trousers of heavy silk. A low-necked silk tunic, navy in background, shot through with lavender, lighter blue, and a silvery gray. She tied the fabric belt loosely, eyes on the mirror over her dresser. One day, perhaps, beer drinking and the sedentary life would catch up with her; but for the moment, the genes of her tall Scots grandfather prevailed.

She had pulled on a pair of soft black boots and was trying to coax her hair into a twist when Katy came in.

"Where are we going, Mommy? What should I wear?"

Hell. In the course of the endless, crazy day she'd forgotten to tell Katy of her plans for the evening. "Sweetie, I'm going to dinner with Chief Gutierrez, Vince Gutierrez, you met him. He's bringing one of his nieces or nephews to stay with you, and I don't think I'll be late. There's some spaghetti sauce in the fridge, I'll cook the spaghetti now. Or I could do you an omelet, how about mushrooms and cheese?"

Wait just a damned minute. She was dithering like a teenager, while Katy, in the mirror, resembled a disapproving parent: arms crossed, body rigid, face tight.

"Katy . . ." Meg pinned a last strand of hair into place, then turned to face her daughter. "I'm sorry I forgot to tell you, but it was a very busy day."

"Mommies don't go out," Katy said flatly.

"Mommies without daddies—husbands—do, or should!" snapped Meg, and regretted her tone instantly. She sat down on the edge of the bed and reached for Katy, who backed away.

"Baby, I'm sorry, but I need to talk to Chief Gutierrez, and besides . . ."

"You could talk to him here. I don't want you to start doing things with men. Cyndi says you'll . . . she says people will say bad things about you, maybe that's why this person is calling us all the time."

And Cyndi is a vicious little bitch who should be staked out over a nest of scorpions. "Katy, I am not 'doing things with men,' whatever that means. I am going to dinner with a friend."

"If he's just a friend, why are you dressed so fancy? In that blouse Daddy gave you for your birthday, I remember when he did that."

"Oh, baby, so do I." Meg's reach was successful this time; she pulled Katy close and stroked her hair. Be very careful, she cautioned herself; don't set up a pattern neither of you will be able to break.

She gripped Katy's shoulders and set her gently away. "And I'll bet Daddy would be delighted to see that it still fits. Now . . . supper?"

"Never mind, I can fix it myself." Eyes down, Katy turned and trudged out, every line of her body proclaiming rejection.

.   .   .

The minutes lurched and stumbled past, and fog began to blot out the summer evening. Meg caught her reflection in the big living-room window. She had tarted herself up for a goddamned small-town cop, and the bastard couldn't even call to say he would be late. Or wasn't coming at all, had better things to do. Surely if Cassie whozit or her friend Jerry had shot him, there'd have been some word of it, something.

Call a baby-sitter, she thought. Call Louise, she'd be glad to help. Get Katy settled, and then go find a quiet corner in a quiet bar and drink until oblivion or closing time, whichever occurs first. No more waiting, never waiting; she'd used up all her waiting skills the night she'd waited for Dan, and waited and waited until the Highway Patrol came to tell her she needn't wait any longer.

The seven-thirty "bong" and the sound of the doorbell occurred together. She stalked to the door, pulled it wide, and said, weakly, "Oh, for heaven's sake." Gutierrez looked weary and far from young, dark face made darker by a starkly white bandage slanted from hairline to cheekbone over his right eye; his right shoulder was held stiffly high, and an empty sling dangled against his chest.

"Apologies," he said, inclining his head as he moved past her. "It turns out that every damned thing takes twice as long one-handed. We have dinner reservations for eight-thirty, I told Jeff to be here by eight. How are you at mixing martinis?"

She accepted the brown paper bag he handed her. "I, sir, am one of the sole surviving practitioners of that ancient art."

In the kitchen, overhead lights deepened the grooves in Gutierrez' face and revealed a purpling smear of bruise at the edge of his bandage. He settled in gingerly fashion onto one of the high stools; as he fumbled with his sling, Meg put the bottles down and moved quickly around the counter.

"Here, I'll hold it. But are you sure you should have a martini? If there's concussion . . ."

"Thanks." His fingers brushed her forearm fleetingly. "No concussion, just contusions, abrasions, and a dislocated shoulder. I told the doctor I preferred gin to pain pills. You look nice."

"Thank you." Suppressing an urge to adjust her neckline to a more modest level, she rattled bottles, glasses, and ice while Gutierrez described a drug raid that had involved a confused tangle of agencies, responsibilities, and motives.

". . . and this particular operation was purely amateur, a bunch of sidewalk cowboys. Poor bastards were ducking at any passing plane, sleeping in shifts to guard against narcs, or competition, or the Mafia, or redneck kids. Even tourists—one lady from Ohio came by the station to complain. She'd wanted a picture of a real California marijuana farm, and those people actually waved a gun at her."

"And at you?"

"Nope, at the D.A. who was standing there in his flak

jacket all ready to call up six armed deputies. I took the gun away. I do not like guns."

Meg handed him a glass, took a sip from her own. Now that she knew he was safe, she could almost wish him elsewhere. The man seemed to fill up a room, consume more than his proper share of oxygen. "Perhaps we should forget about dinner," she suggested. "You should probably go home and get some rest."

"And starve? I've been thinking for hours about cannelloni and veal."

Well. She herself had lunched on an apple and a piece of cheese. Veal and fettuccine; she had last eaten fettuccine Alfredo at Vanessi's in San Francisco.

"And I think you'll find Mary's is as good as any place in San Francisco."

She jumped, then raised her glass quickly to fill her mouth with the icy, aromatic fluid. If her thoughts were so transparent, she'd simply stop thinking. Or deal with business, she decided, and told him of her conversation with Tiny Olsen.

"I don't suppose it's important," she added, "but it does give support to *my* view of Dave Tucker. And the boy must have had scrapes and bruises, how could his father fail to notice?"

"We don't know that he did," said Gutierrez the policeman, making an entry in his notebook. "But we'll certainly try to find out."

Now Chrissie, thought Meg, and then changed her mind. No need to sic the police on poor Chrissie, not until she herself had talked to the girl again.

"... any more letters or threatening calls?" Gutierrez was asking.

"A call here, and one at the library." She explained briefly. "The Tuckers are still away, and Jenny wouldn't talk to me, but I'm sure it's all connected, Dave and the letters and the calls. Gutierrez, maybe it's Jenny! I'd never thought of that, but maybe it's Jenny!"

"I hadn't either, but it's possible. I'll explore it. Kid comes so close to being invisible that she slips your mind."

Like Johnny Stein, thought Meg, and asked Gutierrez whether the missing boy was still the main murder suspect.

"Basically, yes. We've found no trace of him or his bike. The other boarders didn't like him much, he wasn't friendly or helpful. Tucker was at the boardinghouse frequently. Nobody else knew him, and he didn't make any friendly overtures, either, but he was too eye-catching to miss.

"And . . ." Gutierrez gave the gin bottle a thoughtful look. "Better not. Tucker had been giving Stein money, or at least there were matching withdrawals and deposits. Best guess is something shady was going on that led finally to a blowup. I have half a dozen men looking for Stein."

"And I wish all of them the very best of luck." Meg raised her glass in a toast, then turned quickly as the swinging door from the hallway rattled against the wall. Blue eyes like beacons swept the glass-and-bottle-strewn counter, touched Gutierrez, then settled on Meg.

"Katy, you remember Chief Gutierrez? Katy?" Meg repeated her daughter's name in dangerously soft tones.

A twitch of smile in Gutierrez' direction; then, "Mommy, I'm too old for a baby-sitter. Cyndi just called, she can come over, she can even sleep over if you're going to stay out really late."

Not a request, but a confrontation, and damn Cyndi Martin anyway. "No, Katy, I'm sorry. Not tonight."

Katy swung around and stomped out, managing to produce hiking-boot noise with sneakered feet. Meg turned to Gutierrez and spread her hands helplessly. "Sorry. As my world crumbles around my ears, my daughter crumbles with it. She's always had lovely manners."

"If little girls didn't turn salty at ten or so, they'd never make it." The two-note peal of the doorchime brought them both to their feet; Gutierrez drained his glass, then glanced at his watch. "Jeff's right on time. And I promise you, Katy will like him."

Meg swept glasses and bottles from counter to sink board. She reached the entry hall just as Gutierrez closed the door.

"Ah, Meg. And Katy. This is my nephew, Jeff Mulkerrin. Jeff, the Hallorans."

Katy, hands jammed in her pockets, moved widening eyes from enormous lug-soled boots to faded Levi's to clean white tee shirt. Six feet tall, with eyes as blue as her own under a cap of auburn ringlets, Jeff held a flat, square box. Perched on his left shoulder was a black-and-white rat, whiskers twitching as a pointed nose sketched inquiring circles in the air.

The boy grinned at his uncle, nodded to Meg, and said, "Hi, Katy. This is Hannibal. And I brought a pepperoni pizza; that's his favorite. I hope you like it too."

·12·

"She didn't say good-bye," said Meg as she stepped outside. "Gutierrez, my daughter just walked off hand in hand with a boy and didn't even look back!"

"She probably won't do it again for at least a couple of years." He pulled the door tight. "Can you drive a car with a five-speed box?"

"Can I . . . As a matter of fact, I can drive anything from a Harley to an eighteen-wheeler, why?"

"Shifting turned out to be a bitch, just like the doctor

said, but the department's only unmarked vehicle got its radiator ventilated today."

The five-speed box belonged to a Porsche whose paint shone brightly red even in the fog. "I thought you were *police* chief," she murmured. "Gutierrez, how on earth . . . ?"

"Does a poor cop manage to run a Porsche? By having no family, a good head for investments, and a mostly frugal lifestyle. End of quote," he added with a grin.

"Oh, Well, I'm going to feel conspicuous."

He handed her the keys, then opened the passenger door for himself. "Your anonymous caller could probably quote you something about not hiding your light under a bushel."

In the driver's seat, she did a quick instrument check: lights, gauges, side mirrors, gearshift. Pedals: just right, Gutierrez was an inch or two taller but her legs were long for her height. As she put the key in the ignition, she glanced at him, and grinned at the flicker of apprehension on his face.

"Fear not," she told him as she started the engine, "you're in good hands. Dan and I ran rallies in an MG. He navigated and I drove, and we usually finished well up."

"Ah. Well, as navigator I suggest . . . What's that?"

Meg followed his gaze, watched the shadowy figure for a moment, then snorted. "Cyndi, who could miss that waddle? She's out of luck, Katy will surely *not* want to share her prize. Where to, navigator?"

"Mary's is up the coast highway. In this weather I'd drive straight downtown and then take Main Street north."

For several blocks Meg concentrated on herself and the car. As they approached Main she noted that the heavy, wet fog was not keeping the locals from their Saturday-night pursuits. Lights still gleamed in many stores, pick-ups and sedans dotted the curbs, pedestrians wore windbreakers but were for the most part bareheaded. A nod from the sidewalk, a wave, another wave a block later. We're running some kind of damned gantlet here! she thought, and turned to protest; but Gutierrez' running chatter left her no opening.

". . . surprising what you can pull off if you simply smile and stay easy. My mother came to this town with no husband in sight, a flock of little brown kids, and a Mexican name."

"From New England. That's what Miss Luoma said." Meg cast a doubting glance at the fierce profile, and Gutierrez chuckled.

"Right. Emily Butler. Nineteen years old, got sent from New Hampshire to New Mexico for her health and met Esteban Gutierrez. Married in a month, both families hysterical, and my brother Richard appeared just under nine months later." The light above them turned to green; a tall white-haired woman leaning on a cane gave them a semi-bow and proceeded on her slow way.

"Papa was a geologist and mining engineer," Gutierrez went on. "When Mama finally had too many babies to haul all over Central and South America, she moved up here and settled in. She says it reminded her of home."

The road left the business district and swung east to skirt the university campus on its headland. Lighted parking lots glowed under the fog, and building tops poked through like islands in a misty gray sea. "So you grew up here?"

"Right. Papa traveled for the oil companies. Mama stayed here and took care of babies. There are seven of us; Mary Louise was born just about a year before Papa died in a plane crash."

Meg made a little, involuntary sound of sorrow. Gutierrez shifted in his seat, coughed. "Anyway, that was a long time ago. Right now Mama's getting set for grandchild number—let's see, I think number twenty-three."

"Twenty-three!"

He put his left hand up shield-fashioned. "Not me, lady, none of them are mine. I was married once, a long time ago; but we both realized what a mistake we'd made before there were any kids. I am a professional uncle." He leaned forward. "Okay, from this light you go eight and two-tenths miles to the turnoff."

Meg settled the road-hugging little car into high gear and a respectable speed. The highway edged the coastline with now and then a patch of long-grassed meadow intervening, studded with vague lumps, rocks or perhaps sheep. The sea was there, when she rolled down her window she could hear it; but it was hidden from view by a gray wall, a shimmery scrim that might be pulled aside in the next act. The wet, empty road shone under the Porsche's foglights; after a while Meg found her eyes sliding to the right once more. New England mother or not, it was a face to be found on ancient masks, and . . .

"Yeah, I'm the old one, my father's grandfather." He touched her shoulder lightly, as if in apology for catching her thoughts at their source. "I think he was pure Indio; I met him once when I was about ten. I was the brownest one, and something about my face kept getting me into fights. Then here's this old guy looking like some kind of ancient, ageless . . . shaman I guess is the word; I didn't know it then. And looking just like me at the same time. I was scared as hell.

"There's the turnoff, there'll be a left-turn lane." Gutierrez was looking straight ahead, his voice impersonal. "The road meanders a bit; just follow the yellow line right out to the end."

. . .

"Oh—yes, of course it was good. No, it was wonderful, Mary. Thank you." Smiling up at the plump face framed by sweeping wings of midnight-black hair, Meg stifled a sigh. Back to reality; neither ancient Indian magic nor dogged determination can stop the clock for long.

Mary had seated them in one of the several small alcoves created by careful placement of antique sideboards, bookcases, tall plant stands. By the time wine was poured Meg had banished the other diners to murmuring outer darkness and was participating in Gutierrez' scenario. Murder, harassment, civic uneasiness, and political expediency were tacitly but firmly set aside as uncivil dinner-table topics. Instead, baseball, Mozart, John le Carré, Tom Lehrer.

Now Mary Devincenzi chuckled, sending a shimmer over the dull black silk encasing her heavy body. "We been here a long time, my family, we own the place. So we don't have to hurry the cooking or crowd folks in. Now, what? A nice pastry? gelato? zabaglione?" Two heads shook, and Mary went on, "Coffee? brandy?"

Gutierrez pushed his chair back and stretched, carefully. "Mary, has the fog lifted?"

"More like just rolled back, waiting. You can see the boats, though. Ah, you want your coffee in the bar."

Behind the polished bar was a long window, and beyond the window, the sea. Small boats rode at anchor, and a curve of white moon sailed serenely above the fog bank. Meg shortened her focus, saw a reflection of herself, smiled a wry smile. Nothing wrong with a little fantasy. Gutierrez had needed it as much as she, perhaps more.

"Thank you," Gutierrez murmured to the waiter who had just set steaming cups before them. As Meg inhaled an aroma nearly pungent enough to induce sneezing, her companion leaned forward to look at her. "So . . . what about you? This is a nice little town, but very different from Tucson. What brought you here, you and Katy?"

Meg took a sip of coffee and then set the cup aside. "Dan Halloran and I married late, and we used to joke about how smart we were to have waited for each other." She paused to draw a deep breath. "Dan was killed in an auto accident, and for a long time after that I didn't cope with life very well. 'Cope' is a favorite word of my mother's; she is a champion coper, always more than willing to cope for those of us who can't manage it. Mother wanted me to sell our house, Dan's and mine, and move back home. I could have my old room, and Katy could have my sister's."

"Terrific," murmured Gutierrez.

"I was almost tempted," Meg admitted. "I'd have had no responsibilities except to go to work and come home. And drink. So I put the house on the market and came here—my sister's husband spent a year here as a visiting professor and they loved it—and was lucky enough to find a job. At least, I thought at the time it was lucky."

"I believe . . . I *promise* you'll think so again. Trust me."

"Chief Gutierrez?" said a voice from behind them, and Gutierrez turned, frowning. "Telephone for you. Lieutenant Svobada. Mary says take it in the office."

Gutierrez departed with an exaggerated sigh. Meg hunched over her cup, shoulder muscles tightening as if someone was turning a key in her back. Cops were like doctors, always on call; but suppose it was Jeff, and something had happened to Katy. She saw Gutierrez' reflection in the window and turned quickly.

"What's happened?"

"Not Katy." He settled onto his stool, raising one hand in a "just a minute" gesture as he squeezed his eyes briefly shut. "Sorry, I moved too fast, or drank too much. There's been a break-in at the Tucker house."

"Tucker? But Jenny was there alone!"

"She's all right. Svoboda's there. He raised a whole flock of daughters and he's sure she's just scared. Anyway, it was several guys. They blindfolded her and shoved her into a closet. She doesn't know what they wanted. Svoboda made her call her parents, and they're on their way home."

"And you need to get there."

"No ma'am, Svoboda will do just fine and the city has had all of me it gets for today." He tipped his head back for a jaw-crackling yawn. "But it's time to go."

In the car, he rolled down his window and leaned back.

"Meg, would you mind driving me home and keeping the car? I can get it tomorrow, I'll have one of my men pick me up."

Meg inspected his face; the damp-skinned, pasty look had faded to simple weariness. "Imagine that, I get to take this pretty toy home with me!" she said brightly. At his direction, she returned to the coast highway and turned south. The road was clear of fog now, washed by cold moonlight. Meg thought of Jenny Tucker and shivered.

"There." Gutierrez leaned forward. "That goat track up the side of the hill on the left."

Goat track indeed; she geared all the way down and expected every second to hear the undercarriage scrape. A jog to the left, then a wide swing right, and they were before a smallish glass-fronted building stilted high against the side of the hill.

Meg pulled to a stop at a flight of stairs. "Can you manage?"

"I'm fine." Gutierrez laid his palms flat against his temples as if testing his words. "I'm fine, the fresh air got rid of the fuzzy edges. Why don't you come up for a few minutes?"

"Um, well. No, I don't think so. Thanks for a very nice evening, but I'd better get home."

Gutierrez pushed his door open, then turned to look at her. "I enjoyed myself tonight. I don't want the evening to end in sirens and police calls. I want you to come up, see the place where I live, have one beer. Please."

He broke suddenly into his white-toothed, high-energy grin; she threw her head back and laughed. By the time she had opened the door and swung her feet out, he was beside her. She met his extended hand with her own and stepped out into moonlight; he brushed his mouth very lightly against hers.

"I promise you, that's my limit. For tonight." He turned to ease the car door shut. "This late, when there's no traffic, all you can hear is the sea. Listen."

After a moment he took her hand again and began to

move toward the house. "Let's see. I have some Bohemia, I think. And some Anchor Steam."

From beside the steps a shadow uncoiled. Meg screamed, and Gutierrez flung an arm out, pushing her behind him.

"Chief Gutierrez! Jeez, I've been waiting for hours, seems like." The boy planted his feet and stood with wide shoulders slumped, han• loose at his sides. Under tumbled, lightish hair his face was angular and very young, with an enormous arch of nose and pale, short-lashed eyes.

"That's a good way to get hurt, Mike, jumping at people out of the dark." Gutierrez' voice was tight, as if pushed through clenched teeth.

The boy paid no attention. "Look, you've gotta come. There's a truck been down there since last night. And the guy in it, I think he's—I think there's something wrong with him, only the door's locked and I can't get in." The last words were a high wail.

"Down where?"

The wave of a long arm. "Down there on that little strip of rocky beach. See, me and my girl, we've got kind of our own spot down there, where we like to go. I needed to tell somebody, and your place was right close, so I sent Inge on home, and—oh, shit!"

"Ingeborg Olsen. I understand your caution, Mike. Meg, here are my house keys; you can wait inside while I go see what's up."

But Meg was already beside the Porsche. "Squeeze yourself into the back, Mike."

Down the goat track, across the road, carefully along the broad dirt shoulder; and Mike kept talking.

"We was there last night when this truck drove down. A truck or an old car can make it but I don't think I'd take this bomb down, Chief Gutierrez.

"Anyway, just a real old truck; I didn't get a good look but Inge says she thinks there was two people. They drove past our place and on down to the end of the beach. Didn't bother us, probably didn't even see us, so we didn't bother them.

"So tonight we went down there kind of late, after the movie. And Inge says, 'Hey, those guys are back, do you suppose they're anybody that knows us?' She was sort of worried, so I went over to look. It was while the fog was still thick."

Meg had nosed the Porsche as far right as it would go. The three of them piled out, and Gutierrez snapped "Wait!" as he fished around in the luggage compartment. He handed Mike a lantern flashlight and balanced a short tire iron in his own hand. "Okay."

Mike led the way, words spilling out once again. "First thing I noticed, the tailgate was down and the back was empty, I'd kinda thought there was something in there before. Then there was a little flicker of moon, the fog starting to break. I saw the guy was by himself, stretched out like he was asleep but looking sorta funny, I don't know. I banged on the window and hollered, but he didn't move. Man, I'm glad you finally got home, Chief Gutierrez. Can I go now?"

"Not yet, I may need your muscle. Let me have the lantern." He turned the light on the truck, which was ancient and dusty black. The beam of light swept slowly from windshield to tailgate; Meg saw that the exhaust pipe looked peculiar, as if it were flexible and bent back on itself under the vehicle.

"Here, you've got two good arms." Gutierrez handed the tire iron to the boy. "The window on this side isn't tight at the top; set the iron in the crack and pop it." Fumbling, grunting, and a splintering crack; then Gutierrez stepped forward and opened the door.

A long body lay slumped back, head resting well to the right, face turned left. Meg peered past Gutierrez' shoulder to see a dark—unnaturally dark—face. Thick black hair was cut short on top, longer on the sides and probably meant to be slicked back. Eyelashes were very long, the nose small over a small, girlish mouth.

"It's Stein, isn't it?" she whispered; and Gutierrez grunted as he laid the back of his hand just below the boy's jawbone.

"There was . . ." she stopped, cleared her throat, then began again. "There was a picture in the paper, and I thought he looked like Elvis Presley. That little bee-stung mouth." Her own lips felt numb, unwilling to make word shapes.

"He's been dead quite a while, probably since last night," said Gutierrez. "Carbon monoxide." Mike made a gargling sound and fled toward the water. A wisp of wind caught a sheet of paper from somewhere in the truck cab and sent it fluttering to the ground.

Swallowing hard against a nauseating lurch in the pit of her stomach, Meg took the lantern from Gutierrez and knelt to turn it on the paper. White, unlined, perhaps six by nine. Typing, double spaced, errorless; and a scrawled J. S. as signature. "Davey didn't want to be my lover anymore, he was tired of me. So I killed him, but I'm sorry, real sorry, I wish I hadn't done it. You can't make someone love you by killing them."

•13•

Just another Monday after a hard weekend, thought Meg, and blinked against sharp mid-morning light. Except those old Mondays had followed upon too much drinking or talking, while today's hangover had its roots in dreams of murder, of dark dead faces with pouty little Elvis mouths.

She braked the van and turned into the parking lot of the First National Bank. Should have called Gutierrez first. Never mind, he was probably as worn out as she and in as foul a temper.

Cars arriving, cars leaving . . . after one circuit of the lot, Meg pulled into a slot clearly marked Employees Only. This was Mr. Tucker's idea, after all, and she still wasn't sure why she'd agreed to come. As she slid out of the van, she squinted at her image in the side mirror and decided that she looked better than she felt, but not by much.

The bank lobby was bright with polish and sunshine, humming with Monday bustle. Behind a wooden railing a young woman shook back a silky fall of very blond hair and said in breathy tones that Mr. Tucker was expecting Mrs. Halloran, just come this way, please.

It was less an office than an enclosed meadow of grassy green carpet. Tucker rose from behind an enormous desk of dark and gleaming wood, grasped Meg's hand briefly, and settled her into a leather chair before resuming his own seat. "Mrs. Halloran, good of you to come. I appreciate you sparing me a bit of your time; I'm sure we can mend fences if we only . . ."

He peered at her from pink-rimmed eyes, a man who appeared to have dressed in the dark. There was a wispy frill of blondish hair over each ear; the collar of his white shirt was bunched up to one side of a poorly knotted black tie, and the French cuffs were held together by unmatched links.

"Mr. Tucker, I chose to come without my attorney, which may not have been wise. Please tell me what this is all about."

He blinked at her. "Attorney? No need for . . . well, of course, if you wish. Excuse me, Mrs. Halloran," he muttered, brushing his fingers across his eyes. "I'm not thinking clearly, very tired, it's all been too much."

Certainly too much . . . a dead son, the murderer's

suicide, the violation of his home by burglars. This morning's paper had reported the last incident in a separate story on an inside page. "Was Jenny hurt?" Meg asked.

"Jenny?" He frowned, as if he had trouble focusing on his own daughter, then shook his head. "No, no, Jennifer is fine. Apparently the burglars were expecting an empty house and she surprised them. They just put a pillowcase over her head and told her to keep quiet and shut her up in her own closet. She's fine."

Fine. Jenny was just fine. Probably she'd leaped from the closet, tossing the pillowcase aside and proclaiming her fineness at the top of her voice. Gloryoski, Daddy, I am fine! Those fellows did not beat me or rape me or murder me, so I am fine! "I'm happy for her," said Meg. "Mr. Tucker, just what is it you want of me?"

"Mrs. Halloran, I understand that Chief Gutierrez took you with him Saturday night when he went to, um, discover the body of this John Stein."

Disapproval there, but in an undertone; the main issue was yet to be touched. "That's true, I went along to help," Meg said silkily. "Chief Gutierrez was off duty at the time; and as you may know, he'd been injured earlier in the day."

"Injured. Yes, of course, I'd forgotten. Mrs. Halloran, I understand that he showed you the young man's, ah, suicide note."

"No." As the blond head came up sharply, Meg went on. "He didn't show it to me. It blew out of the truck, and I was the first to see it."

"But you read it."

"Oh, yes."

"Yes." The figure behind the desk seemed to sink in on itself; Meg had an image of polished shoes dangling, not quite able to reach the carpet. "Well, it's all over now, my son's murderer is no longer a threat to the community. Time to try to get back to normal." He paused to line up his leather blotter holder with the edge of his desk, to set a gold pen and a notepad perpendicular to that edge.

"I'm establishing a scholarship in David's name. I will start the fund, but of course others will be welcome to contribute."

"Mr. Tucker, this is all very interesting, but what is it that I . . . ?"

He pushed his chair back and rose to pace behind his desk. "A scholarship for a young man interested in the ministry," he intoned. "That's what we wanted for David, a life of Christian ministry. He felt and we felt that he had the call." He shot Meg an anguished look. "From the very beginning David was full of such promise! He was handsome, intelligent, serious. And good, we thought he was good." He spoke these last words softly as he paused behind his chair, gripped its back in both hands, and with obvious effort pulled himself straight.

"So my hope is that you'll be willing to forget past . . . misunderstandings and be kind to us, to Mrs. Tucker and me. Chief Gutierrez agrees that there is no need to make that foul note public. But he says it is not within his power to compel you, a private citizen, to silence. He told me I'd have to speak to you myself, which is . . . what I'm doing now." He paused to lick his lips. "Our only son is lost to us, apparently had been lost to us for some time. I'm asking that you help us to preserve at least his good name."

The figurative light bulb over her head clicked on at last. Gutierrez, nudged along by fate, had handed her a weapon. To turn a potent enemy into an equally potent ally, she had only to promise to keep a secret that she'd had no intention of revealing.

Her thoughts must have been plain on her face. Tucker sat down and drew a deep breath. "Mrs. Halloran, I loved my son. Perhaps as much as you love your daughter. Now I do not advocate shooting homosexuals down in the street, nor even denying them jobs. But I honestly believe, my faith tells me, that what these people do is

abominable in the eyes of God and our Lord Jesus. That
they cannot be saved unless they repent and change their
way of living. Can you understand how that makes me
feel about my son's death? About his salvation?"

He sighed. "Although I suppose it is cowardly of me to
worry about public opinion."

Is bigotry any less offensive for being sincere? Meg
wondered, and decided that somehow, in this case, the
answer was yes. And was it decent for her to take advantage . . .

Never mind. Boy-scout morality is best left to ten-year-
old boys. Cut and deal. She settled back into her chair.
"In the coldest of blood," she told him, "I have to think
that the destruction of Dave's good name would probably
benefit me. Perhaps you can convince me that I'm wrong."

Meg detested game playing of this sort; Tucker, even
in the grip of a deep distress, possessed a good deal of
skill. He gave sober, avuncular attention to each issue as
Meg raised it, offered solutions without in any way ac-
cepting blame. Bobbing and weaving, Dan would have
called it.

If he had voiced anything like an accusation against
her, Tucker said, he had done so in time of personal
stress and sorrow, had been overheard by purest chance.
But he would certainly retract any such accusation and
put a firm stop to any rumormongering among his
employees.

If David had delivered anonymous letters to Mrs.
Halloran, and evidence the police had found suggested
that David had, Mr. Tucker was sorry and ashamed; but
he had no idea, none at all, whose hand had actually
shaped those words.

And as to Bible-quoting phone callers, he had never
made an anonymous call in his life nor had his daughter.
He had asked Jenny and he believed her denial and so did
Chief Gutierrez. Tucker spread his hands and shook his
head. Honest concern? Meg was past judging.

She nodded and rose. "I promise you," she said to him, "that I have no intention of revealing the contents of Johnny Stein's letter to anyone. But further assaults on my privacy or my reputation might very well weaken my resolve. No, don't bother to get up, I can show myself out."

· · ·

Arm extended to press the doorbell for a third time, Meg peered through black iron grating into a dark hallway. Of course Jenny Tucker was not her anonymous enemy, that was a stupid notion and she was embarrassed about it. Jenny, whose privacy had been violated but who was now, once again, at home alone, because her mother was "resting" at a resort some miles inland. Approaching Mariposa Street on her way home, Meg had made no real decision, had simply turned left.

If Jenny was at home, she was either sound asleep or hiding. Meg stepped off the porch and peered up at second-story windows, already half regretting her impulse. She'd go home and call Gutierrez, ask him to have Svoboda or somebody check on Jenny. Or perhaps he could rustle up a spare niece to keep a frightened girl company.

"Nobody here. And we don't need no more reporters."

Meg spun around to meet the baleful glare of a squat, dark man holding a pair of hedge clippers.

"Oh, I'm sorry. I'm not a reporter, I'm a friend of Jenny's, a teacher." The man tipped his head back to inspect her face as she hurried on. "I just spoke with her father, and I thought she might be still frightened. I wanted to make sure she wasn't alone."

"She *was* alone, except for her pooch, that poodle. Her mother's off someplace again. Jenny fixed my lunch and put it in the fridge; then she lit out in her little car."

Meg's eyebrows lifted in polite query. He looked at her for another moment, then shrugged. "Went to the beach,

I expect. She takes the dog there most days. Now I got work to do."

• • •

At home, Meg found a note on the kitchen table. Katy had made her bed, practiced her guitar. She had then gone shopping in town with the Martins, who would probably head afterward for a beach. Louise would feed everyone, Meg was not to worry.

Gutierrez was not available, either. Meg declined to leave a message. "Nobody loves me, everybody hates me, guess I'll go eat worms," she sang softly. Then she opened the back door and braced herself as Grendel came to weave lumbering happy circles about her legs. Somebody loved her. He also loved the beach; and as everyone else had apparently discovered, this was turning into a fine day for the beach.

"Since we are good citizens," she advised the dog a few minutes later, "we will go to the appropriate beach. Get down, you dolt, I can't see." She backed carefully onto the street, then pointed the van west. "Yes indeed, to avoid giving offense we will go to Driftwood Cove, otherwise known as dogshit strip. You remember that place, tiger. Dogs are legal there. It's where you took on two huskies at once."

And it's where Jenny Tucker, who courted invisibility, would take her dog to run. Meg still felt a niggling need to see Jenny. How, she wondered, could anybody feel fine after having been captured and blindfolded and locked up in her own house? Katy had been cornered, captured in her own house, by Dave Tucker; Katy hadn't been fine for a long time after that. And Meg was sure that if Jenny *had* been raped, or mistreated in any embarrassing fashion, Mr. Tucker would do his best to conceal that fact, deny it. Never mind, dear, it didn't really happen.

The sandy strip at Driftwood Cove was an unofficial beach, one of many dotting the North Coast; and two pieces of flat empty ground which happened to border the road there had become unofficial parking lots. More than a dozen vehicles were there today, from pickups and vans to several nondescript imports, any one of which might be "Jenny's little car." As she clipped the dog's leash into place and let him out, Meg made a bargain with herself: she would settle for just a glimpse of the girl, would not bother her. "Now heel, lummox! Don't lunge!"

There were a good many people on the beach, most with dogs. A tiny gray poodle pranced by, towing a tiny gray lady. A preteen girl with a vaguely familiar face pulled her cocker up short, listened, and shook her head. Sure, she knew Jenny Tucker, but she hadn't seen her today.

With a rumble of exasperation Grendel tugged hard at his leash. "Why not?" she muttered, peering south at a stretch of beach untenanted except for shorebirds. She let Grendel off lead, then set off smartly after him; down to the end of the cove and back, for the leg-stretch she and the dog both needed.

"Grendel, come!" she called suddenly; he had shot off toward something large and black playing in the surf. "Come!" Grendel never looked for fights, but his size and manner often moved other animals to defensive action.

There was a burst of yapping, then a deeper yelp. The black dog, a standard poodle in a rough kennel clip, had dealt smartly with Grendel and was now venturing further out into the surf. As Meg drew closer, she heard a whine, then a single bark. She followed the dog's line of sight, and saw a head out beyond the breakers, uncomfortably far out.

"Shit," she muttered. There was no one nearby, and none of the distant walkers was looking in her direction. She recalled the signs at the top of the path: Caution, hazardous water, no lifeguards.

"Shit!" She kicked off her sneakers, unzipped her jeans.

JANET LAPIERRE

A strong swimmer, she'd had lifeguard training many years ago, training in pulling people out of *pools*. She couldn't be sure it was Jenny Tucker out there. If it *was* Jenny, she was probably enjoying her solitude. Meg stepped ankle-deep into the surf and caught her breath at its chill.

How to get out? Twice she attempted to leap through chest-high waves; then she took a deep breath, set her jaw, and launched herself headfirst, going so deep that she felt swirling sand against her face. Scraping of knees, a push with both feet; she was up and out on the other side, facing an endless swell of dark green, oily-looking water. Little lashings of white danced here and there, surely not foam but ice.

Instant retreat of blood, with the beginning of numbness in feet and hands. She snapped her head sideways to fling wet hair from her face, snatched measuring glances beyond and behind. A single, frog-kicking breast stroke brought her body level; then she threw herself into a churning crawl, battling aslant up an endless hill to a nauseating drop and the same hill again. Physical rescue was out of the question; if she kept moving as hard and fast as she could, she might come to within calling distance of the girl and still be able to get back.

Head up for a look; back to churning, each stroke requiring more effort. Another look, and there, ten feet ahead, was the figure she'd seen . . . no, the head she'd seen. Long wet hair clinging and then frothing with the water's movement, just a black-and-white cork bobbing.

"Jenny!" she shrieked, taking a mouthful of water. The head jerked; not a cork, not drowned.

The girl turned, arms moving languidly, body nearly upright in the water. Half-hidden by plastered strands of hair, the white face was without expression. "Leave . . . 'lone," she croaked.

As if she had a choice, thought Meg grimly. Warmth was only a memory, a dying ember somewhere deep in her belly; her numb limbs would soon be beyond

120

her commanding. "Right!" she shouted. Then, "But look!"

Both dogs had managed to get past the breakers and were paddling slowly but steadily out; the poodle was leader by several feet, curly black head high out of the water. Jenny's face twisted in some emotion, pain or perhaps anger. As Meg began to stroke beachward, she looked over her shoulder and saw long white arms rise and fall, their awkwardness nearly as terrifying as the girl's earlier stillness.

Surely the waves should be helping now, she told herself. Why weren't they, why were her arms so heavy, what made her feet continue to sink? kick, goddamn it! Behind her, Jenny's arms were still flashing . . . wrong word, they stuck up and then fell down, slow windmill blades. Just keep it up, Jenny, I'm going to make it and I think you can too, I think so.

Here are the dogs, good dogs, all insulated in nice woolly coats; Grendel, if you get in my way I'll kill you, where the hell's your collar?

She realized that her heavy feet had touched bottom. Determination and her grip on the dog's collar brought her upright, carried her forward in stumbling steps. By God I did it! I'm walking out! She let go of the collar and fell forward to hands and knees. Ignominious scramble forward, to get clear of the icy foam; hanging head, heaving lungs, and all the while her mind playing and replaying a prayerful apology to Katy: sorry, baby, sorry, just about blew that one.

Up rear end first, like an old and very weary cow. Absolute blind foolishness, behaving as if she were still a teenaged athlete. And where was that damned girl? She swung around, and the warming flare of anger died. Jenny was coming out of the water on her feet, moving slowly and awkwardly like an ivory doll jointed only at the hip. She wore nylon running shorts and a tee shirt; her skin was blue-white and goose pimpled. Meg moved to meet her and put her arms around the shaking shoulders; but the two of them were two sets of bones rattling against each other, with no heat to share.

There wasn't a towel in sight, only the jeans Meg had discarded. "Here, Jenny, put these on and we'll get to my van, my towels."

Jenny shook her head. "You'd . . . better put them . . . on," she said through chattering teeth. She clutched her own elbows tight and blew out her breath. "Teachers . . . better not run around in their underpants." Almost a giggle.

"Well, screw *that*." Meg tugged her shirt as long as it would go, picked up her shoes, draped the jeans over her shoulders. Then she gripped the girl's hand. "Come on, everybody run!"

• • •

Wrapped in two beach towels, Jenny huddled in the van's passenger seat. The girl's skin was still bluish, and spasmodic shudders continued to rack her narrow body from entwined ankles to clenched teeth. Meg kicked the throttle hard to disengage the engine's fast idle, then bent to adjust the heater vents.

"You're in no shape to drive, Jenny. You can get your car later." Without waiting for agreement, she began to edge the van backwards from between its neighbors. By the time they gained the highway and turned north, Jenny had untwisted her legs and was sitting straighter, head up.

"Mrs. Halloran, I'm sorry you had to . . ." Her voice caught and she faked a cough. "I always like to go out there where nobody is," she began again, her voice wispy. "I usually wear a wet suit. But it wasn't in the car today, and I didn't want to go back in the house for it." A pause, and a deep breath. "So thanks."

Meg shot a quick glance sideways. She had no idea whether or not Jenny had intended to return to shore;

she doubted that Jenny herself knew for sure. "I'm glad I was there," was all she said.

Sliding another glance toward Jenny, she met a wide gray-eyed gaze. Limpid, she thought. And innocent. Lie to that face and your nose will grow six inches.

"I saw your father this morning, Jenny." The girl's mouth stretched thin, corners tucking in. "He mentioned the break-in and said that you hadn't been hurt, but it seemed to me not a good idea for you to be home alone."

"I really wasn't hurt," Jenny said flatly; "just scared. I woke up and heard a noise, and when I went out in the hall somebody grabbed me. They put something over my head and pushed me in the closet and shoved a big dresser up against the door. They told me if I tried to get out they'd make me real sorry. Then, not long after I heard them leave, the cops came. They wanted to talk to my dad about a . . . body."

"Jenny, did you know Johnny Stein?"

Jenny's chin went up. "No, but I saw that note. Johnny Stein was pretty dumb if he thought my brother loved him. Dave never loved anybody. Besides, Dave hated what he called 'queers'; he said they were an abomination in the eyes of the Lord. So how did you find me, Mrs. Halloran? Did my dad tell you where I'd be?" A determined change of tone, and of subject.

Meg shook her head. "I went by your house and I met your gardener, I suppose he is. But he said you'd be walking your poodle, and I was looking for something small with a topknot and pompons."

Jenny made a sound that would have been a snort from a heartier specimen; her left hand reached sideways to rub the curly black head that had poked between the seats. "Hey, Feef. This is Feef."

The girl drew her legs closer. "For my birthday last year I wanted a dog, a Lab or a golden retriever. Or maybe a rottweiler. My dad said I could have a poodle, he signed a blank check and told me to go buy a good poodle.

"So I brought this dumb poodle home, she was only eight weeks old and real little, I told him her name was Fifi. He thought that was all just great and he didn't even look at her again until she was four or five months old and up to about forty pounds; she's fifty now. My dad never heard of standard poodles. I tried to find a royal standard."

Passive resistance of a very inventive sort, thought Meg in surprise. "Hi, Feef," she murmured. The poodle cocked its head at her, then turned to give Jenny's ear a lick and a nibble.

"She turned out to be okay," admitted Jenny, eyes straight ahead. "She's not tough or even very smart, but she's funny. And she really likes me. Where are you going?" she asked in a sharper tone, sitting straight to look around.

"I thought I'd take you home first, and . . . whoops, wait a minute!" Meg pulled the van over and braked hard as Jenny scrambled free of her towel cocoon.

"Let me out, I'm not going back there!"

"Jenny, stop that!" Meg's sharp command brought the girl to a momentary, quivering halt.

"Sit down. I'll take you wherever you want to go. Do you have an aunt? A friend?"

Jenny simply stared at her, tears welling and then spilling in great slow drops.

"Jenny, please stop that! I catch tears the way other people catch yawns." As she spoke Meg felt her own eyes fill. Jenny peered, blinked, and produced a tiny ghost of a giggle.

"All right, I'll take you home with me, if you like. Do you like?"

A sniffle, and an abrupt nod.

"Fine. I'll find you a dry pair of jeans and a sweatshirt, and something to eat; and you can pay me back by brush-

ing the sand out of my dog, how does that sound?"
Another nod.

"And Jenny, we'll have to let your father know where
you are, but not to worry." She extended a cupped palm
and gave it an imperious look. "For the moment, I have
the man in the palm of my hand."

◦ 14 ◦

Gray and cold. She must be very deep, and her arms and
legs refused to move. The sea was winning after all, held
her in an icy clasp she would never break.

"Mommy? Telephone."

Not the sea. Meg lurched upright and waited for her
pounding heart to slow. Stretched in a beach chair in her
own backyard, she'd slept the sunlight away, had finally
been covered toe to chin by the chilly shadow of the high
board fence. "Coming, Katy."

"I'm aware that you didn't leave a message," said
Gutierrez. "Apparently the man on the desk recognized
your voice. What's the problem?"

She propped a shoulder against the wall and rubbed a
bare sole against a bare instep. "Never mind, it wasn't
important." Her circulation and her mental processes
seemed equally sluggish; what had she said or done to
bring that note of irritation to Gutierrez' voice? A glance
at her watch, and she spoke quickly, overriding his next
words. "Hey, it's time I did something about feeding the
troops. Would you like to come join us for whatever it
turns out to be?"

His "Sorry" was perfunctory. "I'm tied up here. Just

tell me what you called about, and let me be the judge of its importance."

The blast of wrath or humiliation that swept her proved wonderfully warming. "Thank you very much, Chief Gutierrez," she said, biting off each word, "but I'll try to manage my life without official assistance." She set the receiver into its cradle with exaggerated care. Close mouth, inhale through nose in quick hard sniffs, lungs full, Haaaa! And again. Thank you, Amrita, she told her long-ago yoga teacher, the cleansing breath *does*.

"Jenny? Let's go get your car. Katy, you come, too, and we'll get something to eat on the way home. I'll bet Jenny knows a good hamburger place."

"Mommy?" Katy trailed the other two through the kitchen. "Mommy, the phone's ringing."

"Never mind, baby. I'm sure it's no one we'd care to talk to."

. . .

Perhaps a crime wave had developed. Meg's eyes were on the small tan Toyota she was following, but with only casual attention; Jenny was, as she had insisted, a good and careful driver. The Toyota's right rear light began to flash, and Meg flipped her own signal lever, noting that Jenny's idea of a place to eat looked less than promising. Well, once couldn't hurt.

Or perhaps Gutierrez had come across another nasty rumor, a convincing one. She followed Jenny past several big rigs to park head-in against a concrete-block building.

The Hungry Wheels cafe had dust-blurred windows, a grayish floor pocked from many boot heels. Burgers, fries, milk shakes, proclaimed one plastic-lettered sign above the counter. Hot roast beef sandwiches, apple pie, said another, with pictures.

"Mommy, can we stay and eat here? This is a neat place, it smells wonderful."

Frying onions always smell wonderful. Meg looked

around at the eight or nine large men bent over plates, noted that the woman behind the counter had a broad, cheerful face as well as a reasonably clean apron. The woman turned, flipped meat patties on a grill; there was a spitting sizzle, a cloud of steam. More than onions smelled good.

At the counter a burly diner pushed his plate away and turned toward the newcomers. He gave Meg a long look and an appreciative grin that showed a lot of large white teeth.

The better to eat you with, she thought. Bastards.

With a polite nod he picked up his coffee mug and slid one seat to his left, leaving a row of three empty stools. Meg felt her face grow warm as she nodded in return. "Sit down, girls," she muttered, "and decide what you want."

She watched the woman flip meat, push onions about in the grease, set open buns facedown to toast. Gutierrez wasn't a bastard, either, and she wanted to know what was troubling him. "Double my order, please," she told the cook, unwinding her legs from the stool support.

"You two stay here to eat if you like," she said, handing Jenny a bill. "I'll take mine with me, and pay a visit to a sick friend. See you at home in an hour or so."

. . .

"This police station is not a model of efficiency," stated Meg as she closed the door of Gutierrez' office behind her. "For all that man out front knows, I could have a bomb in this bag."

Gutierrez sprang up from behind his battered metal desk, sending his chair careening against the wall. "He probably hopes you have." A flush darkened his face, exaggerating the old bruise above his right eye. "I've been trying your number every five minutes since you hung up." He came around the desk, hand extended; she thrust the paper bag at him and settled into a nearby wooden armchair, face fixed in an expression of polite inquiry.

"Well. The thing is, I've been taking shit all day, and like any good commander I've passed it on to the troops." He paused to sniff. "A bomb with onions. And then you got into the line of fire. I saw the note and returned your call without giving myself time to change modes. I'm sorry as hell." His gesture in her direction was impeded by the bag. "Um, Meg. Is this for me?"

"Half of it, if you're hungry. Otherwise I have two kids and two dogs who aren't fussy about leftovers."

"Two kids. And two dogs." Gutierrez opened the bag, lifted out a grease-stained paper parcel, and inhaled deeply. "Jesus, you're a lifesaver. I haven't eaten since breakfast."

Meg accepted the proffered burger and laid it on the desk. "French fries in the bag, and a couple of beers here," she said, rooting around in her big shoulder bag. "Although I suppose liquor might be illegal in a police station."

"Never mind, I'm thinking about blowing this chicken outfit." He settled his rump on the edge of the desk and opened the second parcel. "Tell me about the extra kid and dog."

"I've managed to collect Jenny Tucker and her standard poodle." Gutierrez glanced up quickly; she considered relating her beach adventure, then decided against it. "Jenny is . . . I thought she shouldn't be alone at home. And she and Katy hit it off at once. Do you know who broke into Jenny's house? Or why?"

Gutierrez' raised eyebrows swooped into a frown; he resumed chewing and shook his head. "Jenny said they blindfolded her right away, and didn't talk much where she could hear them. Males, two or more. Her father thinks they took a camera of Dave's, an inexpensive cassette recorder, and an old sleeping bag. He's not positive, because Dave had a lot of gear and may have disposed of those things himself."

Meg fished several french fries from the bag and inspected them. "As you probably know, Mr. Tucker has decided that I'm quite a respectable person after all. Which is why he didn't mind my taking Jenny home with me."

Gutierrez took a sip of beer. "I was going to call you after I saw Tucker earlier. Then I decided you'd do better if his proposition came cold."

"Proposition is not quite . . ." Hearing the sharpness in her tone, Meg began again. "All he asked of me was something I was quite willing to give. It wouldn't have occurred to me to talk to anyone about that note."

Gutierrez' face was bleak, his eyes down.

"I have a child to raise, after all," she said, pushing the words past a tight throat. "And a job I need. Unfortunately, Mr. Tucker's good opinion—his public good opinion—is of importance in this town. We all do a little whoring to survive, Gutierrez."

"Yeah, but we don't have to enjoy it." At the hiss of her indrawn breath, he looked up. "Hey, I'm talking about me, not you. I don't have a kid, but I like my job and I think I'm good at it. I get seriously pissed when some officious civilian interferes." He spread his hands and shrugged.

"So what is Tucker asking of you? That you conceal the note? That doesn't seem so awful."

"More than that." Gutierrez glanced toward the closed door as he pulled his desk chair around and sat down beside her. "He insists that I accept the note."

"*Accept* the note? As what?"

He tipped his chair back and stared glumly at the beer can between his hands. "As real. As evidence that Johnny Stein was both a murderer and a suicide." His eyes met Meg's.

She closed her gaping mouth, then closed her eyes. How very odd; she'd known that Stein's confession was too convenient. Life never tied itself up that neatly. Besides . . . She jumped at Gutierrez' "Yeah," and watched his mouth shape a sour grin.

"Jenny says Dave didn't love Stein, or anyone else," Meg remembered aloud. "And she says Dave hated 'queers.' "

"Okay. And I've come across no suggestion, here or in Oakland, that Stein was homosexual. Or that he'd ever been violent." Chair legs and boot heels hit the floor together; Gutierrez leaned forward, elbows on his knees.

"Then there's the gun, what happened to the gun? It's not in the truck or on the beach or in his room. No gun, no bullets, no greasy rags or grease spots in drawers or in his suitcase. Where's the bike, Stein's bike, and how did he come by an old truck with no registration? And my biggest question, where was Stein himself for a whole week? How did a strange city kid stay invisible in a small town that long?"

"Wherever he stayed, there was a typewriter," noted Meg. "I thought that was strange, a typed suicide note with an initialed signature. Could he even type? I don't remember a single error in that note. You should find out whether he took typing in school."

"Yes ma'am, I should find that out, that and a lot of other things. But according to Mr. Tucker, former mayor, confidant of most members of the city council and holder of their mortgages and mine, we have here a solved crime. Neat and tidy. No need to spend any more city time or money."

"What about his family, Johnny Stein's family? Surely they'll insist on further investigation."

"Mommy is still out of reach, Daddy wires regrets and funeral money. Aunt Betty is coming up tonight to make a formal identification. Mr. Tucker is personally meeting her plane and will bring her here around eight."

"Aunt Betty will be impressed."

"Damn right. Aunt Betty may even wind up somewhat richer."

Meg rose to play housewife, sweeping wrappers and napkins and beer cans into the paper bag. "But don't you have some autonomy as chief of police?"

"Yes ma'am, I certainly have. And the city council has the autonomy to fire me, too."

"Gutierrez," she began, then paused. "To put it in the very simplest of terms. If Stein didn't kill Dave, then someone else did."

"Right. Then somebody killed Stein, probably the same somebody."

"Jenny?" Transfixed, Meg stared at the policeman but saw the Toyota, and her daughter's imploring face at the back window.

"Meg, all I can tell you is that I really don't think so." His fingers circled her wrists and clamped tight. "In more than twenty years of police work I haven't seen a single instance of a girl murdering her older brother." He released her and got to his feet. "In fact, when teenaged girls do get involved in violence it's nearly always with a boyfriend or a gang. So far as I can find out, Jenny is a loner."

"Yes, all right." She picked up her bag and settled it over her shoulder. "Then who?"

He shook his head and began to pace the small room. "Sunday a couple of my men told me they'd begun to pick up a flutter," he said, holding a hand before him and tipping it from side to side. "Little waves from a kid or two, suggestions that they might after all have something to say about Dave. Then the Stein story hit the news, and zip, everybody's dumb again."

"If you like, I'll talk to Jenny." Or even if you don't like, she thought.

"Yeah, good. She has to know more about her brother than she's been willing to say. And if the guys who broke in were locals, which seems likely, she probably knew them, too." Meg fished car keys from the outer pocket of her bag, and took a step toward the door.

"Meg." He stepped in front of her. "Only Jenny, please, and be careful there." At her frown, he sighed loudly. "Never mind wide-eyed innocence, just don't play cop any further than that. If Stein was murdered, it was a cold-blooded setup. You don't want to irritate the person who did that. *I* don't want you to."

"Oh," she said weakly. "Yes, I see."

•15•

Meg drove very carefully and considered civilized options. Plead the onset of a cold, flu, measles. Tell her you'd forgotten you were going to Tucson. Go to Tucson. Caught at a red light, she worried a hangnail with her teeth until she tasted blood. Gutierrez doesn't suspect her.

Tell her you think her father needs her. Tell her the truth, that you're not sure she isn't a murderer. Meg blinked and saw Jenny lurching out of the surf, blue-white and shaking. This is nonsense, that skinny little girl couldn't have killed two big strong boys.

The service porch was full of dogs. "Katy, Jenny? Grendel, Feef, knock it off! Okay, enough. Out, both of you!" She opened the door again and boosted both dogs outside.

"There. I'm sorry I was so long, I should have called. What on earth is the matter with the pair of you?" Katy's face was bright pink, surely with rage; and Jenny looked like a tall sad ghost, eyes brilliant with tears. "What's happened?"

Katy opened her mouth to speak, but Jenny was quicker.

"Katy's friend Cyndi just left. She was really . . ." Jenny

swallowed. "It turns out she thought she was supposed to sleep over tonight. I'm really sorry, Mrs. Halloran. I offered to sleep on the couch, and she could have the other bed in Katy's room, but that wasn't enough. And I don't want to go home."

Goddamnit! thought Meg, as Jenny's voice quavered to a halt. "Jenny, of course you won't go home. Cyndi Martin is a wretched little . . . Cyndi can be very difficult," she amended.

"Cyndi just acts so dumb sometimes, I don't even know why I like her!" Katy wailed, blinking hard.

"Oh, baby," Meg murmured, sweeping her daughter up in a hug. "Here's one of your mother's precepts about life: your best and dearest friends will seldom like each other, no matter what you do about it."

.   .   .

The girls were making music, Katy with her guitar and Jenny with the flute she had fished from a tangle of clothes and other personal belongings in the trunk of her Toyota. Meg listened for another moment, then stuck her head into the living room. "Miss Luoma has asked me to come to her studio for a cup of tea," she told them. "I won't be late. And please keep the dogs in. They were making a terrible racket out back."

Jenny gave her a smile, Katy an abstracted nod. "You watch," Meg told Grendel as she went out the front door.

Behind Miss Luoma's one-story shingled cottage was a tall building that had once been a garage. Was still a garage, Meg reminded herself as she eyed the wide wooden door. A flight of steps ran up the side of the building to a railed porch rimming three sides of the upper structure.

The door at the top was open. "Come in, come in," called Miss Luoma. "The water's just on the boil."

Meg stepped into a single room, lofty and spacious, with floor-to-ceiling bookcases, redwood paneling, and two large skylights. On the north wall, beneath a row of high windows, was a long built-in table strewn with spiral notebooks, pages of typescript, sketches. The wall above the worktable was cork, and a forest of pushpins held more sketches there, and maps, and old photographs.

"That's Port Silva about 1880," said Miss Luoma from behind her, pointing to a line of false-fronted wooden buildings looking out on a dirt street. "Suomi in my books, of course. And there's a schooner being loaded by chute, right out in our harbor. People got on board in much the same way, in a basket sliding down a wire anchored to a buoy beyond the ship.

"That's my dear father," she said softly as Meg moved to look at an enormous man and a smallish woman standing on the front steps of a tall wooden house. "And poor Mama beside him. At the Luoma place in Covelo, my farm."

Another house, a squat-looking structure of dark wood with a wide porch, the small woman, looking even smaller, sitting next to a baby basket.

"My mother again, at her family home, and I'm in the basket. Mother died when I was twelve, and I kept house for my father until he died, my goodness, it must be twenty years ago. But look, here's what I wanted to show you."

Miss Luoma pushed papers about and finally came up with a single sheet, which she held out to Meg. It was a simple head-and-shoulders sketch of Katy, nearly full face; her eyes were wide, and a half smile curved her mouth.

"Miss Luoma, that's wonderful!"

"Yes, I'm quite pleased with it. If you'd permit me, I'd like to use her for a model." More rustling of papers, with mutterings; Meg was reminded of the White Rabbit. "The book I'm working on has some Portagee children in it. My editor suggested that, and of course none of those people appear in my mother's picture albums or sketch books. But with just a little change, see?"

The second sketch was the same pose, but Miss Luoma's

pencil had darkened the eyes, deepening their bottom curve to give them a heavy look; and the dark hair was denser, coarser. It was Katy as she might have looked had her name been Silveira.

"I'd be happy to pay her, of course."

Meg shook her head, trying to restrain what she knew must be a fatuous grin. "I don't think so. But that's between you and Katy. If she wants to sit for you now and then, it's perfectly all right with me."

"That's lovely, thank you. Katy is very easy to catch, nice clear features, good bones. And she's capable of sitting absolutely still, an unusual trait in a child. Mostly I draw from photographs, you see, because it's less trouble. Now, you may keep that original sketch. I'll go get the tea."

After a moment Meg pulled her eyes away from her daughter's face and looked around the room once more. The bookcase wall had a glass-fronted section, she noted; and framed sketches hung against the redwood paneling. Deep blue lined draperies of a coarse-textured, nubby fabric bordered the windows. There was a round oak table at one end of the room, and Windsor chairs with quilted cushions, one of them occupied by a dozing calico cat. Above the table glowed a Tiffany lamp, a gently-flared inverted tulip in scarlet, white, a touch of green, and gold.

"It is nice, isn't it." Miss Luoma set out flowered bone-china cups and saucers. "The wood for the paneling came from my grandfather's oldest house, which was mostly destroyed in the 1906 earthquake. Someone had used that wood to patch another house and a barn, if you can imagine. The lamp is a copy I had made from my mother's descriptions. I hope Darjeeling is all right?

"I indulged myself ruthlessly when I had this place built; but I could afford it." Miss Luoma filled the cups, set the pot on a trivet, and tipped the cat off her chair. "Off, Clytie, go find your own bed."

"It's beautiful, a refuge." Meg sipped the tea, delicately

dark and smoky compared with the anonymous-teabag product that she herself occasionally brewed.

"Refuge! You're quite right, it's my refuge. And I hate to leave it, but . . ." she sighed and shook her head. "My agent is flying to San Francisco from New York. He's been insisting we need a conference, and I've been putting him off, but now that things are safe and normal once more, with the murder solved and the murderer . . . Oh dear."

Miss Luoma set her cup down and reached across the table to pat Meg's hand. "I'm sorry, I'd forgotten that you were with Chief Gutierrez when he discovered the body. It must have been awful. I suppose Vincent must be used to bodies. He was in the service and he's been a policeman for ages. But I'm sure it was terrible for you."

"Yes, it was."

"Terrible," Miss Luoma repeated softly. "But that poor boy did us all a kindness, you know."

By murdering Dave. It was a thought Meg herself had ruthlessly suppressed; did that make her the better person, or merely the less honest?

"He saved the town from a great deal of misery," Miss Luoma went on. "People were becoming suspicious of one another, and resentful of the police investigation. No one likes having his life laid out for public inspection. We all have our little secrets. So by his confession we were all spared. And surely, he wouldn't have wanted to live his life in prison."

People not in prison were always saying that; Gallup or someone should do a survey of inmates. Perhaps Stein, if he'd taken time for a second thought, might have decided . . . No, remember that he may not have done the deciding at all. Meg was sure none of this confusion had moved from thought to tongue; but Miss Luoma cocked her head and narrowed her eyes.

"Unless, of course, there is still some doubt. Vincent is satisfied that this Stein person's death ended things?"

Certainly ended things for Steinperson. Stop that! "Chief Gutierrez is far too old a hand to be indiscreet with police information," Meg said, choosing her words with care. "I do know, however, that Mr. Tucker is satisfied."

"Ah! Well, then, that's it, and Port Silva can stop holding its breath. But are you and William Tucker on speaking terms now? It seems to me I've heard . . ." She paused delicately.

"Mr. Tucker and I spent some time this morning working out our differences. In fact, his daughter Jenny is staying with me for a day or two, while her mother is away."

"Jenny Tucker?" Miss Luoma's face wavered and then stilled, as if a deep-moving fish had disturbed, briefly, the surface of a pond. "Jenny Tucker, with Katy? Do you think that's wise?"

A jolt of fear along her spine brought Meg's teeth together sharply; she blinked hard, twice. "Jenny couldn't have . . ." She swallowed, then began again. "Jenny was one of my students, and she's having a bad time. And Katy is crazy about her."

"Well, of course you must decide for yourself, and you're experienced with youngsters. But I don't suppose you know a lot about local history."

"That's true, I don't. Should I?"

Miss Luoma tipped the pot over each cup, her face thoughtful. "Jenny is the fourth of them, of the McKissick women. The first was a Jennifer too; she ran a logging operation with her husband. After he was killed she ran it herself. There was a time when a neighbor had a boundary dispute with her; the surveyor he sent in disappeared, never seen again. The neighbor sold up and moved, I believe."

"But . . . isn't there a McKissick Grove just north of town?"

"Oh yes, the old lady became a conservationist toward the end of her life, when she had no need for more money." Miss Luoma smiled. "Elizabeth was Jennifer's daughter. When she was, oh, eighteen or so, Elizabeth had an affair with a married man, a Portagee fisherman named Duarte. He wouldn't leave his wife for her, so she shot him."

"Just shot him?"

"One of her brothers officially took the blame, but there were witnesses. Duarte survived, and insisted the whole thing was an accident. Elizabeth went away for a while, and then she came back to town and married Burns Feed and Grain. Jim Burns, that is, he was one of the few young men around in the early forties, because he was a cripple. He'd had polio."

Miss Luoma pushed her teacup aside and folded her hands in her lap. "Elizabeth turned Feed and Grain into Feed, Grain, and Nursery, and she had Abby. Ten years later Elizabeth got her share of the family money; she packed one bag and left town. She's in Florida now, I believe."

"She left her child? A ten-year-old?"

"About that. From then on Jim raised Abby all by himself. Elizabeth's mother, old Jennifer, wanted to take the child, but Jim hung on."

"Poor baby," Meg said softly. "And she's Jenny's mother, she's married to William Tucker."

"Yes indeed, poor thing. People do say that she drinks; I wouldn't know about that. What I do know is that Abby was a burner."

"A burner?" Meg was irritated to find herself becoming an echo. "What do you mean, a burner?"

"Fires happened wherever Abby was, when things didn't suit her. Finally, when she was seventeen and Jim wouldn't let her go to San Francisco to study piano . . ." Miss Luoma looked at Meg with a shrug and a sigh. "Well, all that's known for sure is that the nursery burned down, right to the ground."

She'd fallen into a framing tale, weary travelers sitting

around the table telling each other ghost stories. Soon the landlord would pour a last drink, lock the door, distribute candles. "Miss Luoma, I don't . . ." Her chair clattered as she pushed it back from the table. "It's getting late, I have a few last-minute chores at home. What about Jenny?" The last three words came of themselves, unbidden.

A slow, thoughtful shake of the white head. "I have never heard anything specific. But she surely has Abby's looks, and her habit of solitude. Blood tells, you know. In cattle, or field dogs, or people."

· 16 ·

"Miss Luoma says eleven is the proper time for morning tea," Katy proclaimed as she pulled on her blue nylon anorak. "Only I don't like tea, so she'll make me hot chocolate. And she says the light should be good for drawing. I told Jenny I'd see her at lunchtime." Her last sentence tilted up in implied question.

"Mm," Meg replied. "You're almost late, little. Better scoot."

" 'Bye, Jenny," called Katy, and scooted. Meg closed the door and was tempted to lean her head against it, for just a minute or two. Never mind, old lady, get it in gear.

Jenny Tucker was at the sink, a frail silhouette against the window. The hot water was on full force, and rising steam had given the girl's straight hair a frill of wispy curls. "Well," said Meg in hearty tones, and Jenny turned the water off. "Well, you appear to have been left with the dishes."

"That's all right, Mrs. Halloran, I like doing dishes, I

like hot water. And Katy did the cooking, I only know how to make pancakes from a box."

"Katy has learned to cook in self-defense, poor baby." Meg looked at the coffeepot and felt a warning lurch at the bottom of her stomach. "I hope she isn't wearing you out, Jenny. Katy missed having brothers and sisters, so she gets pretty high on visitors."

"No, she's a really nice little girl." Jenny shook water from her hands and turned to face Meg. "I think it's incredible that she likes me, after what my brother did. And you too. I wouldn't think either of you would want me in your house."

"Even a ten-year-old knows you can't choose your relatives."

"I used to pretend that Dave was adopted, or that I was," said Jenny. "But he hadn't really bothered me since I was eight years old, when Granny chopped up his bike."

"Chopped . . . your grandmother?"

"Granny McKissick, she was really my great-grandmother. I was staying with her, and Dave rode out on his new ten-speed to tell me he drowned my kitten because it was sick. Granny got a great big axe from her shed," Jenny said with a tight little smile, "and she chopped that bike to pieces. Then she told him that next time she'd shave his head and burn up all his clothes. She would have, too."

"How old were you when she died?"

"Practically grown-up, fourteen. She said she was tired and ready to go, so I sat beside her bed and held her hand all night." A small shrug, with a lifting of both palms as if setting something free. "She was Jennifer, too."

As Jenny wrung out the dishcloth and moved to wipe up the counter, Meg took a long breath. Here's what I think now, Gutierrez: I think she had no reason to kill her brother, although she might, she just might, have been able to do so. If she thought it was necessary.

"Suppose," Meg said softly, "suppose Johnny Stein didn't kill Dave?"

Jenny shook her head as she moved back to the sink. "I don't think he did; that note was dumb. If you'll tell me where to find a dish towel, Mrs. Halloran, I'll dry these."

"Jenny." Meg reached out to touch the girl's shoulder. "Chief Gutierrez isn't completely convinced, either. Do you know anything, about anyone, that might help?"

"No." Jenny faced Meg once more and stood very straight. "Not anything. I stayed out of Dave's way, out of everybody's way. Do you want me to go home now?"

"Good heavens no! Katy would be terribly upset. And I'm sure your father can manage for himself. But perhaps you should call your mother."

"My mother?"

"She may not know where you are; if she calls your home and gets no answer she'll probably worry."

"My mother's up at her cabin. She won't have a phone there, she doesn't like to be bothered."

"Oh."

"But she won't be worried. She isn't interested in anything but her piano, and the woods a little bit, I guess. She didn't want to get married, and she didn't want to have kids."

"Jenny . . ."

"I know that because she told me. She thought I had a right to know why she wasn't like other people's mothers. She said my dad got her pregnant, and so she married him. I can't see why she ever let him do that." An expression of polite distaste flitted over Jenny's face, replaced almost at once by one of concern.

"Hey, Mrs. Halloran, it was okay, really, because I had Granny. And Dave had old witch Addie. He even liked her, he still goes . . . went . . . to see her in the convalescent place. So we weren't orphans or anything, honest."

Meg brushed a hand over her face; quick change, erase pity or distress or anything of that sort and substitute calm. Or curiosity: Addie? "Why 'witch'?" she asked.

"That's what Granny called her. Addie came to help my mother when Dave was little, and she stayed. She was somebody my dad's mother knew, another church freak. Oh, excuse that, Mrs. Halloran." Meg shook her head impatiently, and Jenny went on.

"Well, Addie thought Dave was God's own special angel or something. She taught him Bible verses and took him to church on weeknights and sang hymns with him in the kitchen, and they prayed a lot, she used to make me get down on my knees with them. She didn't like me, and I hated her."

Meg moved to the dining-room bookcase, reached up for the *Oxford Quotations;* Gutierrez had returned the letters to her Saturday night. "Jenny, would you recognize Addie's handwriting?"

. . .

Addie Bengsten had been a resident of the Evening Star Convalescent Home and Geriatric Facility for some three years, said the hefty, chatty woman whose white uniform had the name "Grace" embroidered on one pocket. Old Addie started out in one of the cottages, then had to move to the main building after a fall put her in a wheelchair. That Tucker boy had been her only regular visitor, practically like a grandson to her, she'd be happy to talk to someone who'd known him.

"But I think I'll just send you up on your own. Don't like to leave the desk, and besides, she'll just be after me about something or other; she always is. Room eight, off the front."

What had obviously been a porch across the front of the main building was now enclosed, and carpeted in green indoor-outdoor stuff, so the numbered doors opened onto a corridor of sorts. Room eight was at the end on the right, its door ajar.

The figure occupying the big wheelchair was short,

with a compressed look, as if someone had set a heavy hand on the white head and pushed down hard. Broad but no longer fleshy, she had probably been a powerful woman in her youth. At Meg's rap on the doorjamb, the head turned with no movement of the shoulders; a tiny white topknot danced at the motion, bound by a ribbon just a shade pinker than the scalp gleaming through thin hair. Big-knuckled hands gripped each other against a fringed plaid lap robe; in the hooded eyes there was only faint delineation between white, milky blue, and black.

"Miss Bengsten, I am Margaret Halloran." As the woman's head snaked forward, lips tightening, Meg stepped inside. "I learned about you from the Tuckers, and now I've come to insist that you make no more vicious calls to me or about me. And send no more of these," she added, pulling one of the letters from a pocket.

"You're an ungodly woman!" The old voice was harsh and breathy, familiar enough to make Meg's spine tingle. "Davey knew, I taught my Davey about the ungodly."

"Whatever Dave told you about me . . ."

"He told me you're a whore, a Jezebel! You'll be thrown down for the dogs to eat, you and the others. 'But they found no more of her than the skull, and the feet, and the palms of her hands.' Second Kings 9:35."

"What Dave told you was a lie, Miss Bengsten." Meg made her voice slow and calm. "And people can go to jail for repeating lies, even very old people."

"No lies, not from Davey. He was God's divining rod to know the sinner where he stood, whited sepulcher full of dead men's bones." She drew a raspy breath. "Davey brings the box in, and closes the door. Then he shows me pictures he took, people whoring and thieving and committing abominations."

Meg pictured that topknot dancing beside Dave's smooth, golden head as the two of them leafed like grandmother and grandson through their own grotesque version of the family album. "Why?"

At the crack of Meg's voice the old woman jerked back in her chair.

"Why did Dave take pictures? What did he want?"

"It was his mission to save the sinners."

"Save . . . ? We're all of us sinners in one way or another, Miss Bengsten, even Dave."

"No, no, not since he was a baby. When he was a tiny little mite I taught him to know mankind is vile, filthy and vile and depraved in his very nature. Why, at age four Davey could kneel and pray with me for an hour! And if he weakened, if he reached out for the toy or the cookie there on the floor in front of him, he'd quick pull his little hand back." She lifted her own gnarled hand from her lap, shook it loose where woolly fabric clung to rough skin, turned it palm up.

"For me to spank it with the wooden spoon. Then he'd say 'Davey good boy,' and hardly ever cry. I made Davey proof against sin, he could no more sin than a . . . a cat could fly."

Meg moved to a window and cranked it open. "There is some evidence that Dave did sin, that he became the lover of another boy." To hell with her promise; and she hoped it was true, that he had however briefly loved *somebody*. "His parents are very troubled about that."

Addie went still as stone; then, only her lips moving, she said, "Lies."

"Lies or the truth, the Tuckers would prefer that the town not hear about it." She turned her head for another draft of clean outside air. "I have agreed to respect their wishes so long as the anonymous calls and letters cease. Otherwise . . ." She spread her hands and shrugged.

"Yes, we'll respect their wishes. Your wishes." Addie made herself smaller, peering up at Meg from under bristling eyebrows. "We mustn't let lies be spread about Davey, he prayed to be good and he always was. He'll be here soon; he'd never forget his Addie. He brings my cough syrup, and pralines, the kind with just one nut on that I can pick off and throw away."

It was not an act, nor a sudden lapse into senility, but an exercise in self-delusion; tears were welling from under closed lids to lose themselves in furrows in the ancient skin. You might even pity her, until you remembered that kneeling four-year-old. "Where is the box?" Meg asked. "The box of pictures; what happened to it?"

A shrug. "Just an old green metal box. Davey always locked it up and took it away with him. He said he kept it in one of his high places; he always had a rooftop or a tree house or something. He liked being up high."

"Who were the people, the ones in the pictures?"

"You. I only remember you."

Meg stared at the old woman, who stared back.

"No more calls, no more letters," Addie said in her near-whisper. "But I'll pray for you."

. . .

There was a pay phone in the office, she could see it through the rear window. But she could see Grace there as well; Gutierrez would have to wait yet a while for this latest information. She nodded and waved as she skirted the building, picking her way through untrimmed, patchy grass to the parking lot which overlooked the highway.

She climbed into the van and rolled down both front windows. Whether from moral conviction or simple lack of opportunity, she had committed no sins of the flesh in Port Silva . . . unless you counted smoking and quiet, at-home boozing, not very riveting subjects for a hot camera. If Dave had a damning picture of her, it must be a pasteup of some kind, and surely detectable as such. Or perhaps she had a doppelganger, a stranger who went about in her guise committing public indiscretions.

Let's not get fanciful, Margaret. She gazed out the windshield and over the roofs of a housing tract at the Pacific, very blue today, innocent. She could not, she admitted after several minutes, absolutely could not think herself into Dave's head. Perhaps he had taken money from his victims, and Addie had chosen not to mention it. Perhaps he simply wanted power over lesser mortals, or a bolstering of his sense of superiority: they were sinners while he was in a high place.

She sat up sharply and slapped the steering wheel; her hand hit the horn, causing a low-flying, curious gull to take himself quickly higher. The break-in at the Tucker house was a search for Dave's box. Had the searchers found it? Probably not, not if he'd tucked it in the rafters or up a tree or something. Tell Gutierrez.

Just north of the Evening Star was an intersection busy with gas stations and convenience stores, and she thought she remembered one of those pillar-box telephones. Although she had already put in a morning several years long, it was only half past noon; perhaps Gutierrez could join her for lunch.

A Sergeant Findlayson informed her that Chief Gutierrez was away for the day at least, on personal business. Instructions were that if Mrs. Halloran called, she was to be told he'd be back late today or early tomorrow. Was there anything he, Findlayson, could help her with?

"Personal business" probably translated into police business, not authorized, in Oakland. A pox on banker Tucker and his heavy hand, Meg thought; had Gutierrez taken any of his men into his confidence? Maybe the one with the odd name, Svoboda.

Lieutenant Svoboda, Sergeant Findlayson was sorry to say, had the day off and was unavailable except in the event of an emergency. No emergency, Meg assured him, not at all, thanks very much.

She put the key in the ignition, then sat quite still for a moment, staring out the sun-dazzled windshield. Lunchtime, but she wasn't a bit hungry. Jenny might know more, but probably not, and Katy would be home by now. There should be something . . .

Chrissie, she thought suddenly, and kicked the van to life. Poor Chrissie, who took refuge in the toilet at the very mention of Dave Tucker's name. On a day like this, at lunchtime, Chrissie the dedicated runner would be running somewhere, probably on the school track. Wanna bet, she said silently to her mirror, that Chrissie's not in Dave's little green box? What odds?

·   ·   ·

The high school was at this end of town, but several miles inland. Meg pointed the van east and drove just slightly faster than the speed limit, enjoying the breeze that whipped through the open windows. No smog, no fog (for the moment), no unpalatable human smells. There was a whiff of horse as she swept past a corral; and somewhere nearby, earlier, there had been a skunk.

Whoring, thieving, committing abominations: was the old lady's list specific or symbolic? Chrissie's father ran a construction business reputed to be the most successful in the county. The girl had told Meg that Art Maldonado expected all his kids to work for the firm, but paid them well. Chrissie had very nice clothes, and Meg had seen her driving a sporty new car.

No need for "thieving" if you have plenty of money, thought Meg. Nor for whoring either. Except of course Addie had not meant whoring, she'd meant sexual activity of any kind at all. An empty lumber truck rattled up behind the van; she slowed to let him pass, took note of her surroundings, and braked harder in preparation for a right turn. Chrissie might be stunning in five years, but at present she was relatively nonsexual, a girl who'd grown up with a troop of brothers and still saw herself as one of the guys.

The faculty and visitors' parking lot was empty; behind

it, the sprawling, bastard-Spanish main building was closed and silent, an abandoned mission. The newer classrooms, single-story brick buildings in a neat row, were similarly deserted, teachers still catching their breath elsewhere.

Summer-shaggy lawns on the left, student parking lot on the right, empty, with sawhorse barriers protecting bright new striping. Never mind; like other runners of Meg's acquaintance, Chrissie would drive as close to the track as possible. In front of the gym, right beside the big plaster panther, squatted a grubby machine that gave off visible waves of heat; new roof, thought Meg, wrinkling her nose at the smell of tar. The workmen were apparently on a lunch break, lounging in the shade between a pickup and a larger truck.

Tennis courts, baseball diamond, then the stadium; she swung right, to the south stadium lot. No barricades here, just a flame-nosed pickup and an open-topped blue Fiat. Quarry in view, she thought. Or within earshot at least; as she slid out of the van she caught the sound of pounding feet.

She stopped next to the end-zone bleachers, shaded her eyes, and mouthed a quiet "Aha!" Long, long legs, long, thin pumping arms, flying hair a glossy blue-black in the sunlight: Chrissie Maldonado, no doubt about it. At the opposite end of the stadium, coming into the homestretch, the girl extended herself in a final burst. She hit an imaginary tape at the fifty-yard line, seemed to lurch and flail for several strides, then settled into a fast, loose-limbed walk toward Meg's end of the oval.

Metamorphosis! thought Meg, remembering the pale and staring waif of—lordy, only three days ago. What an advertisement for fresh air and exercise. "Chrissie, that was beautiful," she called as she stepped out from the bleachers.

The girl flung her head up and saw Meg. In an attempt to reverse directions she stumbled over her own feet and fell, her rump meeting the cinders with a bounce which made Meg wince.

"I'm sorry, I didn't mean to startle you." She moved forward to offer a hand to the sprawling girl.

"Shit shit *shit!*" Chrissie wailed, and she scrambled backwards in a dusty flurry of arms and legs. "Go away! I don't want to talk to you!"

"Stop that or you'll hurt yourself!" snapped Meg. "Now get up out of the dirt." Chrissie gripped the proffered hand this time, and lurched to her feet; she brushed herself off, sniffed, and began to jog in place. "I'm your friend, remember?" Meg went on. "At least I thought so, and I thought you'd rather talk to me than to the authorities."

Tears spurted from Chrissie's eyes, and a kind of sobbing whinny escaped her clenched teeth as she jogged back and away from Meg's reaching hands.

"Chrissie, it can't be that bad!" Except of course it could; murder was about as bad as it got. Suddenly Meg remembered Gutierrez' caution, noting that nothing else was moving in the sunlit stadium, and there was no noise except their breathing and the soft thud of Chrissie's feet. I won't do this again, she promised silently, and cleared her throat. "Whatever Dave Tucker was holding over you, whatever pictures he may have had in his little green box"—another whinny from Chrissie—"you can't go on making yourself sick over it. Let's go have a cup of coffee, Chrissie, and see what we can work out."

Chrissie was gripping her own elbows now as she bounced up and down, and her teeth were beginning to chatter. "Maybe," she muttered, and then, with a great, rough-edged sigh, "Okay. But I gotta take another lap, or my legs will cramp."

"I'll meet you in the parking lot." Chrissie nodded and turned away; after a few shambling steps her head came up, her shoulders lifted, and her stride took on its natural easy grace. "Good girl," said Meg aloud, and hoped Chrissie's was a small sin with a manageable penance. She sighed and turned to move past the bleachers, her own head down. Messing about with other people's lives made her feel grubby.

She had taken several steps on the graveled surface of the parking lot before registering the presence of a group of boys directly in her path. "Excuse me," she said and checked her next step as none of them moved. An acid remark formed in her mind but remained there as she remembered her isolation; the campus was deserted except for Chrissie and the distant roofing crew.

She stepped smartly to her right; one of the boys moved just as smartly to his left. Then all of them . . . four of them, she noted numbly . . . shifted and closed, making a half circle before her, around her. She looked from one unfamiliar face to another, in warm, heavy air which stank of sweat, and beer, and tar.

◦17◦

Strangers to her, all four. Two were young men rather than boys and well over six feet tall, one lean and the other beefy. Dark eyes, high-bridged noses, black hair. The arc tightened and she stepped back. The third was a gangling, sandy youth who'd be another behemoth when he finished growing; the last a whippy, jittery boy, smaller than the others and dancing with barely suppressed emotion.

Tiny's football teammates? Then the largest one shook his hair back, a glossy mane which glinted blue in the sun, and she thought, Maldonados! "You must be Chrissie's brothers," she said brightly. Disarm a potential enemy by using his name; what had she heard Chrissie call them? "Pete, isn't it? and . . . ?"

"Artie," said the slimmer, probably younger of the pair. Then he shot an embarrassed glance at his brother.

"Artie. And your friends here?"

"Nemmine that," growled Pete. There was a flanking, turning movement, as if the quartet had devised a rough dance; Meg moved on her heel, took several steps back as they moved forward, and found that she was facing the stadium and school buildings. She snatched a glance over her shoulder: a wall of greenery, the forest which backed the campus.

"You're just a real nosy lady. It's a good thing we were here to protect our sister." Pete thrust his head forward; the motion set him off balance, and he teetered for a moment, eyes blank. "Our little sister."

He's drunk. Meg took a quick step, intending to slip between him and the small boy; but Pete lunged, gripped her upper arm hard, and spun her around.

" 'Cause you're trying to get her in trouble." The hand tightened, fingers meeting around her arm. "We don't let nobody bother our Chrissie." He was moving in great clumsy strides into the forest, pushing her before him as the others followed.

"Chrissie's in trouble already; I was trying to help." She stumbled, but Pete held her up and carried her on.

"Then why'd you knock her down?" demanded the sandy boy in her ear. "And make her cry?"

"And why were you at the police station?" The small one capered along beside them. "You went there Monday, I saw you."

"You gotta understand . . ." Pete stumbled, caught himself. "You need to learn to mind your own business, see?" The last word came out more like "shee." As he stumbled again, his grip broke, and Meg bolted into the dank, brush-choked woods.

Stupid, stupid! her mind screamed, but her body paid

no attention, committed to flight. Uneven ground slippery with needles; whipping, clutching branches; light and dark of mottled sunlight. Young trees in a tight line plucked at her as she slid through; then she dodged left around a thick, branchless trunk, heard the thud of heavy feet behind her, swerved right.

A hand grabbed at her shoulder, slid off. She stumbled, lost control of her own momentum, met rough, solid bark with her face and then her right shoulder. Hands and knees for just a moment; then a twist, a lunge upward and around. *Don't* fall down.

The Maldonados stood flat-footed, arms hanging loose, faces wet and white. There was space between them; she sucked in a great draft of air and aimed herself. A single slow-motion step, two, and a medieval torture instrument locked itself around her, one steel arm across her ribs, the other over her breasts.

"Gotcha!" said the sandy boy as he lifted her clear of the ground. He gave another, harder squeeze, and the figures before Meg's eyes wavered in a blurry, dark blue twilight.

"Hey, Jerry," breathed Artie, "hey, man, you better put her down."

"How come?" As Meg's feet touched the ground, she tried to pull away, but the arm gripping her ribs tightened once more and she gasped in pain. The boy giggled and moved his other hand in a tentative grope. "What's the matter, you guys chicken?"

Artie's eyes were white rimmed in a face going a dusky red; Pete hunched his shoulders, moving his head slowly from side to side. As Jerry's attention focused on his audience, he relaxed his grip slightly; Meg shoved hands and forearms under the encircling arms and broke free.

The four gaped at her, then swung around as Chrissie burst into the small clearing, eyes flashing. "Are you out of your minds?" She banged the heels of her hands against Pete's chest, then slapped both his ears. "You just *had* to pull another fuckup?" Artie next, but Artie got his hands up to protect his ears.

Slap, slap. Whap! "You know what Daddy's gonna do to you two dummies?" A stiff-armed push sent Artie reeling. "Redding. He'll put you both on that supermarket roof in Redding and have you pouring tar until your brains melt!" She punctuated her words with a thudding fist against Pete's shoulder. "Soon as you get off crutches!"

With a wordless squeak the smallest boy turned and fled. Chrissie put her hands on her hips and began to advance on Jerry, her clenched jaw thrust forward. "Good riddance. Now you. You get out of here, Jerry denBrunk, before I . . ."

"You dumb cunt, who do you think you're ordering around?" He had an arm raised to deliver a backhanded blow but thought better of it as the male Maldonados moved past their sister.

"Pete! Artie!"

One on either side of Jerry, they turned to look at Chrissie with identical sheepish glances.

"Okay, you get him out of here and go on home. Or maybe you better stop at Saint Joseph's on the way and light a candle and say a prayer that Mrs. Halloran will maybe decide not to tell Chief Gutierrez about this, even if he does happen to be her boyfriend."

Boyfriend! thought Meg wildly, pressing the back of one hand against her trembling mouth. Boyfriend, what an absolutely ridiculous term.

"Mrs. Halloran?" Chrissie's outstretched hands stopped just short of Meg's shoulders, and her enormous dark eyes were suddenly bright with tears. The termagant had departed, and a tall, frightened child remained. "Please, Mrs. Halloran, let me talk to you."

Nice switch, she should certainly take advantage of it. Except her face hurt. Meg touched the edge of her jaw cautiously and blinked at the smear of blood on her fingertips.

"Yeah, we'd better take care of that, you're kind of . . . Jesus, which one of them hit you?" Chrissie whispered.

"A tree hit me. No. I hit a tree." Meg looked around and felt her lips begin to tremble once again. Trees, and trees, and trees that way too, muffling sound and filtering light greenly. Where was the sun, and the parking lot?

"Here, this way." Chrissie linked her fingers with Meg's and stepped out confidently; in a matter of seconds they had found the open sky and the sun. Well, it *felt* like the depths of the forest, Meg told herself. Catching sight of her van, she lifted her head and restrained her impulse to break into an undignified lope.

"Please, Mrs. Halloran, you have to listen to me."

I don't have to do anything. From behind the barricade of the van's half-open door, she surveyed her face in the side mirror: raked, seeping patches at brow, cheekbone, and jaw, where bony structure had met tree trunk. Not deep, but ugly; she'd have to stop somewhere and clean up before going home to Katy.

"Here," Chrissie thrust a dripping cloth at her. "It's a clean towel, I dipped it in my ice chest." After a long moment, she said, "We could sit in my car and talk, I've got some beer in the chest."

Meg cast a quick glance around the parking area. The pickup was gone, but for all she knew the other trucks could still be at the gym. "No." The raw patch near her right eyebrow was free of grit and bark now, as was the scrape over her cheekbone; she folded the cloth to find a clean spot, then worked at her jaw with gentle, patting strokes. "Not here."

Chrissie hooked hands like pleading paws over the window. "You ought to go home, or maybe to the doctor. Let me drive you. I'll walk back for my car later."

It's a trick, thought Meg, as she watched the big eyes grow bigger, darker, more sorrowful; she does it by holding her breath or biting her tongue. She turned her attention to her own scraped and filthy hands.

"I can drive." She handed the cloth to Chrissie, then stood straight and still. Nothing moved, there was no close sound. The air was thick and dead, as if the brassy sun had weight and thickness. She smelled dust, and dry grass, and tar.

A soft "Mrs. Halloran?" reminded her that the girl was there and vulnerable. Yes indeed, but she herself was vulnerable, too, her spirit as raw as her face. She needed a sharp salty breeze, and freewheeling gulls. And people. "If you want to talk to me," she said, flexing her hands slowly, "follow me to the highway parking lot for the state beach, the beach the abalone fishers use."

. . .

As her front tires touched the log marking the edge of the lot, Meg was shaken by another chill, remnant and reminder of terror. Next would be a sweeping, sweaty flush of angry humiliation, the opposite reach of the emotional pendulum she was riding. She gripped the wheel and waited. A dozen vehicles, several boat trailers, divers in wet suits, a number of darting children—all brushed the barest edge of her attention. But she nodded grimly at the telephone booth; Chrissie would by God cooperate, or else.

Eyes on her rearview mirror, she saw the Fiat pull off the highway. "Come into the parlor, little fly," she muttered. "There's a hungry spider here." The little car disappeared from the mirror as it slid up to park beside the van.

"Here, Mrs. Halloran." Chrissie opened the passenger door and shoved a small tilt-top cooler across the seat. As the girl scrambled in, Meg tilted the top: melting ice, half-a-dozen cans of Coors. Matter of survival, she told herself, and fished one out.

Chrissie pulled the tab on a can of her own as high, hurried words began to spill. "Pete and Artie were way out of line, Mrs. Halloran, way out and they know it, too, they feel just terrible. Or they will when they have time to think it over," she amended, and sniffed. "My daddy expects them to work like men but mind him like good little boys, and they're . . . they're not too smart anyway, I guess." She blotted tears with the sleeve of her sweatshirt. "But they're not mean, not really bad mean."

Meg had once had a friend who insisted that her hundred-plus-pounds doberman, Rommel, was merely being playful when he took a visitor's arm in his mouth. "Your brothers set out to terrorize me," she said flatly. "They trapped me, they herded me into the woods as if I were a sheep. 'Mean' is not precisely the word I'd use."

"Mrs. Halloran, they wouldn't have . . . they'd been working in the sun, and then they had a few beers, and . . ." Chrissie looked at the can in her own hand, grimaced, took a quick gulp. "They were just trying to protect me."

"Oh? From what?"

Chrissie merely bent her head, hiding behind a fall of glossy black hair. "Look, sweetie, the game playing is all over. Either you answer my questions, or I call Vincent Gutierrez and tell him to arrest your brothers for assault."

Chrissie drew a long, shuddering breath and sat up, shaking back her hair. "And if I tell you, that's all? You won't tell anybody else?"

Meg drew a long breath of her own. No game playing for anyone. "I'm afraid you'll have to leave that to me. Now. From what, exactly, were your brothers trying to protect you?"

Chrissie closed her eyes and her face went blank; Meg had a sense of whirrings and clickings, internal rear-rangement. Then the girl sighed and stretched her legs out before her. "Shit, it isn't . . . excuse me, Mrs. Halloran. It's just not that big a deal now, nothing worth hurting anyone over or going to jail. Except I really hate having you know. I don't mind so much about Mr. Engebritsen."

And what did the clod who taught U.S. government have to do with all this? "Know what?" Meg prompted.

"That I, um, well . . . During Christmas vacation I

broke into the school office," she said in a rush, "and found the final exams for English and government, and made copies. So I'd make B's. I had provisional acceptance at Vassar if I got B's in those two courses."

Personal outrage stiffened Meg's spine, froze her face. Chrissie glanced sideways and muttered, "See, I knew you'd hate me."

"Oh, for heaven's sake." Meg tipped her beer can, then cast a guilty look around the parking lot. No one was paying any attention to the van or its occupants.

"My grandmother went to Vassar," Chrissie said in sorrowful tones, "and so did my mom, and she says I have to, too. I don't want to, I'd a whole lot rather stay right here and maybe go to junior college. But see," she said earnestly, turning sideways in the seat, "my dad is this terrific guy. He works really hard and makes lots of money and he loves us all but he's crazy about my mom. And when things don't go the way she likes, she treats him like shit practically for years, even when it's not his fault."

Meg's sympathies didn't rise, didn't even twitch. "So you broke in and stole the finals, and Dave Tucker found out about it."

"Hunh! It was mostly Dave's idea. He's the one told me where the tests were." Chrissie made a wry face. "But whatever, I'm the one that did it. Christina Mary Maldonado, big as life, both hands grabbing in the file cabinet, this scared-looking face and right there in the school office, you can see the clock and everything. I didn't even know he had a camera."

"And what did Dave want from you in return for his silence?"

She gave a little chuckle. "Well, he sure wasn't after my bod. Except I think he did get off on praying over me, talking about what a sinner I was. That was the worst part, the praying. When he'd kneel down, and bow his head, and wait for me to get down there, too. Weird."

In a flash of horrid insight Meg saw the golden head, bent yet arrogant, and remembered what Gutierrez had told her about the bullet wound. Dave must have played his game once too often, with the wrong person. She took a swallow of beer and asked, "What was the other part? If praying was the worst," she added as Chrissie looked at her inquiringly.

"Oh. Tithing. He asked me how much money I made, and then I had to give him ten percent of that every week. It was for his ministry, he said; he was going to build a big TV station here and preach, save the country for God."

Extortion for Christ. Nasty if far from original. "Did you get the picture back?"

"Huh?" Chrissie looked startled.

"From Dave's house. Saturday night."

"No! And that wasn't me, that was my . . ." Her face closed tight, and she turned to stare straight ahead.

"Your brothers. Did they think it up all by themselves?"

"Yes." Chrissie blinked rapidly. "They found out about the picture. I was scared the police would find it and think I killed Dave. They could see I was crazy scared and they kept at me and I told them. So they went charging off, just like today, to rescue their little sister."

She took a deep breath. "But that time they didn't hurt anyone. Please don't tell."

"They didn't find the picture, or the little green box?"

"No. You're going to tell, aren't you?"

You bet, thought Meg. What came across with raw sincerity was Chrissie's concern for her brothers; all the rest could be truth, hogwash, or something in between. No, she believed the part about Dave.

"I think it would be wise for you and your brothers to tell your father," she said slowly, "and I'll decide later about pressing charges."

"But Mrs. Halloran, my father will *kill* them!" Chrissie wailed.

CHILDREN'S GAMES

"I doubt that," snapped Meg. "But someone else might, someone who decides to defend himself the next time those two go marauding. One more thing: who else was Dave blackmailing? And it's far too late for that look of innocent stupidity."

Chrissie sniffled, wiped her eyes, and then sighed. "Well. Okay. This is not for sure, only what I think from watching. Arnold Kindelstadt. And Peggy Gruen. And maybe Guido Santori."

"Thank you." Meg leaned back against the seat and stifled a groan; her body was threatening to lock itself tight like that of the rusted Tin Woodsman. She spread her hands and inspected them; the abraded palms were ugly and beginning to swell.

"Time to go home," she stated. "What you'd better do is track down your brothers and make this very clear to them: they are to leave me strictly alone."

"Yeah." Chrissie opened the door, slid out, reached back for the cooler. She slammed the door, stepped away, and gave Meg a long, sober look. "I guess you're doing what you think is right, Mrs. Halloran. See you."

• • •

Drive with your fingers, not your palms, she told herself a few minutes later as she eased the van onto the highway. She would call the police from home, after she'd had a chance to collect herself. Gutierrez was a man who would expect a request of his to have the force of an order; he was likely to display some irritation when he learned that she'd gone hunting.

And been caught. Her hands tightened on the wheel, and pain arced to her shoulder, to her jaw. An irascible Gutierrez faded from her inner vision, to be replaced by Pete and Artie, sweating and furious. Could their sister persuade them to restraint? Would she even try?

She slowed, waited for a red light to change, and swung right. She was sure she'd seen . . . ah, yes, there it was. In

159

the window of the shop a bright orange sleeping bag spilled out of a canoe before a wall displaying crossed fly rods and crossed rifles.

A notice taped to the window reminded prospective handgun purchasers of California's fifteen-day waiting period. No matter, she'd be more comfortable with a long gun anyway, and she already had one, courtesy of the pot-farming wench in the old truck. All she needed was ammunition.

Light was dim in the body of the store, bright in back where a counter ran the length of the wall. Behind the counter a middle-aged, leathery-faced man in a plaid flannel shirt lifted his head, smiled, and then frankly stared.

She stood straighter and thrust out her battered chin. Take a good look, Buster, she told him silently. And feel free to mention my purchase to anyone who might inquire. "Twenty-gauge," she said.

"I beg your pardon?"

"Give me a box of shells for a twenty-gauge shotgun. And a cleaning kit, please."

·18·

It wasn't the scabs, but the bruises. Who'd have thought flesh could get that color, red and purple like a dying sunset? Rather interesting, if you didn't take it personally. She picked up an unfamiliar gray paper bag from her dresser top, and it was moments before her mind registered the bag's heft as shotgun shells. Extraordinary what serious sleep could do for the spirit.

Well, sleep and relief. Margaret Halloran and Chief of Police Vincent Gutierrez had agreed that Mrs. Halloran would make no further attempts at crime solving or information gathering. Furious with her for her carelessness, with the Maldonados for their treatment of her, Gutierrez had settled into his hunter's guise as she told him Addie's tale, and Chrissie's. He would deal with Addie, and with Chrissie, and with Pete and Artie to their sorrow. He would talk to the three kids Chrissie had mentioned, and any others whose names he could wring from that sorry girl. And Meg would stay home and be quiet and cultivate her garden.

Absolutely, no argument, Meg thought now as she pulled on old sweatpants, a thick sweatshirt . . . everything soft, no zippers or buttons to surprise a bruise. Chin up, shoulders back, and pick up your feet, not too bad. No worse than, say, a marathoner the day after, or a catcher who'd worked a full nine innings.

Toast crumbs on the cutting board and a smeared, buttery knife; in the sink, glasses with shreds of orange pulp, bowls with clinging bits of cereal. Maybe coffee was all she wanted.

She turned at the sound of slow footfalls on the back steps; the door from the service porch swung open, and Katy trudged in, Grendel on her heels. Katy looked up at Meg, blinked, caught her breath. "Oh, Mommy," she whispered.

"I know. Pretend it's rubber, a mask for Halloween. Easy, baby, the ribs are a little tender."

"I *hate* all the things that are happening to us!" Katy's voice was high and thin. "I'd like to *kill* those guys!"

"I know, baby, I felt the same way and so did Chief Gutierrez." Gutierrez, jaw whitely clenched, had threatened to castrate the Maldonado boys with a rusty chain saw. Probably not the image to suggest to her daughter. "They *are* being punished, and their father assures me that they're very sorry; he called this morning."

"I don't know why you like Chief Gutierrez, the way he was yelling at you last night." Katy's lower lip was out. "And I don't see why Jenny had to go home. I miss her and Grendel misses Feef."

"Jenny's mother needed her." Meg filled the teakettle and set it on the stove. "I'm sure she'll be back to visit. Are you going to Miss Luoma's this morning?"

Katy sighed and shook her head. "She's getting ready to go to San Francisco. Sitting there for somebody to draw you gets kind of boring, anyway."

"Katy . . ."

"Besides, I think we should both stay home. If we're both here maybe nothing else will happen."

"That is just what Gutierrez . . . Chief Gutierrez suggested, that we stay home."

"Okay. So I'm going to go practice my guitar now. Jenny says I should practice at least an hour a day."

Which is exactly what your mother has been saying for the past year. Restraining a sigh, Meg made a single cup of coffee and was about to sit down when she realized that the morning paper was nowhere in sight.

Well, it was in sight, she acknowledged a moment later as she leaned over her back gate. It was lying in full view at the end of the driveway. Way down there.

"Grendel, would you go get the paper?"

Nose on paws, the dog rolled his eyes at her and sighed heavily.

"I thought not. Well, who needs the newspaper anyway. Shit." The muscles were willing enough, she found as she picked her way down the slope; it was the spirit that was fragile. One confrontation, just one set of astonished or even sympathetic eyes . . . All is vanity. Trophy in hand, she had turned to climb back to decent privacy when the squeal of brakes spun her around in her tracks.

Maria Mazzini came across the street at a trot, leaving her dark blue sedan at the curb with its door ajar. "Meg, oh you poor thing! When I heard about it, I told Ben those Maldonado boys should be horsewhipped."

"How on earth did you . . . ?"

"Oh, Ben's done the plumbing in most of Art Maldonado's projects, and the two of them are always going off fishing, or deer hunting—those things men like to do."

"Katy told *me* about it," said another familiar voice. Felicity Luoma stepped through her gate, dressed for the city in dark trousers that might have been silk, a white shirt that definitely was. "Those boys are drunken louts and belong in a work camp."

"I think their father has something of that sort in mind for them," Meg said, and noted that her audience had increased by one. Tom Emery. No, two, here came Eleanor Nordstrom in a ruffled pink maternity smock. Perhaps she should ask them all in for coffee. Or sherry? Or beer?

More expressions of awe and sympathy. Tom Emery would bring home a special salve for her, and Eleanor remarked that her own doctor recommended sunshine as the universal healer. "Thank you all. It really looks much worse than it is." Might be a good idea to print that on a piece of cardboard and pin it across her chest.

"Hey. Friends." Sweat-drenched from rusty curls to wool crew socks, Mark Haywood brought his knees high in a run-in-place while he gulped air. In the street, Louise Martin's Volks van had just pulled up behind Maria's car. "What's up? Latest bulletin on the murder investigation? Whooo. Jesus, Meg! What happened?"

"An accident," said Meg, and was interrupted by Louise before she could elaborate.

"That's what I wondered, Meg. What the hell is Vince up to? I thought they had a confession or something, and then today a cop is on my porch practically before dawn, wanting to hear one more time what I knew about Dave Tucker."

"If you are interested in what Chief Gutierrez has in mind, why don't you call him and ask?" said Meg.

"No, but any little bit of news, from the horse's mouth so to speak, would be appreciated, Meg." Mark was no longer running, only dripping. "With a murderer loose people get paranoid, even sensible people. Marcia's on a tear now about locking up every time we so much as step outside. She decided the other night, on pretty flimsy evidence, that someone had been in the house while we were away."

"Ben, too." Maria Mazzini clasped her hands against the neck of her blue linen dress. "He came home late, while I was in Sacramento, and nothing was gone, but old Brucie was upset, he kept whining and sniffing around in corners."

"Probably just rats," said Felicity Luoma, drawing a faint shriek from Eleanor Nordstrom. "If you need a trap, Eleanor, I have one you may borrow. But I believe I'll check my own locks once more before leaving town. Margaret, have you any information you can share with us without feeling you're violating a confidence?"

Polite phrasing had somehow transformed a rude question into a reasonable request. "I believe Chief Gutierrez has information that, uh, makes him less sure that Johnny Stein was the murderer." Like the word from Stein's Oakland acquaintances that Johnny was absolutely, whole-heartedly straight; or the report from the schools that Stein was moderately dyslexic and had taken no typing course. "So he is continuing the investigation."

•   •   •

"Where were you?" demanded Katy as Meg came in the back door.

"I went to get the paper and stopped to talk to some of the neighbors."

"Oh. Okay." Katy opened the refrigerator door and stood peering inside. "Can I have a Coke?"

"Before lunchtime? How about a glass of orange juice?" Meg reached past her daughter for the carafe, pushing the idea of a beer firmly from her mind. Same rules.

"Could I have some ice cubes, and some Calistoga to make it fizzy?"

Meg set small glasses back in the cupboard and took a pair of tall ones down. "Why not. Get a bottle from the pantry. How is Miss Luoma's new book coming along?"

Katy shrugged, her eyes on the glass into which she was slowly pouring mineral water. "Okay, I guess. Those Portagee people seem kind of boring."

"Portuguese, Katy." Katy's reply was a silent shrug, and Meg reined in tongue and temper. "Like Kimmie's grandfather. Mr. Silveira is Portuguese." Perhaps the Maldonados, too, but she wouldn't mention that possibility. And Johnny Stein, or at least his mother; Gutierrez said the boy had searched for local relatives named Carvalho. Portuguese persons all over the landscape.

"I wish Kimmie would come home."

"Me, too," said Meg fervently.

"Kimmie and I just play; she doesn't ask weird questions all the time. Like about you and that policeman. I don't like it and I told Cyndi to quit it."

" 'That policeman.' Katy, the fact that *Chief Gutierrez* is a friend of mine is absolutely none of Cyndi Martin's business."

Katy jammed her fists into her jeans pockets and lifted her chin. "Cyndi said that you and Mr. Gutierrez . . . she said she was going to see if I could come live with her at her grandmother's and go to a private school and maybe have a horse."

"And why did she think you'd want to do that?"

"Because she said you and Mr. Gutierrez were doing it, and you'd have a baby and then you wouldn't want me anymore."

Meg's flare of anger was tempered by a flicker of pity for Cyndi, who had so bleak a view of life. She reached out, took her daughter's cold hand and led the way to the breakfast-room table. "Come here, little." She settled into a chair, pulling Katy onto her lap and brushing her cheek against silky, ruffled hair. "Now, let's clear this up, in reverse order. I will always want you, I promise."

"Okay. That's what I thought."

"And I am not going to have a baby."

"That's what I told Cyndi." Katy shifted position, looking up expectantly.

There was a giggle building in Meg's chest; she stifled it ruthlessly. "And, although it is none of Cyndi's business, I am not presently 'doing it' with Mr. Gutierrez."

Katy, no dummy, caught the qualifier and frowned. "But strictly speaking, kid," Meg went on, "that really isn't any of *your* business either."

"Well, okay." Katy sighed and leaned her head against Meg's shoulder. "I think that's all really gross anyway. I don't know why anybody would want to do that."

"Mm."

The sound of the telephone brought Katy bolt upright, quivering. Meg wrapped both arms around her and hugged her hard. "Remember, baby? No more phone creep, I took care of that."

"I forgot." Katy slid to her feet and trudged across the room to the wall phone. Apparently the caller was Cyndi, and all she was getting from Katy were monosyllables: no, no, not now, I can't.

"What was all that about?" Meg asked when Katy had hung up the phone.

"Cyndi wanted me to come over. I told her I'm just going to stay home for a while, with my mother."

.   .   .

Checkers. Lunch. Cribbage. A double recipe of chocolate-chip cookies. Several phone calls, none of them anonymous nor threatening. By five-thirty Meg saw signs that the siege mentality was wearing off, being vanquished by boredom. "Heavens, it's getting late," she remarked cheerfully, "and Grendel hasn't had a walk, and I'm much too stiff. Would you mind taking him around the block?"

"Okay, if you want. If you think you'll be okay by yourself. Maybe I'll call Cyndi and ask her to come along."

.   .   .

"Katy, I promise you, I don't mind being alone," Meg found herself saying again some two hours later. "Just have a good time, and I'll see you tomorrow. Let me talk to Louise for a moment. And good night, little."

"Louise," she said softly, "are you sure she really wants to stay? This afternoon I thought she'd never leave the house again."

"She seems fine to me," said Louise in cheerful tones. "She and Cyndi got out the folding bed and made it up, and now they're playing Monopoly. And Flower is perfectly happy because Grendel will be *her* overnight guest. I think I'd better start looking for a dog. Where did you get Grendel?"

No, no, no! "From Hungary, more or less by accident. Honestly, Louise, I think you'd be happier with a nice retriever."

Lordy! Meg thought as she set the receiver back on its hook. Just imagine two of them in one neighborhood. She turned the night lock on the front door and stood listening to silence, a house wrapped in the cotton wool of heavy fog. Up and down the street her neighbors were no doubt turning locks, too, building up the fire in the mouth of the cave. All talking about prowlers, or perhaps about the trouble-prone Hallorans. At least most of them had someone to talk to.

"Poor little me," she muttered, and set off on her nighttime secure-the-premises circuit. Passing the kitchen window, she glanced out, gasped at the sight of a shadowy face, realized it was her own reflection. She yanked the flimsy curtains together and remembered summer nights on the desert, hanging stars and sharp shadows and the warm breath of the cooling earth. And coyotes.

The Hallorans hadn't kept a cat, or chickens, ducks, any of the other small creatures their desert neighbors rounded up protectively as dark fell, so Meg had felt free to enjoy the night sounds of the calling coyotes. Unlike human prowlers, coyotes did not peer through windows or creep into houses. She closed the door to Katy's bedroom, wishing Katy and Cyndi were giggling and whispering here rather than at Louise's house. In the entry hall she paused to stare at the obstinately silent telephone. Why hadn't she heard from Gutierrez?

She carried a chaste glass of white wine into the living room, set it on the coffee table beside a stack of books. With a footstool and several extra pillows she built herself a nest in the couch corner and settled into it: peace and quiet at last.

At 10:00 P.M. she decided that the mystery suffered from inadequate plotting and was peopled by characters no one could possibly care about. By 10:30 she found herself furious with Mrs. Proudie and irritated with gentle Mr. Harding; perhaps *Barchester Towers* was a daytime book. Perhaps another glass of wine would help.

The eleven strokes of the clock's bell were followed at once by the telephone; hand on the instrument, she waited for it to complete its second ring.

"Meg?" Gutierrez, his voice fuzzy.

"Yes, hello. Where are you?"

"I'm . . . I'm in town. I can't talk from here, just wanted to see how you are before I head for home. First chance I've had all day."

"Oh. Well, I'm fine. I guess."

"Has anything happened?" His voice was sharper.

"Of course not, what could happen? Or not much, anyway. I suppose it's quite safe tonight. The fog is too thick even for prowlers."

"Look, if you like . . . Meg, do you want me to come by for a minute on my way home? That's where I'm . . ."

"Yes," she said before he could finish.

·19·

Engine sound, and this time it did not fade but simply stopped. Meg opened her front door, stared into the fog, and watched the dark figure surface, head bent and shoulders slumped. Not until he turned to face her in the hall did she see the puffy, discolored flesh around his left eye; by morning he'd have a spectacular shiner.

She closed the door and leaned against it. "Sometimes, in Arizona, whole weeks went by without anyone I knew getting beaten up."

He shrugged out of his jacket and handed it to her. "Yeah. I have this fantasy of you and me in bed . . . only it's a hospital bed, and we're both in traction."

"That's not fantasy, it's prediction." She pointed him at her pillowed couch corner. "Relax and put your feet up, while I see what I can find to revive you."

"Brandy? Great!" he said a few minutes later, reaching eagerly for the glass. "Aren't you having some?"

"I can't stand the stuff; I keep it for friends." She set the bottle on the table beside him, then pulled a hassock close and perched on it. "Gutierrez, is it over? Do you have the murderer?"

"No. At least, I don't think so. We're still sifting a bunch of shit-scared kids, but what we've got so far is lots of motive, no hard evidence."

"Did you get anything from old Addie?"

"Hah!" Gutierrez took a sip of brandy, rolled it around in his mouth, swallowed. Sighed. "One look at me, and

Miss Addie Bengsten rang for the attendant and then passed out. Miss Bengsten, according to her doctor, has a serious heart condition and must not be subjected to stress. That may even be true. She looked bad."

Meg had serious doubts but kept them to herself. "So, you were left with Chrissie's names?"

"Right, those she gave you plus several more she figured as possibles."

"What about Dave's green box?"

He shook his head, winced, and said, "No. Jenny Tucker stuck to what she said the other night—that she'd never seen it. I had two men turn the Tucker house over from cellar to rooftop, and the garage as well: nothing. Mr. Tucker never saw a green metal box in his son's possession. Mrs. Tucker knows nothing of green metal boxes, her son's or anyone else's."

"And the Maldonados?"

Gutierrez' wide white grin seemed all canines. "Pete and Artie Maldonado got nothing from the Tucker house but grief. No green box. Their father assures me of this absolutely, and I believe him absolutely. You hear from Art?"

"About nine this morning. He was practically in tears on the telephone, wanted to come over to apologize, and I told him it wasn't necessary. Then he wanted to send Pete and Artie over to apologize, and I said absolutely not. I told him I was feeling better and didn't intend to prosecute."

"Probably the boys would have *preferred* jail. Actually, you are looking better. Pretty good, in fact."

"So my neighbors say. They're an attentive lot who manage to know everything that happens to me, sometimes even before it happens. Katy and I are considering a move to the safe metropolitan anonymity of, say, Santa Rosa. Okay, Gutierrez, I want to know what happened to you. To you and your face."

"What happened is I pulled a royal fuckup and a kid

nearly got killed." He poured an inch of brandy into his glass, sank back against the cushions, propped his ankles on the other hassock. "I had a 4:00 A.M. commitment to the narc patrol this morning, so I asked Svoboda to track down the list of high-school kids. Some of them are graduates now."

"Did Svoboda frighten somebody?"

He grimaced. "Svoboda's the kind of guy, little kids make him sit down so they can crawl in his lap. No, he and Chang found three of the kids on the list, talked to them quietly, persuaded them to come in and give statements. Number four is working in Eureka for the summer. Chang's seeing him tomorrow. Fifth one was Guido Santori. Guido's dad, Joe, is famous for going off like a rocket, but I've known him for years, so Svoboda decided to leave that job for me."

"Oh."

"Right. I came down from the afternoon helicopter run, shed the goddamned flak jacket, made an end run around William Tucker, who is very unhappy about rumors he's hearing. Then out to the Santori place, where Guido is chopping wood and fretting and falling all over himself to talk to somebody. Did you know Guido?"

"I didn't have him in class, but I knew him by sight. Absolutely gorgeous, dressed straight out of *GQ*, always talking a mile a minute and waving both hands. He usually had half-a-dozen girls with him; did he get caught in some kind of female cross fire?"

A sad, slow shake of Gutierrez' head. "Guido was having a love affair with a man, an instructor at the university he met when they both took a drawing course at the Art Institute. He figures Dave Tucker must have seen them together and suspected something. Anyhow, Dave photographed them saying good night on the porch of the guy's cottage."

"Oh," said Meg again. She pulled her knees close and locked her hands around them. "And I don't suppose Joe

Santori is the kind of man who'd take kindly to having a homosexual son."

"Jesus." He leaned his head back and closed his eyes. "Like a jackass, I was talking to Guido out there by the woodpile, which is not far from the back of the house. Joe's wife was in the kitchen and heard just enough to decide something funny was going on, something Joe should know about, so she trotted right in to wake him up from his nap." He picked up the brandy bottle, hesitated, then carefully measured out another inch of the golden-brown liquid. Meg sat still and watched him.

"So, Joe's screaming that he won't have a goddamned faggot for a son, Guido says what the hell are you going to do about it, Joe says he'll kill the son of a bitch who buggered his boy. Then Joe charges Guido, who's about half his size but has an axe in his hand. And I jumped Joe." He touched his darkening eye.

"And while we were thrashing around, Guido hopped in his truck and took off, yelling that he might as well be dead." He drained his brandy glass and set it aside. "And if somebody hadn't already killed Dave Tucker, I'd get in line."

"But he's all right—Guido?"

Gutierrez sighed. "He's in the hospital; he got drunk and crashed his truck out on a forest road. Punctured a lung, crushed his spleen, broke a collarbone and some ribs. The only reason we got to him in time was that we located the boyfriend and he helped. The boyfriend, Jeffrey's his name, would have donated blood, too, but he was the wrong type. Joe and I were the only O-negatives right at hand."

"Gutierrez." Meg leaned forward to scrutinize his face. "Are you telling me that you donated blood within, what, the last couple of hours?"

"Yes ma'am, seemed the least I could do." He pushed his shirt sleeve up and inspected the strip of flexible tape encircling his forearm. "I can probably take this off now."

"I wouldn't do that. Ninety-proof blood must be quite thin."

"Ah." He looked at her, put his feet on the floor as if to rise, sank back against the cushions. "But I'm not really drunk. It's just too many motives and no evidence. That kind of thing makes a cop very tired. Guido, incidentally, says he didn't kill Dave. He was with his boyfriend Saturday night. Not the greatest alibi going."

"So you're still . . . Louise said you had men on the street here today."

"Men here, men everywhere. Can't forget Stein, see? One of these kids could have killed young Tucker, and small loss. But Stein . . . like I said the other day, he had to be somewhere for six or seven days. Somebody hid him, and then somebody killed him."

Meg shivered, and Gutierrez said, "Right. So we'll do everybody all over again. And get a second opinion on Addie Bengsten. I'd sure like to talk to that lady."

He sighed. "Meg, do you suppose . . . could you drive me home, do you think? I hate to bother Svoboda this late. His wife is sick."

A few minutes later she pulled bed covers back and watched him settle himself gingerly on the edge of her bed.

"Meg, the couch would be fine."

"Only if you want to wake up with permanent spinal damage. Gutierrez, I often sleep in Katy's room. Now, lie down and I'll bring you some aspirin. Please."

When she returned with two white tablets and a glass of water, he was perched where she'd left him, but had reduced his garb to white cotton underwear and black socks. She handed him the glass, tipped the tablets into his other palm, watched as he swallowed.

"Gutierrez? Should I let anyone know where you are?"

He shook his head, waving a hand at her as if she were a departing friend, or perhaps a fly. "Svoboda would know to try here if he couldn't get me at home."

*   *   *   *

The plot of the mystery had somehow improved; Meg read at it in snatches as she prowled the house, listening for sounds of intruders, breachers of the enclosing fog. Now and then she found herself standing completely still, all sensory wires down, as she considered Dave Tucker, Dave and his victims, Dave the victim. Malice, like energy, was never destroyed, simply changed in form. Guido Santori had turned it inward, against himself; someone else had sent it back to its source.

Later, eyes on print that danced and then blurred: How often do adolescents plan and carry out a murder? two murders? Flaring anger and the snatching up of whatever weapon came to hand, yes. But plan? Gutierrez had complained of too many motives and no evidence; so none of the kids had yet been singled out as main suspect. Chrissie? Her numbskull brothers? Tiny Olsen? Jenny?

" 'Can't believe it, lived next door for years, such a nice quiet kid,' " Meg recited aloud. She decided that the phrases were commonplace because ordinary persons, most of humanity, look at others and see themselves. And ordinary persons do not become murderers. Killers yes, probably most people could kill if the terror or threat or outrage were great enough and a weapon available. But a murderer ... perhaps a murderer feels only his own separateness, looks at his fellows the way an anthropologist looks at chimpanzees.

Three stately bongs sounded from the dining room. Knock off the morbid ramblings, lady, and get some sleep.

Jenny had stripped her bed, nice well-trained girl, but Katy's would do. Meg padded into the front hall to check the night lock one more time, then paused at her own room, where the bedside lamp still burned.

The white underwear was on the floor. Gutierrez lay on his back, blankets drawn up to his lower ribs, one arm flung above his head. About to reach for the lamp switch,

Meg dropped her hand and looked at the sleeping man. Skin a warm, even brown, a light furring of dark hair on the forearms, none at all on the broad chest. The upflung arm was solid and firm, but without the sharp muscle definition of youth. The gently moving chest was thick, more massive than she'd have expected, dropping sharply from rib arch to flat belly.

"Sorry, but I never could sleep with anything on."

Meg stepped back out of the light, feeling a blush sweep her from toes to hairline. "It's late. I came in to turn out the lamp."

He rolled up on his left elbow, reached out his right hand; one step, another, and she touched his hand, wrapped her fingers around.

"Is Katy all right? Will she mind that I'm here?"

His fingers tugged, and she sat on the edge of the bed. "Um, Katy isn't here. She's spending the night with Cyndi Martin."

"Holy saint somebody!" Teeth flashed and eyes glinted as he pushed himself higher on the pillows, shoved the covers back. "Meg, my love, it would give me great pleasure if you could come here to me. I'd hope it would give you pleasure, too."

Without giving her mind time to intervene she stood up, turned out the lamp, dropped her robe and pulled her short nightgown over her head. "Don't look at my bruises."

"It's dark. Besides, as far as bruises go we're a matched set." Still lying on his side, he pulled her full length against him, stroked her back in long, slow strokes, nibbled gently at her mouth. His skin was satiny-smooth to touch, with a faintly peppery smell. His fingers were smooth, too, and warm and urgent; she arched tighter against him, tucked her face against his neck, remembered something.

"My neighbors. They'll know about this first thing tomorrow morning. Probably they know right now."

"Probably. But most of them won't object." He kissed her throat, then stretched out again, to look into her eyes. "Not in this time of the world, not even in Port Silva." He settled back slightly, away from her; the hand which had rested on her hip moved to her breast. "I promise." His palm made slow, delicate circles against her nipple, and she caught her breath.

"Gutierrez . . ."

"Do you suppose," he said plaintively, "that you could call me Vince? At least when we're making love?"

"You're taking . . ." rather a lot for granted, she'd intended to say, but a giggle of pure pleasure caught her. He lifted his head in surprise, looked at her, chuckled; then, bruises forgotten, the two of them grabbed at each other like a pair of teenagers, rolling and nudging and holding and encircling.

Wordless murmurs, the gentle sibilance of the comforter as it slid to the floor, a groaning squeak . . . not her bones, but the familiar protest of her old bedstead hard used. Meg smiled, blinked up at a ceiling oddly pale and high, blinked again and felt her neck muscles go rigid. A stranger was astride her, hands hard on her shoulders, face dark and sharp and damaged.

"Meg?" Gutierrez leaned forward into a faint wash of light from the half-open door.

"I think so. Yes," she whispered, and reached to pull him down.

· · ·

Katy! Meg came bolt upright in the dark, heart pounding. She had pushed the entangling covers aside before she remembered that Katy was not at home.

As her own breath slowed, she heard deep, even breathing from the figure beside her, the tick of the bedside clock, the soft night sounds of an old house. One night sound was missing, the click of Grendel's toenails on the hall floor as he did his patrol. Tonight he was patrolling the Martin house, guarding Katy. While she herself was neatly tucked in bed with the chief of police. *There* was safety for you. She slid back down against her pillow, pulling the covers tight.

But after such an all-out, sudden waking, sleep proved elusive. She turned, closed her eyes, then sighed and turned again, carefully. The double bed was too small; or she had simply grown unaccustomed to sleeping around another body. Gutierrez was not a neat sleeper; she met a foot or a shoulder with every turn.

Give it up and let the poor man sleep, at least. She edged out from under the blankets, found her robe and slippers on the floor, and crept out of the room, closing the door softly behind her.

The clock over the sink said almost five; she pushed the curtains aside to find that morning light was beginning to glimmer through the fog. What a shame, she thought absently as she filled the teakettle. Anyone up this early was surely entitled to a sunrise. Windbreaker over her shoulders, hands wrapped around her second mugful of coffee, she was sitting on her back steps watching the early sunlight combat the fog when she heard soft footsteps. "The paperboy, praise be!" she said aloud, but softly.

As the figure emerged from the mist, Meg realized with annoyance, embarrassment, and a distant flicker of amusement that it was Louise Martin. Breakfast for three, perhaps? Or, ho ho, look what I've got?

"Meg! I saw your kitchen light was on." Louise fumbled with the latch, kneed the gate open. "Come on, Flower," she snapped to the small figure trailing in her wake.

"I knew it, I just knew they'd be here, the little . . . Jesus." Louise dug both hands into her damp, tousled hair and yanked as if to pull her mind into order. "Jesus, when I looked in and saw those two empty beds, I think my heart stopped!"

·20·

"Empty." Two beds. And here was Flower. "Katy?" said Meg, her voice high. As she stood up, the coffee mug slipped from her fingers and shattered on a flagstone.

"Oh, shit. Okay, they've gone for an early walk or something. Just wait until I get my hands on Cyndi."

"Katy wouldn't . . . it's not even daylight yet. Katy always sleeps late."

"What's up?" said a quiet voice, and Meg turned to find Gutierrez standing in the doorway. She ignored Louise's "Hey!" of astonishment and gripped his arm with both hands. "Katy's gone. Vince, she was staying at Louise's last night, and she's gone."

"Cyndi, too," said Louise, and followed the others into the kitchen. "Come on, Flower."

"Let go," said Meg. "I have to get dressed, I have to go look for her."

"In a minute." Gutierrez kept his encircling arm clamped across her shoulders. "Louise?"

Louise ran both hands through her hair. "I got up maybe half an hour ago, had an idea about something I'm working on. I had a shower and then on my way to the studio I glanced in the kids' room. Flower was in the folding bed, but the other two beds were empty. Katy and Cyndi were gone."

There was a murmur from the corner, where Flower had climbed into a captain's chair.

"What?" asked Gutierrez.

"And Grendel," the little girl said. "Grendel was gone, too."

Grendel was with them. Meg collapsed onto a stool.

"Any idea how long they've been gone?" Gutierrez asked Louise.

"Look, I didn't go in and feel the sheets or anything. They were there when I went to bed last night at, oh, just before midnight. And I'm not a real light sleeper," she admitted, "but I'm sure nobody came in and carried off two big strong kids and their dog. I guess probably the dog woke up and wanted to pee, and the kids decided to make a walk of it."

"Maybe," said Meg. "Flower?" She stood up and moved across the room, to kneel beside the chair where the child sat. "Flower, did you hear them go out?"

"No." Flower pulled her knees up under the kitty-and-bunny print of her nightgown, leaned her forehead on her knees. Long pale hair fell forward and hid her face.

"Flower?" Meg said again. Louise started forward, and Meg waved her off. "Flower, this is important. Are you sure you didn't hear them leave?"

A slow back-and-forth roll of the head. Then, "Not this time."

"Oh, shit," said Louise very softly. "Okay, baby, sit up and look at Mommy. Nobody's mad at you, I promise. What about the other times?"

Flower sniffed and spoke to her own knees. "Cyndi goes out, nights. Out the window. After it's already dark. But always before, she was back when I woke up."

"So they may have been gone all night." Meg stood up, bracing herself for a moment with a hand on the table, keeping her eyes away from Louise. "I'm going to get some clothes on and go out looking."

"Meg, I'm sorry," said Louise. Meg snapped her head around and met the other woman's glance, and Louise flushed.

"They'll probably turn up in ten minutes asking for

breakfast," said Gutierrez. "But let's get descriptions, just in case. Height, weight, eyes and hair, what they were wearing."

Meg listened to Louise's halting description, then listened to her own voice, her clear crisp teacher's voice. ". . . Levi's and a plain white tee shirt. She doesn't like clothes with writing or pictures. Blue sneakers. A blue nylon anorak."

"And the dog?"

Grendel. Grendel was with Katy. "He's a komondor, long coat like a dirty-white mop. Thirty inches at the shoulder, probably a hundred twenty-five pounds. Strong. Strangers . . . it would be better not to approach him, just to phone me."

•   •   •

For what seemed hours Meg drove her van around, whistling her shrill through-the-teeth whistle again and again. She questioned everyone she came across, some of them probably more than once as she retraced paths: Have you seen two little girls and a big white dog? Every now and then, when she came upon a phone booth, she called her house, and then Louise's house.

By eight-thirty the streets were busy with going-to-work traffic and her mouth was too dry to produce a whistle. She drove back to Rose Street and parked the van at the curb before her own empty, silent house. She found one of her yellow pads, wrote "Katy, I am at Louise's, please come there!" and left the pad on the kitchen counter.

Louise's front door was open, and Louise was in the kitchen. "Nothing," Meg said, and added, "Yes, thank you," when Louise gestured toward the coffeepot.

"Nothing here, either. Vince has two guys going door-to-door on Rose, and they'll do Azalea and Elm next. What we think is, Cyndi may be the prowler the neighbors have been talking about. So the kids might have gotten into somebody's house and maybe been trapped there."

Meg considered this for a moment, and found she could not imagine her own daughter as a housebreaker. Moral aspects aside, Katy was noisy and straightforward with no talent for subterfuge. Cyndi, now . . . "Be awkward, with a dog," was all she said.

"Yeah, that's right." Louise brightened. "Goddamn, I am going to blister that kid's butt when she gets home. She won't be able to sit down for about a year."

The coffee managed to be both weak and bitter. Meg set the cup aside but kept her eyes on it to avoid looking at her neighbor. Not Louise's fault, nobody ran an hourly bed check on kids the age of Katy and Cyndi. Just because Louise is a basically careless person who doesn't like her own daughter, who virtually abandoned that same daughter . . .

Stop that. Grendel will protect Katy. If the girls had been in *Katy's* room last night, they could probably have gotten out with no trouble. Meg thought of Gutierrez and their lovemaking: two long-forgotten actors in an old black-and-white movie.

Footsteps from the front of the house, and a figure in the doorway, a dark, trim man with graying hair, in a brown uniform. Meg blinked and saw Gutierrez and closed her eyes for a moment.

"No one has seen them, everyone is looking," he said, and brushed the back of his hand against Meg's cheek before moving to the counter, and the coffeepot. "Did you find anything in Cyndi's room?"

"Nothing that didn't belong to her, or to the library. She spends a lot of time writing in a notebook, but she must have it with her, in that shoulder bag she always carries."

"Flower didn't remember anything more?"

Louise shook her head. "She's only five, for Christ's

sake. She didn't like her sister, so she was pleased to have Cyndi go out. I guess she thought I didn't like Cyndi, either, so I wouldn't care. Flower isn't as smart as Cyndi, but she really picks up on undercurrents."

Meg straightened and rubbed her burning, gritty eyes. "I think I'll go home."

A sharp triple rap from the front of the house brought them all around like bird dogs, quivering. Another rap, and a voice: "Chief Gutierrez?"

Gutierrez moved toward the voice and Meg followed, a part of her mind registering for the first time a slick shine of black leather, the belt and the holster it supported. She'd never before seen him wearing a gun. She'd never even been in the same room as someone wearing a gun. The floor seemed very far away as her feet moved across it; she could hear Louise's breathing behind her.

The man in the doorway was well over six feet tall, with a mane of wiry golden curls making him appear even taller. He had a blond toddler on his right shoulder, and another at the end of his left arm, and his blue eyes were wide and round in a very white face. He looks frightened, thought Meg, and felt her stomach give a sick lurch.

"Excuse me, Chief Gutierrez? My name is Armistead, Tom Armistead. Officer Englund told me I'd find you here."

"Yes?"

The two men exchanged glances; then the giant swung the riding child to the ground and herded both his small charges in ahead of him. "I own the old water tower over on Elm, 1520 Elm Street," he said, keeping his eyes on the children and his voice very soft.

"Um, I went there this morning to figure out what I'd need to use to cut the grass. The neighbors have been complaining. And I brought the boys along just to get them out of the house. So they're playing around in all that long grass, and they found this . . ." He stopped to swallow; there were beads of sweat on his forehead.

"See, there's a girl there, and I think she's dead."

Meg put her thumb in her mouth and bit down hard. The buzzing in her ears swelled, then subsided and she held her breath.

". . . pretty sure, but I didn't actually touch her or anything. Not very old, kind of chubby. Light curly hair, and gray sweat clothes. Looks like she fell from the tower."

·   ·   ·

Meg ran the four blocks and was there to pound on Gutierrez' shoulder when he climbed out of his car. "I want to go up into the tower. He won't let me go up there."

Gutierrez looked past her to the uniformed policeman, a broad-faced man with brush-cut gray hair. "Svoboda?"

Wide shoulders lifted in a slight shrug. "I promise you, missus, there's nobody up there, no kid and no dog either."

"You'll have to take his word for it, Meg. Or mine. I'll go up and have a look if that would make you feel better."

She shook her head and stepped back, hunching her shoulders and hugging her arms close.

"Mrs. Martin will be here as soon as she gets her younger daughter settled with a neighbor," Gutierrez told Svoboda. "Anything yet?"

"Kid must of fell, no sign of anything else. Probably six, eight hours ago, clothes are real damp and she's fairly, uh, stiff." He flicked a glance at Meg, who hugged herself tighter and said, "But where's my daughter? Where's Katy?"

"She isn't here, Meg, and there's no immediate sign that she has been, she or the dog." There was a squeal of brakes, and Meg made herself turn to look, but it was only the big man, Armistead. The man who owned this death trap. Weren't there laws about maintaining such properties?

"I had to take the boys home," said Armistead as he reached them. "Chief Gutierrez, I can't figure how this happened. I nailed a barrier of two-by-fours halfway up the first flight of steps, and I had a locked gate across the bottom, I checked that padlock at least once a week."

"Just a minute, Mr. Armistead," said Gutierrez, and took Meg's arm. "Do you want to wait for Louise?" he asked her.

Stay and be moral support to Louise. Should do that. "No."

"Okay. Then I want you to go home. Katy is not here, so we assume she's alive, and the dog with her. You should be at home waiting for her."

"Waiting . . . Gutierrez, I can't."

"Yes, you can. I'd come with you, but I think I'll be more useful working."

"Yes!"

"But I'll be in touch. You'll hear immediately if we learn anything. Do you want me to drive you home?"

"No."

• • •

Coffee on the stove, cold and murky with a slight oily scum on its surface. She poured it down the sink and scrubbed the pot out with hot water, running water that sent up a good loud noise to banish the echoes of an empty house. She filled the teakettle, set it on the stove, turned on the flame, turned it off. Only 10:00 A.M. but so what. Seven brown bottles of beer in the fridge. It made a little song in her head and she had her hand on one and then thought, dumb shit, you'll be driving again, searching. Orange juice? No.

Coffee. Shiny clean pot, clean cone, pure white filter set neatly in the cone with no bulges or wrinkles, dark coffee in a neat even mound, exactly centered, no messy grains trailing up the clean white sides. Where are you,

Katy? she asked in her head, and wondered why her jaw hurt and unclenched her teeth.

Two cups of coffee later she heard footsteps and lurched up from her chair and as quickly sat back down. Too heavy for Katy, and slow, slow and sad . . . Gutierrez?

"Hey, Meg." Louise Martin came in the back door, dropped into the opposite chair, and stretched her forearms out on the table. That's what "glassy-eyed" means, thought Meg. The wide eyes were blue marbles, unmoving, unreflecting; their lids closed and opened, and Meg listened for a click.

"Vince asked me to tell you that there's no word on Katy yet, and no sign of her. I didn't go up in that fucking tower but lots of other people did; apparently they can tell Cyndi fell from there but that's about all." She paused to draw a long breath. "Meg, do you have any gin, or . . . no, I plan to get seriously drunk later, but for now just beer. Have you got a beer?

"Cyndi looked . . . thanks." Louise took the bottle from Meg, tilted it, swallowed, sighed. "Her head was crooked, her neck that is, she broke her neck. But except for that, she looked almost normal except, you know, a little flat? Like one of my figures if I'd been unhappy the way it was going and dropped it hard." She looked at the bottle in her right hand, turned her head to inspect her uplifted left palm, and snapped her wrist toward the floor.

"Like that." She turned the marble-eyes on Meg, who watched them fill with tears. "It probably didn't hurt much, Vince says. But that's a long fall. Wouldn't you be scared while you were falling?" Before Meg could form an answer, Louise shook her head and blinked several times. "No, not Cyndi. Cyndi never thought anything bad could happen to her. She probably went the whole way knowing an angel or something was waiting to catch her. So maybe one was.

"Oh, but what I meant to say." She took a sip of beer

and then wiped her eyes. "I think it probably went this way. Cyndi and Katy got up in that tower somehow, in the dark and the fog. And Cyndi fell, she always was clumsy. But Katy's quick and agile, she wouldn't have fallen. But she'd have been really scared. She'd have run off. Don't you think?"

"I don't know. But I hope so," Meg said, and cast a look at the telephone on the wall. "If that's what happened, she'll get herself in hand before long and come home, or call."

"That's what I'd have done, headed for the next county," said Louise. "In fact, I still might. Except I'd better go see Flower. She'll be wondering. She's at Maria Mazzini's house."

Meg lifted her head at a faint sound. Gutierrez was standing in the doorway, his face so grim that she stumbled to her feet, sending her chair over backwards. He shook his head at her, spread his hands.

She set the chair carefully back on its four feet. "Gutierrez. Shouldn't that man be prosecuted? The one who owns the tower?"

"I don't think so, Meg. He seems to have taken the normal precautions."

"Normal was hardly sufficient, if two children could breach them."

"They didn't. Someone else already had, had changed the padlock and sawed through the two-by-fours. Louise, are you ready to go home?"

One problem at a time here, thought Meg. Her weary mind was like molasses, slow but sticky. "Who?"

Gutierrez sighed. "Dave Tucker, or at least that's the way it looks. There's a big open room at the top of the tower, and a sleeping bag there with his name on it, and a camera, some other small stuff. And his green metal box, full of money and pictures and tapes."

Dave Tucker was of no interest to Meg at the moment, not the slightest. She was about to tell Gutierrez so when

Louise said "Goddammit to hell," and dropped her head to the table between her outstretched arms.

"God*damn* it! Do you think Cyndi saw that picture?" Louise asked without raising her head.

"The box was unlocked, and the keys were in her pocket."

Louise pulled herself upright and sat back in her chair, making no attempt to stop the flow of tears. "Boy, the kid had a great last view of her mother, didn't she?"

Louise had, she told them, been paying blackmail to Dave Tucker. While modeling for her, he had familiarized himself with her house and her habits, then had taken a disgusting photograph. Every Saturday she put a payment in her mailbox; every Saturday night he came to pick it up, and sometimes to talk to her, although not, she insisted, on the last Saturday of his life; he had merely picked up his payment that night.

Slow and sticky, Meg's mind caught and held at one item, the photograph, perhaps because Louise described it with an artist's economy. Night, big moon, sharp shadows. Familiar driveway. Small naked child in the foreground, thumb in mouth, eyes wide. Behind her, in the backyard, a very unchildlike tangle of bare bodies on a garden lounge.

"Dave had made friends with Flower. He got her out of bed that night and set her out there. He didn't have to take her clothes off, she does that herself every chance she gets."

A distracting little mystery here, something for the sluggish mind to nibble around while important things were beyond imagining. "What for?" asked Meg. "Even here, they probably wouldn't burn you at the stake."

"See, ol' Chaz has failed to knock up his new wifey, and she is, according to his letters, interested in meeting *his* other child, the younger, prettier one. If that picture got . . . gets into the paper, or into Chaz's possession, I'll lose Flower. Too."

Louise rose and moved quickly to Gutierrez, to put a hand on his arm. "Vince? What will happen to it?"

While he did not actually smile, the hard set of his face softened perceptibly. "All the pictures are now police property. Which means my property. Eventually I'll return most of them to their, uh, subjects."

To the subjects who are not murder suspects, thought Meg. And where were you that Saturday night, Mrs. Martin?

"Vince, I want to go get Flower! Please, will you come with me?"

"If you'll wait in the car a few minutes while I talk to Meg." When she had gone, he came to stand beside Meg's chair.

"Gutierrez," she said, "that box, Dave Tucker . . . was there something about *me*? Something that might have frightened Katy?"

"There was a shot of you on your front porch with a man, both of you wearing bathrobes. Not exactly a damning picture to anyone but me," he added with a half grin. "Meg, what I want you to do now is call your friends, Katy's friends . . ."

"I did. There aren't that many, and no one has seen her. Or heard from her. Gutierrez, I want to go out in the van again."

"Let us do the looking. You go over your list of friends again. Try to think where she might go if she were running away. But stay here. Would you like me to leave a policeman here with you?"

"No! I'd rather have him, all of you, looking for Katy."

"A neighbor? Anna Wingate?"

"Gutierrez, I do not need my hand held. Anyone who wants to help me can go find my daughter."

"Right. I'll be in touch."

·21·

Jenny Tucker came, sometime in the middle of the afternoon; the last of many well-meaning visitors, she was the first one Meg was glad to see. Meg beckoned her in, laid the shotgun down on the kitchen table, wiped her oily fingers on a rag.

"I thought maybe I could stay with you for a while?"

"That would be nice." Meg pushed the shotgun against the wall and lined the other things up neatly: rags, oil can, bottle of red wine, glass. "I've been meaning to clean that gun. And I'm permitting myself one glass of wine an hour," she added, glancing at the clock. "Can I get you some orange juice?"

Jenny shook her head and sat down in the opposite captain's chair. "I brought some cards. Do you play gin? But I'd better warn you, I'm pretty good."

· · ·

Jenny excused herself to go to the bathroom; Meg shuffled the cards and glanced at the lopsided score. She had done this one time before, played cards while waiting for Katy; she and Dan had played for hours the night their daughter was born. Cribbage, with Dan doing the pegging for both of them, until the pains grew so intense that riding them out took all her concentration.

And where was Katy now? Meg closed her eyes, exhaled, tried to slow her blood. If Katy were dead, wouldn't she know it? feel the lack of connection as if her reaching hand had closed on air? A telephone bell jarred her, brought her halfway to her feet before she registered the faintness of the sound. Not her phone, but Felicity Luoma's again. Three, four rings sent chilly nerve-echoes the length of her spine. Hang up, you bastard, she's not there. Ten, and silence.

She poured a glass of wine. If there was an inner knowledge, a truth in the blood, it sang beyond her hearing. So, Katy was not dead because she simply couldn't be. Lost, hurt, abused . . . any of those she would survive, and Meg with her. "Fight, Katy!" she whispered.

"Mrs. Halloran, I know she'll be okay." Jenny came back into the kitchen, and paused beside the corkboard where Meg had pinned Miss Luoma's sketch of Katy. "Look at her; she's a really strong, smart little kid."

Meg stared at the small firm mouth, the square chin with its deceptive dimple, the direct gaze. "Yes. Yes, she is. Okay, Jenny, my deal. Time for me to catch up."

She was in fact gaining ground and ready to gin half an hour later when Miss Luoma's phone began again, and went on for the inevitable ten rings. "That is by God enough," she snapped, and set the cards down. "Katy told me where Felicity hides a set of keys. I'm going to unplug that damned telephone."

"Want me to do it for you?" asked Jenny.

Meg shook her head. "If one of us is accused of breaking and entering, it had better be me. You know," she added, looking once more at her daughter's face, "Katy sat for her several times. I'd like to see the other sketches."

"I think you should go look," said Jenny promptly. "I'll stay right here, and come to get you if anyone calls."

It was just after four; the sky had been gray and overcast all day, and the air was growing chilly. Meg picked her way down her own driveway and skirted the wide iron gate across Miss Luoma's drive in favor of its smaller counterpart directly before the house. The little gate swung silently open, then closed behind her of its own weight.

She followed the walk to the front porch, stepped over a pile of soil and broken branches that must have come from a pair of now-empty hanging baskets, and took the footpath around the side of the house to the studio. The studio staircase had treads of metal, each with a lip projecting back to make a shallow shelf. Within Katy's reach, she reminded herself, and her exploring fingers brushed one space, tried a second, and found a ring with four keys.

Heavy curtains drawn tight, air thick and still; the big room was sullen, unwelcoming, very much someone else's place. Someone who belonged, who had old family paneling and an authentic reproduction of an old family lamp; bookcases full of old books, a wall of family photographs in faded sepia tones.

And here was the outsider, the newcomer, housebreaking. "Tough shit!" she muttered, and noted with some surprise that she had no real fondness for her illustrious neighbor. Childish self-interest quickly lost its charm, especially in someone sixty years old.

She wanted those sketches; she had a right to them. It would have been nice to find them right out in the open, but since they weren't . . . Meg drew a deep breath and moved past the work table, bare except for a blank sketchpad and a jar of pencils, to try the twin doors of the tall wooden cupboard. Locked.

Keys. Probably somewhere close; she turned quickly to the table. Three drawers at the left end contained no keys, nothing of immediate interest; on the right was a bank of wider, shallow drawers, flat storage places for sketches in charcoal or pen or occasionally pastels. Halfway down the bank Meg found a twelve-by-fifteen-inch paper folder marked "Portagee Flats."

She set the folder on the table, opened it, reached quickly for the nearby wheeled swivel chair and sat down: Katy nearly full face, looking up, smiling lips parted on the edge of speech. Meg set the drawing to one side without turning it over, and found beneath it the amended version, heavy-eyed Portuguese child in a high-necked dark dress with a white collar, a white pinafore apron.

Another, and another. Meg set aside each true Katy, left the storybook child in the folder. She was intent on her discovery, taking breath only in shallow drafts; when the phone rang, on the wall over the desk, she frowned in irritation and reached for the receiver without taking her eyes from the pictures. "Yes?"

"Felicity! Felicity, you naughty thing, where have you been? I had to pay for an empty hotel room last night, and we had reservations for dinner at Ernie's!"

Meg gaped wordlessly at the telephone, and the man spoke again, in softer, coaxing tones. "Felicity, love, please don't be silly. We've done it before, no problems and no one the wiser, why fuss over a second time? And I've found someone new, she's talented but young and quite poor, and very earnest; she won't even think of herself as a ghost, just a helper. So . . . ?" Silence, then an exasperated sigh.

"Ghost?" She spoke the word which had snagged her mind, and heard a harsh intake of breath at the other end.

"Felicity? Who is this?"

"Margaret Halloran," she replied automatically. "I'm a neighbor, I'm, um, keeping an eye on things here for Felicity." San Francisco, Miss Luoma had gone to San Francisco to meet her publisher or agent or somebody, yesterday.

"Oh my God!" The voice in her ear slid high, horrified.

"We've had . . . we've had heavy fog," she told him slowly. "If she was driving the coast highway . . ." Fog, and fast drivers, and bodies in a ditch, a child and a big dog; she groped for the folder of drawings, fumbled it, and watched its contents spill across the table like a fanned-out deck of cards.

The man said "Oh my God!" again, faintly, and Meg whispered, "Just a minute," through numb lips. From two sheets at the back of the folder, Johnny Stein's face gazed up at her.

"Look, Ms. Halloran," the caller said, his voice gathering strength with each word, "perhaps I got my dates mixed. I do know that Felicity would be terribly upset if she thought anyone were meddling in her life. Let's just leave her to her own shy ways, shall we?"

Meg squeezed her eyes shut but the face was still there, darker now although the moon was very bright here on the beach. She swallowed hard and swiveled the chair, turning her back on the table. "I'm afraid I can't do that, Mr. . . . ?" She let the silence lengthen, and finally he sighed and gave in.

"Farrar, Roger Farrar," he murmured.

"Felicity's what—editor?"

"Agent."

"Agent. And she was to meet you in San Francisco yesterday. But she didn't."

"That's true, but—"

"Has she called? Been in touch at all?"

"Well, no."

"Have you looked for her? Notified the police?"

"Good heavens, no! No," he sighed, "I just keep calling, there where you are and her farm. Ms. Halloran, it appears that I was a bit indiscreet; I hope that as Felicity's friend you'll forgive me."

What you mean is forget. "Certainly, Mr. Farrar. Where are you staying, please? In case Chief Gutierrez needs to talk with you."

"Oh, God." It was a near-whimper this time. "Felicity will be absolutely . . . all right. I'm at the Hyatt Regency."

Meg left the folder open on the worktable, picked up her pictures of Katy, and unplugged the phone. Presumably Mr. Farrar would not call again, but someone else might.

Minutes later she stood with her own phone pressed to her ear and listened to Gutierrez tell her that they had no news about Katy. "Well. I'll be here; Jenny Tucker is with me. But I just found out something odd. Felicity Luoma must have known Johnny Stein; she made some sketches of him, and not from the photo in the paper. And her agent says she did not get to San Francisco yesterday. He's been calling her house here and her farm in Covelo all day."

"She's not at the Covelo place," said Gutierrez.

"Oh. That's interesting. That you know that, I mean."

"We, my people and I, are seriously interested in the whereabouts of everybody in your neighborhood," he said in grim tones. "Meg, did you get the agent's name?"

"Roger Farrar, and he's staying at the Hyatt Regency in San Francisco. From what he said, I think someone has been helping with her books, helping write them."

Gutierrez did not reply at once; Meg glanced at Jenny, who was pinning the new sketches on the corkboard. "Vince, it's getting late, and it's cold, and Katy has just that light anorak. Please find her."

"We're trying, Meg. There's something . . . I was going to come there, but since you're not alone I'll tell you now. Cyndi's fall was probably not an accident. She'd drunk chocolate loaded with a barbiturate."

He was still talking, but she hung the phone carefully on its hook and then leaned her forehead against the wall. Katy had not run away. No surprise, that was a ridiculous notion. Cyndi and Katy together. Somebody killed Cyndi; the rest of the equation wasn't hard to figure out. But why leave Cyndi there and take Katy away? And what became of the dog? as a deadweight he'd be nearly unmanageable.

"Mrs. Halloran?"

The words finally penetrated her daze. Looking up to meet Jenny's eyes, she sniffed and realized that there were tears spilling down her face. That's useful, she thought; she wiped her eyes with a paper napkin, blew her nose. "Sorry, Jenny, I guess I forgot you were here."

"Mrs. Halloran, I couldn't help listening."

"That's all right."

"No, but do you think there was something funny about Miss Luoma knowing Johnny Stein?"

"Funny." Meg propped a shoulder against the wall. Funny, odd, a puzzle . . . a problem to distract the mind's eye from unbearable images. "Yes, I guess there was. Not that she knew him, but that she didn't say anything about it when the whole police force was looking for him." She frowned. "Of course, she could have seen him on the street and drawn him from memory. But I don't think she works like that. I think she draws from photographs or from life," she added, and turned to stare at the corkboard, at the various faces of her daughter.

"Felicity Luoma, you heard that part, Felicity Luoma was supposed to turn up in San Francisco yesterday, but didn't. Now Cyndi Martin was killed in a fall, but she had barbiturate-laden chocolate in her stomach when she fell. That tower was your brother's high place. Jenny, isn't that weird and interesting?

"Chocolate," she murmured. "Felicity Luoma had Katy in for tea the other morning, but she gave her hot chocolate instead; Katy said it was very good. Katy trusts her, Grendel knows her as a friend." Meg pounded the sink board with her fist, once and again and again. "If she'd driven up and opened her car door, both of them would have hopped right in."

"Mrs. Halloran, if there was something funny, I bet Dave was in it some way," Jenny said, her voice cold. "And if he was, Addie knew."

• • •

Meg retrieved Miss Luoma's keys and did a quick search of house and garage. "I've already been in the studio," she told Jenny. "Perhaps it will all count as one crime. And Gutierrez would have to do it legally, with warrants."

She found nothing, not that she had expected to. So

she left her own house unlocked and a note to Katy on the counter, and then she and Jenny headed for Evening Star. "Gutierrez couldn't do this, either," she said as they turned off the highway. "Addie's doctor felt the police might be hazardous to her health. Let's just hope we can get in without being noticed."

"Don't worry, just let me talk."

Meg pulled the van to the edge of the lot. As she slid out, the pockets of her windbreaker slapped heavily against her thighs, and she glanced back to make sure the shotgun was out of sight behind the seat. Carry that thing into a hospital and they'd net her like a rabid dog. "Lock your door, Jenny," she instructed. "And cross your fingers."

Grace, the attendant from Meg's earlier visit, was not in sight today. Their first break, thought Meg, and let Jenny precede her into the office where a sharp-faced woman in her fifties sat behind a desk.

"I'm Jennifer Tucker, William Tucker's daughter. My father asked me to call on Addie Bengsten, who used to work for our family."

"Tucker? Oh, of course." The woman stood up and produced an ingratiating smile. "May I have an attendant take you up?"

"Thank you, but we know the way."

"Very good," Meg said softly as the two of them set off on the path to the upper building. "Jenny, I hope this doesn't get you into trouble."

"Nobody bothers about me. Besides, I want to see Addie; I want to find out if she still scares me."

She scares me, thought Meg grimly. The door at the end of the hall was open, and she strode toward it.

Addie looked smaller and older, her mouth hanging slack as her head rested against the back of her chair. Meg rapped on the doorjamb; the white-tufted head came up, eyes opening wide and then narrowing. "You! What do you want?" She turned in her chair, reaching toward the bed and the call button; but Meg pushed past her, lifted the cord free of the headboard and set the device on the floor.

"I want to know about Felicity Luoma." Addie's face showed no emotion at all, and Meg locked her knees against a sudden weakness; this malicious old woman was the only key she had. "You're one of Port Silva's oldest citizens," she said softly. "You must have known Miss Luoma when she was a child."

"Miss Luoma!" snapped Addie. "I knew Miss Aili Makela before she was *Mrs.* Luoma, and I knew *Miss* Luoma when she was just Felicity. Not Port Silvans, them or me, we all come from out Bacheller way." She paused for breath, wiping her mouth with the edge of a fringed shawl. "Them Finns think they're better than anybody else, bunch of Lutherans living in a commune like filthy heathens!"

"What did you tell Dave about Felicity?" Meg asked, leaning forward to meet the old woman's eyes.

Silence, for a long moment. Then, "Davey, Davey," Addie crooned. She shrank back in her chair, tugged her shawl close, let her head fall to one side. "Davey's gone, he's left poor old Addie alone. Poor old Addie."

Pure performance. Meg clasped her hands before her, squeezing them hard together to keep them from seizing the doll-sized figure and shaking it until its eyes rolled. "Davey was murdered. Don't you want his killer caught?"

"Davey's gone, carried by the angels into Abraham's bosom, he's waiting there for Addie, and she'll be with him soon, soon." Addie swayed as she sing-songed the words.

Jenny had remained in the doorway, stiff and silent. Now she came to stand beside Meg. "My dad is just finding out about what Dave was doing," she told Addie in a clear, cold voice, "and he hates it. If he finds out it was all your fault, you'll be out on the street."

Addie straightened, opened her eyes, dropped her hands to her lap. She stared hate at Jenny, who looked calmly back; then she sighed. "Davey always brought me the newspapers. I don't see so good these days, and he'd read me what was happening. He read this story about Felicity Luoma and her books, how wonderful they were and how they were going to get printed again, how she was starting a new one about the people in Portagee Flats. Hah!" Addie's snort rang with derision.

"See, they weren't her books. They were Aili's, her mother's. Aili wrote stories down in notebooks all those years she kept losing babies, six I think before she finally had Felicity. But no stories about Portagees, you can bet on that. Even the Finns didn't mix with people black as niggers and Catholic to boot. Any story about the Portagees Felicity would have to make up herself, or try to."

"She's missing. Felicity's gone and we can't find her," Meg said. "Where would she go?"

Addie shrugged. "Anywhere."

"Addie . . . Miss Bengsten, I think she has my daughter. Katy's only ten." Jenny had said an appeal would be useless, but Meg had to try.

"Anywhere," Addie repeated tonelessly.

"She killed Dave." Jenny's voice seemed to fill the small room; Addie pulled her head down between her shoulders.

"I told him," she whispered after a moment, "he shouldn't have taken that notebook. I believe she kept the old Makela place . . . out Bacheller Road, like I said. She knows," Addie said to Meg, tilting her head in Jenny's direction but not looking at her. "I took Davey out there a time or two when he was a little fella, and she was along. Our old shack was just this side of Ten Mile Ridge; the Makela place was another half mile on, up and back in some redwoods."

·22·

"No, I need to drive. It will keep me from exploding." Meg backed the van around and headed it down the driveway. "But I can use a navigator, Jenny . . . so long as you promise to stay low if we hit trouble. North or south?"

"South four or five miles, there'll be a sign. I promise."

Meg turned across the highway, settled into the left lane, gripped the wheel hard with both hands. Forty-five here, it wouldn't do to offend a passing policeman. Gutierrez! she thought, and slowed briefly as a service station phone booth caught the corner of her eye. But that one was out of order, receiver wire dangling loose; and the one a mile further along was occupied by a hulking, pimpled youth who ignored her and held the door shut by propping his spine against it. She gave up and hurried back to the van.

Fifty-five now, don't push it to sixty, not right here on the main highway. "Jenny!" she said suddenly, and felt Jenny turn to look at her. "Jenny, I saw that house. There was a picture of the Covelo farm on her wall, and then a picture of a different house, with her mother and father and Felicity as a baby. A wooden house, I think, and dark, a porch across the front."

"Probably redwood. I remember houses like that out there, really old houses with lean-to kitchens and garages that used to be sheds. There's Murphys Road, so the Bacheller Road's next, maybe another mile."

The Bacheller Road was straight and smoothly paved for perhaps five miles; then it began to wind and dip and present long stretches of graveled surface. Reluctantly Meg slowed her pace, squinting against a dusty glare reflected from the western sky behind them. They had just passed the gas station–grocery store crossroads that was Bacheller when Jenny cried, "Hey!"

Meg hit the brakes and felt the rear wheels break free for a terrifying moment. "Jenny, what . . . ?"

"Back up."

She edged slowly backwards into a dust cloud until Jenny put a hand on her arm and whispered, "Look. Grendel. I thought I saw him, but he went back in the bushes when that truck came by."

Meg slammed the brakes on and was out of the van almost before it stopped, meeting the dog as he labored up from the shallow ditch beside the road. Head down and right hind leg trailing, he was smeared with dried blood and oil and dirt; each breath he drew was labored. Meg stroked the filthy head, ran her hands lightly over ribs that were probably broken. "Grendel, where's Katy?" she whispered.

He whined, leaned his shoulder against her heavily, then crept to the open door of the van.

"Jenny, where are we?"

"Maybe halfway to Ten Mile Ridge? I don't know, it's just a brushy gully where Grendel was. There's a fence on this side, pasture."

"Where's Katy?" she asked the dog again; he whined, tried to climb into the van but failed. "Jenny, what was he doing when you spotted him?"

"I think he was coming toward us, you know, going along the road toward town. And he headed across the ditch and into the brush when he heard that truck."

Christ! Had Katy and the dog been thrown down into the gully, or had the dog been kicked out of a vehicle, which then took Katy on? The only sure thing was that dog and child had not reached this point on their own. "You wouldn't have left Katy if she were down there, would you?"

"Do you want me to climb down and look around?" Jenny asked.

Meg shook her head, scanning the roadside. She moved slowly along the ditch in the direction from which the dog had come, examining the thick brush for evidence of disturbance, calling her daughter's name. Twenty yards, and another twenty; she scrambled across the ditch three times, gaining nothing for her efforts except some painful scratches.

"Mrs. Halloran?" Jenny called, and a howling yelp from the dog drowned out her voice. Meg turned and hurried back.

"I can't hold him without hurting him," Jenny said apologetically. "He's trying to follow you. Maybe if we put him in the van?"

Meg closed her eyes, tempted to send forth a howl of her own. "The brush is so thick I could walk right past her and never know it. We'll call Chief Gutierrez from Bacheller; and then we'll go on. Come on, old boy, let us help you in."

•   •   •

"Tell him I found my dog not quite a mile east of Bacheller; he'd been hurt, probably hit by a car. There's no sign of Katy, and the area is woods and brush; a search will need lots of people. I'm going on to the Makela place."

She hung up and ran out to the van. "Gutierrez is on his way already. Somebody at the Historical Society remembered the Makela family and their old farm. And there's Ten Mile," she said a short time later, speaking over her shoulder to Jenny, who was riding in the back, trying to keep the dog from sliding about.

"None of it looks especially familiar to me," Jenny said. "I was too little, I guess. But Addie said about a half mile on."

Meg drove slowly, approached the half mile on the odometer, slowed still more; six-tenths, seven-tenths. "Jenny, I don't see it, the brown house."

"Redwoods, she said."

"Yes! And there was a stand of them just before that creek." At the next wide spot Meg turned the van.

"There!" A circle of old trees stood close to the road, behind a fence of dark, mossy stakes strung on wires. Beyond the trees a gap in the fence gave access to a track leading up and around a shallow hill. Meg eased the van through the gap, then swung in close under the trees and stopped.

"Stay, Grendel," she said, and stepped down onto a muffling carpet of debris from the trees. No human noises reached her ears, only a rustle of breeze in the high branches, bird sounds, the whisper of water from the nearby creek, the metallic snap of the cooling engine.

She slid out, reached back in for the shotgun, eased her door shut. She broke the gun, fished two shells from her pocket, thumbed them into place. Lifting the gun as if to close it, she changed her mind and hung it open over her right shoulder. "Jenny," she said softly, "please, either stay here or keep well behind me."

Meg picked her way up the rutted track, following it behind the hill to another stand of trees, a wide, open-faced shed, and finally the house from the photo. The door of the house was closed, nothing stirring behind any window, but in the shed stood a dusty black Mercedes sedan with a vanity plate: LUOMA.

The three broad steps to the porch bore a thick coat of dust and a muddle of footprints. Careful, she told herself, and took each step slowly, making her own distinct and silent footprints at the left edge. No voices, no sounds of movement; she swung the shotgun down, closed the breech, tucked the stock under her arm. She held her breath as she took the doorknob in her left hand, turned it easily, pushed the door wide.

The air was fresh in the living room, which ran the width of the house; floors and other surfaces were only faintly dusty. In the stone fireplace that filled most of the end wall to the right, a half-burned log had been pushed back from ashes that looked recent.

Three doors on the rear wall; she crept forward, pushed open the first and peered into a large bathroom where water dripped rustily into a pedestal sink, a tub stood on claw feet. Behind the second door was a tiny hall, containing a coatrack, a flight of ladderlike steps leading up, and an open doorway with one step down to a kitchen. There the remains of a fire glowed in a wood-burning stove. Coffee in a metal pot was faintly warm. One cup on the table, with an inch of dark liquid in the bottom. On the wooden sink board a second cup was inverted to dry, next to a steel thermos bottle. The back door stood ajar, and Meg saw a stretch of tall grass leading to thick brush and wooded hills beyond. Nothing moved except a hawk wheeling high above the trees.

She hurried back through the hall to the main room and its last door: bedroom, rumpled double bed, empty. Big old wooden wardrobe, with old clothes pushed tight at either side, a few newish skirts and shirts at center. She dropped to her knees and set the gun aside to reach deep into corners and satisfy herself that only shoes and boots were hidden there.

"Nothing in the car." Jenny was waiting in the living room. "It could be what hit Grendel, that Mercedes. It has a big heavy bumper and a dent in the left front fender. Have you been upstairs?"

Meg shook her head, and Jenny slipped past her to disappear up the ladder. "Nobody here," she called back. "There's a bed been slept in, though. And . . ." After a moment her feet appeared on the top rungs, and she clambered down.

"This," she said, handing Meg a leather leash, "was on a chair. And this was on the floor, like it got kicked under the bed."

Katy's whistle, the whistle Cyndi had given her. Meg thrust the gun at Jenny and swarmed up the ladder to stand very still in the room where her daughter must have been. Bed with old, once-white sheets, two wool blankets; straight chair. Mirror, shelf, a row of empty clothing hooks where sloping ceiling met wall. Twin dormer windows, one of them open; Meg knelt and looked out at the gentle incline of the kitchen roof. There was a path across the dusty old shingles, as if something had slid to the roof edge and then off. Or someone.

She hurtled down the ladder and outside, to circle the house, Jenny at her heels: no crumpled body, no telling depression in the dry grass. "They're out there somewhere," she said through clenched teeth. "Damn it, I need Grendel."

"Let me go search," Jenny offered quickly. "If Miss Luoma shows up you can make her stay. Until Chief Gutierrez gets here anyway."

"Wait." Eyes on the woods, Meg retrieved the shotgun, tucked it under her arm and stepped slowly through the long grass. There was a flash of color in the distance, a movement of branches; a figure emerged from the trees and began to pick its way through the brush.

"What . . . ?" In the dull light Felicity Luoma's hair was cottony-white, her face a blur. She tipped her head up, stopped, then moved forward more slowly. "Margaret. Good afternoon," she called, and slowed her pace further, placing each foot with care. "I don't as a rule receive visitors here; this is a very private retreat of mine."

"Addie Bengsten told me about it." Meg swung the gun up and across her body as she spoke, gripping the barrels with her left hand and sliding her right into place behind the trigger housing. "Where's Katy?" Several leaves were caught in the older woman's hair, and the right sleeve of her plaid shirt had pulled loose at the shoulder seam. Her hands and forearms were dirt streaked; mud smeared the legs of her jeans and clotted her sneakers. Meg tightened suddenly clammy hands on the gun and demanded, "What have you done with her?"

"I beg your pardon?" As Felicity looked past Meg and

saw Jenny, color drained from her face. "Get her away from here!" she cried. "I won't have a Tucker on my land! Get her away!"

In answer came an eerie howl, and then another, long and trailing. Felicity's face went from white to green, and she put a hand over her mouth. "That vicious dog! I let him out and told him to go home, and he just kept jumping at my car."

"Grendel is Katy's dog; it's his job to protect her. Jenny," Meg said without looking around, "would you please go to the van and see if you can keep him calm?"

Jenny made no reply, but Meg heard the whisper of feet and saw Felicity watch the girl away, regaining color with each breath. "Addie Bengsten is a senile old woman," she muttered, turning her gaze to Meg. "Anything she told you was her own malicious invention."

"Perhaps. But I just found Katy's whistle in your upstairs bedroom. She was wearing it the last time I saw her."

"Oh. Yes, but Margaret, you must understand that I was only trying to protect her." Miss Luoma shook her head and sighed: the trouble we go to for others. "You see, she was on her way to that tower, and I knew her friend had fallen. I felt it would be awful for Katy to see her like that. So I suggested a cup of chocolate and a nice ride, and the first thing you know we were here! By then Katy was sound asleep, and there's no phone here, so . . ."

Meg pointed the shotgun skyward and pulled a trigger. When the reverberations had ceased, she asked again, "Where's Katy?"

"Out there somewhere!" A sweeping gesture toward the wooded hills behind them; then the older woman collapsed onto a broad, low stump and sat hugging herself. "I don't know!" she wailed. "She was asleep when I took her upstairs, she should have slept the clock around. But when I went up about noon she was gone, and I've been looking for her ever since. Out there."

Looking for her, or disposing of her, out in that sweep

of brush and trees. Easy enough to push a small body under a bank or against a hill and drag branches and dirt and leaves over it. Meg's heart swelled against her ribs, then contracted to a tiny, hard knot of pain just under her breastbone.

"Margaret, this is ridiculous. Could you . . . I just can't believe you could really bring yourself to shoot me."

Meg met the pale unwinking gaze. "Believe it. And the remaining barrel is full choke, it will cut you in two at this distance. How far back does this . . . this woods go?" She nodded in the direction of the land behind the house.

"A long ways." Felicity moved slowly in turning to look over her shoulder. "We had a quarter section originally, one hundred and sixty acres. Wooded hills, lots of streams, and besides small animals there are bears," she added in a rush of words, "and I've heard that the mountain lions are coming back. Margaret, we should be trying to find her before dark. You could follow behind me with the gun."

One hundred and sixty acres. "Shut up!" Meg snapped. She opened her mouth and sucked in deep drafts of air, trying to cool pain and rage and the intense need to move, to do something. Too much land. The old woman would know it well enough to fool her or lose her or perhaps kill her. Even with Jenny along . . . no, she wouldn't bring the girl to risk again. Wait! she told herself silently. Leg muscles quivered, the fingers of her right hand twitched against metal. Wait for Gutierrez.

"Be careful," Felicity whispered. She huddled into herself, peering up at Meg. "It's so easy to make a mistake, to have a terrible accident with a gun."

"And with a hose attached to the exhaust of a truck? and a bottle of barbiturates? and whatever you used . . ." Meg's throat closed tight as she looked out at the woods, and the older woman hurtled into speech.

"It isn't fair! That preening, sadistic boy was humiliating me and threatening my good name. Don't I have a right to protect myself? I'm all alone. I'm sixty years old."

"Cyndi Martin was thirteen years old," Meg said. Thinking: Katy was ten.

"Be careful!" Felicity inched backwards to the very edge of the stump, her eyes flickering from Meg's face to the gun and back again. "I caught her tearing up my new fuchsias, can you imagine that? And she had questions and questions and that notebook where she'd written nasty fantasies, lies! She was just like the Tucker boy, or maybe worse. Women's natures are more evil than men's."

Absolute childlike simplicity: I didn't break it and besides it was in my way. Meg watched from a great distance as Felicity Luoma set her feet neatly together, squared her shoulders, clasped her hands in her lap.

"Margaret, you can't think I'd want to hurt your Katy. Such a nice child and I was right in thinking she was *not* snoopy or suspicious like that other. I should have asked you before taking her so far, but I was so tired it just slipped my mind."

Upturned, composed face, an errant ray of sun touching the dandelion halo of hair, washing all color from eyes round with sincerity. She would deny everything, and Katy would lie in the woods until time and animals had reduced her to small white bones. Meg's hands tightened, and the gun lifted and began to swing around.

"Meg!" She thought for a moment the sound came from inside her head, but Felicity turned sharply, bracing a hand against the stump.

"Stay where you are," Meg ordered, and stepped back and to one side.

"Meg, here's Katy," called Vince Gutierrez as he appeared between shed and house. "She spent a few hours in the woods, but she's okay."

Katy rode high against Gutierrez' chest, eyes blazing a fierce blue in a scratched and filthy face. "Mommy!" she cried, leaning as far forward as her grip on Gutierrez would permit. "Shoot her, Mommy! She ran over Grendel!"

·Epilogue·

Grendel heard it first. Lying in a patch of late-day sun, he lifted his head, hunched his shoulder muscles, pulled his unbandaged rear leg close; then he slid Meg a glance that said Never mind, and relaxed with a gusty sigh.

She closed the paperback over a finger and listened. Yes, beneath the soft chuckle of the rock-strewn creek and the soprano and alto arpeggios of the little girls' voices, a familiar engine note. Some minutes away yet, low-slung cars don't travel very fast on rutted forest roads.

Company, how nice. She felt her mouth shape a smile. After four days in the woods she was contented but fragile, moving through simple tasks like a person newly recovered from a serious illness. When the Porsche finally nosed in beside the van, she kept her feet on the piled rocks of the fire ring and turned only her head to watch Gutierrez slide out of the car, shake his shoulders loose, and amble in her direction.

"You look good," he told her softly.

Here came the smile again. It was becoming a permanent part of her face. "Thank you," she said, "I feel good. You look different."

"Must be my vacation look. I told the mayor that Svoboda could run the department for a week or for good, whichever." He took a folding chair from against a tree and set it beside hers. "Thought I'd spend some time here, if that's okay with you."

"For heaven's sake, Gutierrez, this is your camp, or your mother's anyway."

He shook his head. "Right now it's yours."

"Well. Actually, I was beginning to get just a tad lonesome," she admitted. "Ten-year-olds, however charming and brilliant, spend a lot of time climbing trees and throwing rocks and telling absolutely awful jokes. And giggling."

"Vince!" Katy ran up to launch herself at Gutierrez, who caught her and swung her high.

"Hi, tiger."

"Did you see Grendel? He's almost better, he'd even run except we won't let him. And we found a place deep enough to swim, and we saw a whole family of ground squirrels. But we're almost out of milk and bread and we're all out of Coke, we might have to go to town."

"No, you won't." He gave her a hug and set her down. "I brought all those and lots more. Hello, Kimmie," he said to the little girl standing quietly a few feet away. "Your mother says things are fine at home but she misses you. I told her I'd bring you back any time you asked."

"Thank you," said Kimmie Silveira, bending her smooth dark head politely. "I don't want to go yet, please."

"Are you going to stay?" demanded Katy.

"I thought I might."

"Good. I have a friend, so Mommy ought to have one, too."

"Right," said Gutierrez, quirking an eyebrow at Meg. "Now, if you and Kimmie would unload the car and put groceries away, older friends could sit and talk. Come on, I'll show you."

He was back in a few minutes, carrying a bottle of beer, a glass, and a slim dark green bottle with a hand-written label. "Brought this just for you. I know a guy who owns a small winery, and his zinfandel is getting damn good."

"Pretty, too." Meg watched the ruby liquid rise in the squat glass.

"Cheers." He handed her the glass, toasted her with his

beer bottle, and sat down, propping his feet beside hers on the rocks. After a moment he reached for her hand and clasped it against his thigh. "So you're enjoying life in the woods."

"Wonderfully. Your mother certainly did things right." The summer camp Emily Gutierrez had built many years earlier was in a mountain forest, in a clearing with a creek nearby. A single wooden building contained kitchen, bathroom, and enough additional covered space to provide shelter in the event of bad weather. Otherwise, living and sleeping went on in tents or in the open.

"Mama had a lot of sense. Still has," said Gutierrez. "If she'd been in town when Dave was killed, I might have plugged into the old-lady network sooner."

Meg turned to look at him, and he sighed. "We, my people, went over Rose Street with a very fine comb, turned up all kinds of blackmail-worthy secrets. Nothing on Felicity Luoma, though, until I talked to one of the old dolls at the historical society. Turns out half-a-dozen people, real old-timers, knew she'd been publishing Aili Makela's stories as her own. Nobody thought it needed talking about."

Shivering, Meg pulled her hand free, wrapped her arms tight, leaned nearer the small fire she'd built against evening chill. Several times each day she hit an image as if it were a brick wall: white-haired woman, taller dark woman, long gun swinging and lifting.

"But I didn't," she said aloud. "Didn't kill. And I wouldn't have. Why did *she*, Vince? Especially Cyndi; however exasperating, Cyndi was still just a kid. Felicity could have brushed her off, intimidated her, even taken those miserable keys by force; who'd have believed Cyndi if she *had* complained?

"Well, except for Katy," she added in a near whisper as she tossed a quick glance toward the building. It was Grendel who had found the keys; he'd chased a cat into the vacant lot as the girls were walking him Wednesday evening, had then dug furiously at a flat stone beside the water tower gate and turned up a key ring bearing the key to the padlock, the key to the green box, and a big pink rabbit's foot which must have carried the scent of Dave Tucker.

Cyndi had insisted on waiting until after dark to explore the tower and the treasure she was confident it held. Cyndi had slipped out in the middle of the night to make the exploration by herself. Katy had waked some time later and followed, taking the dog along because he refused to be left.

"Trouble was, Cyndi knew a lot," Gutierrez told Meg quietly. "She'd been night-prowling for weeks, safe in the fog. She saw Dave Tucker several times, once going to the Luoma house very late. And on the Tuesday after Dave's body was found, Cyndi saw 'a humungous guy on a black motorcycle, in armor, like Darth Vader,' rolling his bike out of Felicity's driveway. Johnny Stein, sure as hell."

"How on earth . . . ?"

"We found Cyndi's diary, that notebook where she wrote down everything: where she went, who else was around, what people had in their houses and closets and drawers. It was buried in Felicity's compost heap, probably because Felicity hadn't had time to destroy it."

Meg drained her glass and held it out for refill. "So they had a confrontation," she said softly, "Cyndi vandalizing because she was mad at Felicity, Felicity caught at home when she was supposed to be away. And I'll bet Cyndi threw some threats around, that was her style. And I'll bet Felicity recognized the key ring."

Gutierrez nodded agreement. "But Felicity smoothed things over; at least she clearly got the kid to sit down for a nice cup of cocoa. Let her get a little drowsy and then said come on let's go up there and look at treasure together. Shoved Cyndi off, reclaimed her own notebook from Dave's cache, and went home happy."

"And came across Katy, and would have murdered her

on the spot if it hadn't been for Grendel, bless him. I wish I'd shot her."

"No you don't."

"Okay, you're right; I don't." She slid lower in her chair and propped the glass of wine on her upraised knees, where it reflected small flames. "Vince, she killed Dave with so far as I could see no regret at all; she was cheery as a sparrow all week long."

"It looks like she shot him in her studio, late Saturday night," Gutierrez broke in. "With her father's .22 pistol, although we're not absolutely safe on that because the bullet was in marginal shape. Anyway, one pistol shot late on a foggy night, in that high studio; nobody even noticed. She tumbled him down the outside stairs; we found several strands of his hair. Got him into the trunk of his own car, drove him to Tanbark beach and dumped him over. Drove the car the three miles back to town, left it and walked home. We think."

"Vince, how could an old woman do all that?"

"Her neighbors in Covelo don't see her as old; they see her as a working lady, a working farmer. Or rancher."

"Okay. But what took her so long to get to the next murder? Why did she wait a week to kill Johnny Stein, if she did?"

"Stein knew about Dave's games," Gutierrez said. "Guido says that a couple of times Dave came to make his collection on the back of Stein's bike. And it was probably Stein who stole the Makela notebook from Felicity in the first place, when he went to her studio to pose. Incidentally, she met him at the Art Institute and got interested in him because of his Portuguese background.

"Anyway, we think he panicked when he heard about Dave's death and ran. But he had no money. And of all the people Dave was blackmailing, Felicity had the most available money, and looked the safest; it probably never crossed the poor bastard's mind that a nice old lady could be a killer."

"Poor dumb Johnny Stein," said Meg.

"Right. Anyway, there's evidence Stein stayed for some time at the old Makela house, no sign that he broke into the place. We know Felicity took five thousand dollars out of the bank the Wednesday after Dave was killed, and put the same amount back the following Monday. The black truck was one her father got from some transient years ago and never registered; she kept it at the Makela place." Gutierrez, who had long since finished his beer, reached out and plucked Meg's forgotten wine glass from her fingers, took a sip, handed it back.

"Maybe Stein wanted more money. Or maybe Felicity just figured he would be a returner, like Dave," he suggested.

"Or maybe she just hated giving away five thousand dollars," said Meg. "I'm sorry, that was a disgusting thing to say. This is so bizarre I can't get a grip on it."

"I know," he said softly. "Whatever her specific reason, she poured him full of booze and got him into that old truck. Drove him to the foggiest scrap of beach she could find and set up the simplest kind of deathtrap and left him there. And I'll bet she went back to the old house on his motorcycle, although I may have trouble convincing anybody else of that."

"Somebody told me Felicity once belonged to a motor-cycle club," Meg said. "Vince, she must have thought she was home free until I cleverly told the whole neighbor-hood you had doubts about Stein's guilt."

"Ah. Well, it was the truth. And it sent her out to her hideaway to try to clean things up, when she should have been on her way to San Francisco. Don't, Meg!" he snapped as she made a small muffled sound. "You didn't do any-thing irresponsible or mean, so stop rooting around in search of your share of guilt."

"Yes, well. There's always plenty of guilt around," she said, and wiped her eyes. "Also self-pity, I've noticed. Although Felicity Luoma seems to be champion in that arena. I know what she's going to say."

"Where?"

"In court. She'll say she was a poor victim throughout. First of Dave the blackmailer, and then of Johnny, who killed Dave but threatened to implicate her. She'll sit there with her white hair and her sweet face," Meg said, pounding a fist on one knee, "and she'll claim insanity or some kind of self-defense. She'll probably even believe it."

"She might have pulled that off," said Gutierrez, "if she'd simply blown Stein away with whatever gun was around. But the kind of planning involved in his death—the long drive with the bike for return, the suicide note expert opinion says she typed, the new piece of hose for the exhaust? I bet we'll find where that came from. No jury is going to sit still for all that as the work of a temporarily deranged mind.

"And then, of course, there was Cyndi," he said flatly. "We can never be sure of a conviction, Meg, and that's the truth. But I think we have a good chance here. And I don't think Felicity Luoma will be publishing any more children's books. Maybe a memoir from prison."

"One of these days," she said, "some television genius will figure out how to do talk shows from prison."

"I think somebody already has. But I didn't watch." He tipped his head back and surveyed the darkening sky. "Be stars out tonight, one of the best things about the mountains. I'll have to dig out my old star book for Katy. Meg, is she going to be okay? I watch her, listen to her, she seems like herself; but I haven't had a lot of close personal experience with kids."

Meg picked up a long stick from beside her chair and leaned forward to poke a half-burned log closer to the heart of the fire. "I have a new maxim: Rage is a great healer. At least for a ten-year-old who knows that anybody who'd deliberately run over a dog is a really rotten person. For the next level, when she realizes someday just what kind of danger she was in: I'll watch for it, and we'll handle it. Katy and I are a pair of tough women, Gutierrez."

"I know."

Meg sighed, stretched, and leaned over to reach for the wine bottle. "Good stuff; one more glass and I'll be ready to forget all about supper. Vince, I'm going to sell my house."

He dropped his feet from the rocks and sat up abruptly.

"Not to leave town," she added quickly. "I still have a job, and Katy and I both want to stay in Port Silva. But not right next door to Felicity Luoma's house."

"Have I got a deal for you," he said. "See, my mother is going back east for at least a year, for various family reasons. She wants me to move into her big house here, the family home, and so I'm thinking, why not . . . ?"

Meg was shaking her head.

"Don't jump to conclusions," he said with a grin. "What I thought was, why not just rent your house for the time being, and move into my little hillside place? It has an enormous sleeping loft, another bedroom on the main floor, plenty of space out back for Grendel."

"That's an interesting idea," she said slowly.

"It would be your house," he told her. "I wouldn't be underfoot, at least not all the time. Anyway, I think Katy's getting to like me."

"Gutierrez, you idiot, she's half in love with you. More than half."

"She is?" He looked both pleased and startled.

"Of course. You rescued her. You helped her rescue her mother. And you're a good-looking man who happened along just as she got old enough to appreciate such things."

"Oh." He blushed, there was no other word for it. "Um, well then. So, how do *you* feel?"

"How do I feel." She cocked her head, contemplated her wineglass. "Let's see. I feel like a very elderly teenager."

"I beg your pardon?"

"On my last birthday, my fortieth, I set my feet firmly on the path of middle age and was bent on creaks, crotchets, and serenity. Mainly serenity."

He goggled at her for a moment before bursting into laughter. "Serenity!" He leaped to his feet, grabbed her hands, and pulled her into a galloping dance around the fire circle, pausing now and then to wipe his eyes on his shirt sleeve without letting go of her. "Serenity!" He bumped into a tree, then set his back against it and pulled her forward, wrapping his arms around her, resting his forehead against hers as he whooped.

"Gutierrez," she snapped, "stop it. Gutierrez!"

"How about . . ." He subsided into occasional snorts, then swallowed and cleared his throat. "Turbulence? excitement? How about passion, I like that." He straightened and pulled her closer. She struggled for a moment and then leaned against him, as giggles set up a tremor in her own chest.

"Right, that's nice," he sighed. "Why not put serenity off for, oh, twenty years? Make it thirty, I come from a long-lived family."